Monster Dogs

The History of the Beast of Dartmoor

Melissa Westwind

Monster Dogs: the History of the Beast of Dartmoor

Melissa Westwind

Copyright Melissa Westwind 2013, all rights reserved.

All text, diagrams and tables © Melissa Westwind, 2013.

The front cover was designed by Amy Norman and based on the original and now public domain Arthur Conan Doyle *Hound of the Baskervilles* cover, courtesy of Wikimedia.

The maps in the introduction are © Google Maps, 2013, but permitted for use under Google's fair usage guidelines.

The Stemma Diagram is © Melissa Westwind, 2013, but uses vector art from http://all-silhouettes.com by permission.

The picture of Lady Howard and the front cover of 'A Straunge and terrible Wunder' are in the Public Domain.

Other pictures are used with permission as noted.

Copyright may be sought from: melissa.westwind@gmail.com

To Yoshi, the 'beast' of my childhood at number 37.
She was my friend.

Contents

Introduction 1

   An Introduction to Dartmoor 1
   What is Today's Beast of Dartmoor? 6
   The Beast of Exmoor in 1983 19
   Format of this Book 25

Beasts of Dartmoor 1929-1830 28

   'The Hound's Pool', by Eden Phillpotts, 1929 28
   'Richard Cabell of Brooke', by Sabine Baring-Gould, 1907 47
   The Hound of the Baskervilles, by Arthur Conan Doyle, 1901 50
   'The Farmer and the Black Hunter', recorded by M.J. Walhouse, 1897...67
   Popular Romances of the West of England by Robert Hunt, 1865 ...73
   'The Devil and his Dandy-Dogs' by Thomas Quiller Couch, 1855.......85
   'Cwn Annwn' by James Motley, 1848 90
   'The Wish or Wisked Hounds of Dartmoor', in *The Athenaeum,* 1847 99
   Fitz of Fitz-Ford, by Anna Eliza Bray, 1830 108

Interlude – From Dartmoor to Britain..121
Monster Dogs of Britain, 1678-c.1127 125

   The Wonders of the Little World, by Nathaniel Wanley, 1678.........125
   A Straunge and terrible Wunder, by Abraham Fleming, c.1577 131
   'Jacob's Well', from Salisbury MS 103, written in Sussex, c.1425...143
   'The Desputisoun Bitwen the Bodi & the Soule', in the Auchinleck Manuscript, c.1300..151
   'Sir Orfeo', in the Auchinleck Manuscript, c.1300...........................157
   'Pwyll', in the White Book of Rhydderch, c.1200 A.D. 161
   'De Nugis Curialium', by Walter Map, c.1181-84..............................167
   The Peterborough 'Anglo-Saxon Chronicle', c.1127. 179

Conclusions 187

Introduction

The Landscape of Dartmoor

Dartmoor National Park stretches across the south of Devon, occupying a large proportion of the south of the county opposite Exmoor to the north-east. It is approximately 20 miles long and 20 miles wide, or less roughly a total of 368 miles squared. This makes Dartmoor 'the largest area of wilderness in the south of Britain' as signs on the edge of Dartmoor proudly claim.

In practice Dartmoor is not as large an area of wilderness as the signs would have it. If you look at a map showing Dartmoor National Park, like the one at the end of the chapter, you will see that although the area of the National Park is supposed to cover most of the land between Exeter and Plymouth, and is bisected by two B roads at right-angles to each other (north-east to south west and north-west to south-east) which cross at Mortenhamstead. In actual fact though, only the western 'High Moor' half; very approximately between Okehamton, and Yelverton, and between Mortenhamstead and the A386; is truly wilderness at all. The southern and eastern portions, or the 'Low Moors' have a small number of villages, which are mainly sustained by commuters or those who work in rural businesses. This area is less steep and frequent transport links and commercial services are available south of Princetown and east of Mortenhamstead.

But the High Moor of Dartmoor *is* truly wild. Weather conditions are unpredictable, high winds, storms and even snow can come very suddenly at any time of year. It is possible to walk for days (in circles) without meeting any people on the High Moor, and those who do go out usually take maps and compasses and dress for hiking.

The High Moor landscape is dominated by very steep hills called tors. 'Tor' is a word inherited from the ancient British language ancestor of modern Cornish and was spoken in the area before English. It referred originally to the large masses of rock which were found on the tops of the hills, although nowadays in colloquial English the word almost always refers to the hills themselves under the rocks. There are tors all around England, and the most famous is probably Glastonbury Tor, near the site of the famous music festival.[1]

Across all of Britain it is the High Moor of Dartmoor which has the densest frequency of places called 'tor'. In this small area alone there are probably over 100 of them.[2] The steep contours of the land mean that although in good conditions you can see for miles, there will always be far more ground you cannot see: behind other tors, in valleys, and over or under ridges. Sound carries very badly, mobile phones do not have a signal and sometimes you can be very close to other hikers without being aware of them at all. Streams and rivers run along the bottom, and sometimes along ridges of tors, and boggy land is very common, potentially hazardous, but also hard to avoid. All in all, although the tors of the High Moor are densely packed into a small area, the relief of the land creates much more surface area for humans to walk across, and the conditions are sufficiently hard that walking from one end to the other of the moor without using one of the two crossing roads is a full day's trek most of the year.

Schools, colleges, youth groups and walking societies in the south west of England have a history of sending hikers to participate in the yearly 'Ten Tors' challenge. To complete this, hikers must walk across 35, 45 or 55 miles of Dartmoor, and climb ten separate tors over the course of two days in summer, carrying heavy rucksacks with cooking and camping equipment along with them. The longer of these walks often form part of training tests for marines and special-forces operatives, and even the 35 mile 'bronze' medal is a test which needs months of training.

---

[1] Many extraordinary things are claimed for this tor. Locals will tell you that the hill is hollow, or that it lies on a 'confluence of ley-lines' and that it is said to contain an entrance to the underworld. During the early medieval period, the area may have been an island, rising over the low-lying Somerset Levels to the west. This might have been what inspired the important medieval monastery of Glastonbury to 'find' (the medieval Latin word used is 'inventum' amusingly), the bones of King Arthur, and to claim that Glastonbury Tor was the 'Isle of Avalon' where Arthur was taken after the Battle of Camlann.

[2] Tim Sandles counts over 400 names for these tors but believes that only about a third of these are true, unique (not nicknamed) tors (Sandles, T. 'The Tors of Dartmoor', http://www.legendarydartmoor.co.uk/tors_moor.htm, *Legendary Dartmoor*, 2010)

Down the centre of the high-moor is an army shooting range, which has its base in Okehampton. It is possible to find bullets and even occasionally live ammunition on the moor, and hikers must always be aware for red flags on the tops of the tors which signify that the army is practicing with live rounds in the vicinity.

Sheep freely wonder the moor for most of the year, and are largely unsupervised apart from when they are sheared, when they are lambing and when they are being slaughtered. Sheep ownership can be distinguished by painted marks on the fleece and cuts on the ear, meaning that even if the animals wander away they can be easily identified.

The moors are also home to a large number of animals apparently unafraid of the unpredictable weather and occasional shooting by the army. The presence of foxes means that lambs are occasionally taken, and sheep are sometimes also killed by broken bones, old age or by falling into Dartmoor's rivers or bogs in the valleys. This means that fragments of bones and especially sheep skulls can be found all over the moors, and when on the High Moors it is easy to imagine this landscape to be home to a vengeful ghost or big cat.

Dartmoor was made into a National Park in 1951. That means that even though the land is mainly privately owned, it can mostly be accessed by anyone, and the area is being preserved for its natural beauty and wildlife. Fires are forbidden and there are also a few areas of Nature Reserve which are forbidden to Ten Tors participants, for example. Dartmoor is an important habitat for reptiles and amphibians as well as songbirds. It is the only place that the Dartmoor pony is found along with mustelids (badgers, weasels, stoats, otters) and foxes, deer, rabbits and hares.

Dartmoor, as a mainly untamed (and unwanted) 'wilderness' is also one of the few places where populations of deer and rabbits are not culled, but are allowed to grow to carrying capacity. These creatures might form a very good diet for a solitary-hunting large cat or dog depending on its size, especially if supplemented with the occasional sheep. Many sheep go missing on Dartmoor each year, and scavengers like ravens, foxes and buzzards will often have found a corpse before humans, making the cause of death impossible to identify. In this romantic context the idea of a 'Beast of Dartmoor' is scientifically easily conceivable, and not outside the bounds of reason, since the physical landscape of the moor makes systematic searches very difficult.[3] Ultimately whether or not you accept the existence of a real beast on the moors today, the existence of a myth about such a beast is very easy to understand.

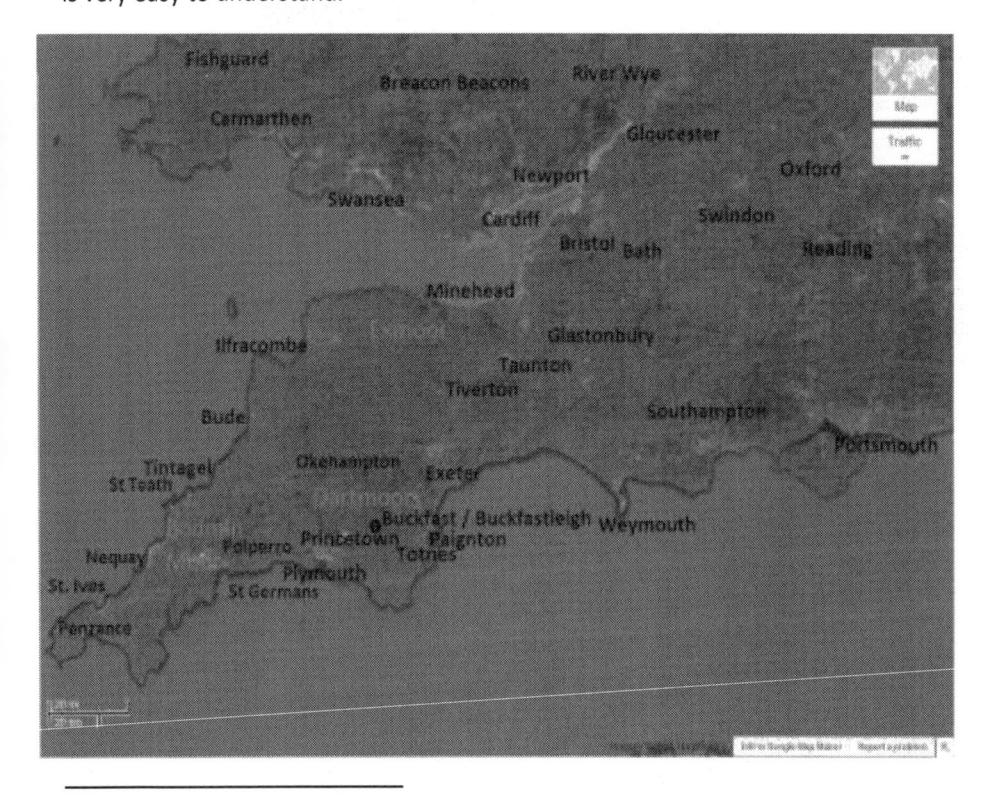

---

[3] The fact that no-one has never been attacked, the rarity and discrepancy of sightings and the fact that cattle are rarely targeted suggests only the absence of the largest cats and packs of wolves, since smaller cats like lynxes, jungle cats and jaguars are far more discreet, never approach humans and only ever target rabbits or small deer.

LOW MOOR

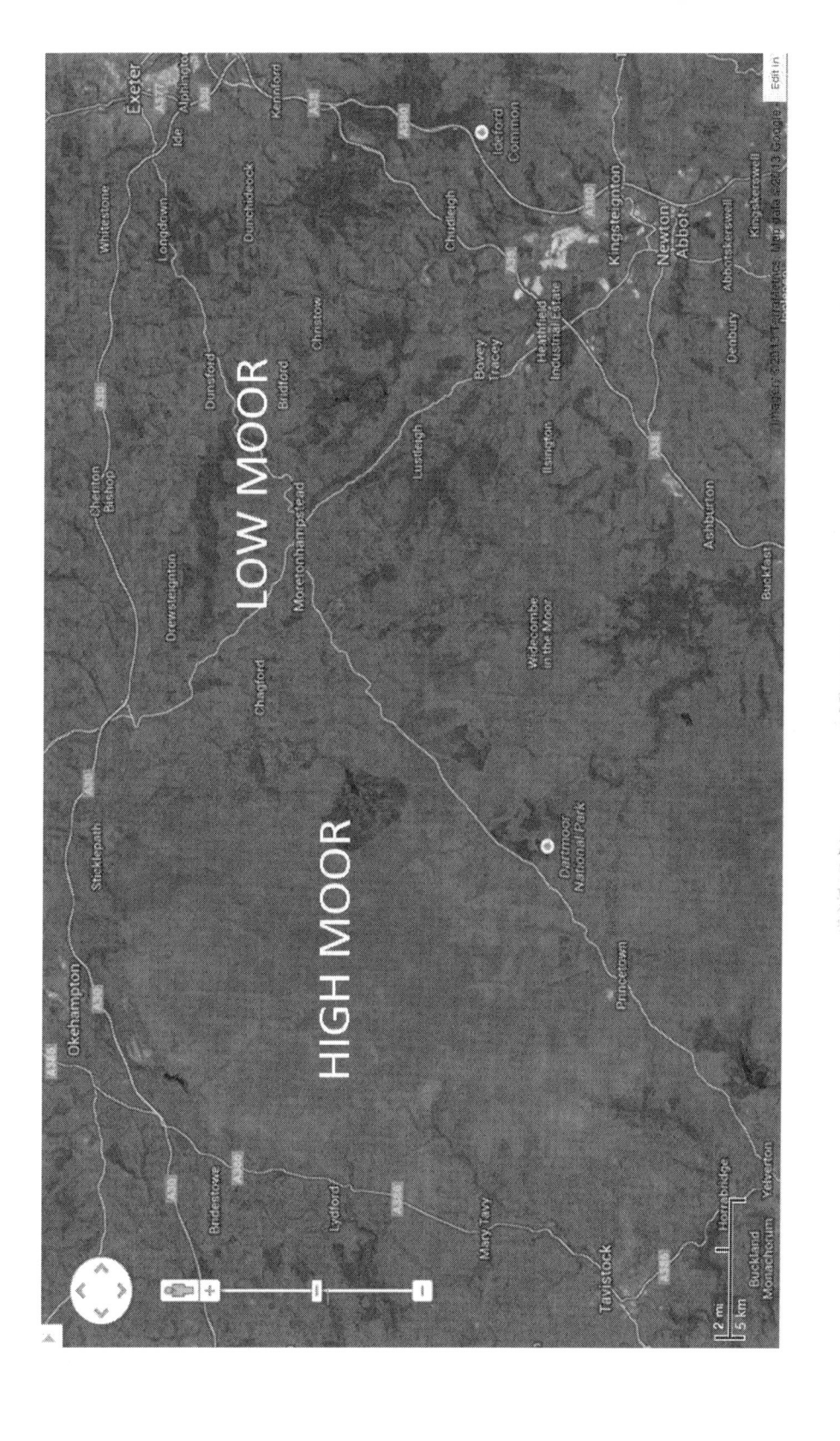

HIGH MOOR

What is Today's Beast of Dartmoor?

Today the Beast of Dartmoor is most usually considered to be a feline rather than a canine. As we shall go on to see, this has not always been the case and traditional stories of Dartmoor's beast tell of dogs rather than cats. However before we look in more depth at the 'Monster Dogs', it is worth considering the most frequently cited origins of the legend.

According to Chris Moiser, one of the most influential researchers writing in the area, there are four possible explanations for the evidence of big cats in Britain:

(i) the cats could represent unknown survivals from Britain's past, wildcats or lynxes;

(ii) they could represent a species unknown to science, especially hybrids between escaped large cats and domestic cats;

(iii) they could represent animals released from captivity (a) in the 18th century, (b) during the 1960s and 70s (c) after the Dangerous Wild Animal Act of 1976 or (d) illegally later on; finally,

(iv) they could represent non-physical entities (which Moiser calls 'zooform phenomena'), either (a) ghosts or thoughtforms or (b) inherited images of human-eating cats in the shared psyche.[4]

Some of these theories are more likely than others, and it is worth spending some time discussing each of them in turn.

The Survival Theory

To start with, the evidence for number (i) has actually gained weight over time, but it remains highly unlikely. This was one of the very first theories considered for the big cat in Britain, and was the idea of Di Francis, whose book *Cat Country* was published right at the beginning of the mystery cat craze in the 1980s. The range of colours and sizes of

---

[4] Moiser, C. (2005), *Big Cat Mysteries of Somerset*, pp.3-6; (2001) *Mystery Cats in Devon and Cornwall*, pp.3-5, (both published by Bossiney Books, Launceston, Cornwall)

reported cat sightings suggested to her that at least one, or possibly two previously unknown but native species of big cat have survived in Britain undetected by modern Britons except in quick glimpses. Di Francis' idea was that Britain's beasts could actually be descendants of a small cryptid population which has passed unnoticed into the modern period. She grouped a large quantity of eyewitness accounts from 1960-1980 into four categories, and then suggested that these categories have all the characteristics that we might expect to see in animals evolving in Britain.[5]

Britain's native animals are those that returned to the country after the 'end of the last Ice Age' or, more properly, the start of the Holocene Interglacial period, which occurred approximately 11,700 years ago. At this point, the climate began to warm up and the ice sheets and glaciers slowly retreated north of Britain. According to currently established scientific theory, in the wake of the ice, in the warmer climate left behind only two species of feline were able to settle: the lynx, (*Lynx lynx*) and the wildcat (*Felis silvestris*) before the melting ice caused sea levels to rise, and made Britain an island. These two animals are therefore called 'native' to Britain, even though the first is no longer found in the country at all and the latter is only found in the Scottish Highlands.

The reason the survival theory is gaining in popularity is that since the 1980s, lynx remains have been found and carbon dated, shifting scholarly consensus about when the lynx became extinct in Britain later and later. When Di Francis and Moiser first wrote the most recently dated remains were from 4000 years ago,[6] but only a few years later Moiser could update his claim to suggest that the lynx survived up until 180 A.D[7]. The latest radiocarbon date published in a peer reviewed journal dates the remains to c.425-600 A.D.,[8] and this creature is unlikely to be the last lynx ever to have lived in Britain.

So is it possible that isolated populations of lynxes have survived around Britain? An analogue for the situation does exist. The pine

---

[5] See: Francis, D. (1981) *Cat Country*, (David & Charles, Newton Abbot, Devon). pp.96-115
[6] *Mystery Cats in Devon and Cornwall*, p.3.
[7] *Big Cat Mysteries of Somerset*, pp.3
[8] Hetherington, Lord, Jacobis., 'New evidence for the occurrence of Euasian lynx (lynx lynx) in medieval Britain' pp.3-8 in: *Journal Quarternary Science Vol. 21* (2005).

marten was thought to have been lost from all but Highland Scotland at the beginning of the twentieth century, although there were occasional sightings and signs of the creature across the rest of the country especially around Snowdonia, Wales and the Lake District in England.[9] However in 2012 a road-kill carcass was found. No previous carcass had been seen anywhere in Wales since 1971, although a single pine marten scat from Wales had been positively DNA tested in 2007.[10] This proves that predator animals can exist very quietly in parts of Britain for decades without humans being aware of it.

However it is highly unlikely that viable populations of lynx could have existed secretly for centuries anywhere in Britain. The mammal predator species of Britain are incredibly well known. The only reason it's possible for us to doubt this is because of the deplorable state of mammals in Britain in the twenty-first century. The reason that Britain's mammals are so poorly known today is obscure, but it worth taking the time to understand because it shows why it is so unlikely that any large mammal could have hidden in the wilderness for all this time.

Basically, from the eighteenth to the early twentieth centuries, most of Britain's countryside was divided into large, private, country estates. The estates' owners, and rich gentlemen on holidays 'in the country' very much enjoyed shooting game like grouse, pheasants and moorhens. In this environment predator creatures were seen as truly undesirable and they were universally despised by the gamekeepers of the time.

This attitude had its root in a hatred of "vermin" species which is peculiar to Britain and too complicated to go into here.[11] It led to a two-century long misguided campaign which aimed to exterminate predators from private land in Britain. The repercussions of this campaign are still being felt today, and have meant out of control populations of prey, uninhibited grazing on commercial crops, and a

---

[9] Lovegrove, R. (2007), *Silent Fields*, (Oxford University Press). pp.276-7.
[10] Vincent Wildlife Trust, 'Pine Marten found in Wales' (http://www.vwt.org.uk/news/vincent-wildlife-trust-blog/vwt-blogs/2012/11/07/pine-marten-found-in-wales-the-first-in-40-years), (November 7th, 2012)
[11] See the *Acts for the Preservation of Grayne* from the sixteenth century and see *Silent Fields* as quoted above.

general 'de-wilding' of the country. Populations of most predators plummeted during the centuries of persecution including pine martens, polecats, stoats and weasels, wildcats and most birds of prey. Almost all of Britain's natural predators by around 1900 were confined to fringe, wilderness areas of Britain with the important exception of foxes, which were actually encouraged to breed so they could be hunted by countryside scions.

Britain's predator species are only now beginning to recover. Wildcats are still confined to the Scottish Highlands and the pine marten is almost as rare. Even people living in the countryside today may not be aware of the wildlife which is native to the island.

But there was a time about two centuries ago when, for example, the wildcat was not 'Scottish' but was found across the full extent of the Island of Britain. Luckily the animals of Britain were recorded by naturalists of the time so that we can trace when almost any charismatic animal or bird was lost from each region of the country. But despite countless records being made, many being categorical in nature, we do not find the lynx mentioned anywhere. Admittedly, a lynx in Britain would live mainly on rabbits and roe deer which would not attract attention, but lynxes do frequently take lambs and sometimes adult sheep wherever there is sufficient cover for ambush hunting. In pastoral areas of Wales and the South West, sheep live almost feral on the moors throughout much of the year, and a lynx would find ample hunting ground here. The number of animals in these areas currently taken by 'mystery cats' has been in almost all cases not sufficient to cause alarm, and unlike the pine marten, historically no-one has ever even wondered if the lynx survived extinction. Actually the very native words for the animal were lost in the medieval period, and Welsh, Gaelic and English people talk about the 'y lyncs', 'an lioncs' and 'the lynx' respectively. All of these words were borrowed from the Latin 'lynx'/'linx' in the twelfth-thirteenth centuries. Surely if anyone at the time was still talking about the creatures, their names would have been remembered.

The Survival theory was the earliest theory to explain Big Cat sightings, and had much more currency when first advocated by Di Francis in

1983.[12] Things have moved on since then however. Francis' predictions for the future have not come to fruition. For example, in 1983 she claimed the following:

> 'If the felling and clearing continues over the next twenty years... the only change it can make will bring it to the notice of the public...
>
> Someone would have photographed it... If the entire population of this country went around with cameras draped round their necks twenty-four hours a day
>
> Once the experts have to accept that the creature is really around our countryside, then they will come out of hibernation, shake the museum dust from themselves and tackle the task of identifying it with enthusiasm'[13]

Well, the countryside has continued to be improved, and experts are still sceptical. We are not quite at the stage where the entire population of the country carry cameras but we are nearly there. 51% of adults carried smartphones in 2013, and the figure is much higher among teenagers[14]. The bar for a phone to be smart is currently quite high (basically it has to be an iPhone, Android or Blackberry) but today even the most basic model of phone still bears a camera, so that according to Francis' predictions, new pictures and videos of big cats should really be a daily feature by now. Option (i) was a good theory in the 1980s but now it seems rather a lost cause.

The Hybrid Theory

Moiser's second hypothesis about the origin of the Beast of Dartmoor is the idea that a creature or hybrid unknown to science lurks the moors. The main trouble with this theory is that there is no evidence that such animals exist at all, or could form a successful breeding population.

---

[12] Francis, D. (1983), *Cat Country*, (David & Charles, Newton Abbot)
[13] *Cat Country*, pp.8-9.
[14] See: Ofcom, 'The Communications Market 2013', (2013), (http://stakeholders.ofcom.org.uk/market-data-research/market-data/communications-market-reports/cmr13)

Quite often you will hear the idea that the Beast of Dartmoor could be a Kellas Cat. This is usually said to be a hybrid between the Scottish wildcat (Felis silvestris) and the domestic cat (Felis catus), although research has shown that the Kellas Cat is just a melanistic wildcat which can have pure wildcat genes as well as being a hybrid wildcat-domestic. This creature was also first discovered by Di Francis and described in her second book, *My Highland Kellas Cats*. There are two main problems with this theory. The first is, as Di Francis has tiredly and repeatedly emphasised, this animal does not fit the description given for the sheep-eating Beasts of Britain. It is not nearly so large, and seems quite incapable of taking down a sheep[15].

The other trouble with this theory is quite how rare this genetic mutation is. Hybridisation between British wildcats and domestic cats has been the object of intense research over the last few decades, as it has become clear that wildcat numbers in Scotland are not improving. The reason for this is the inter-breeding between wildcats and domestic cats. Because of the unnaturally high density of feral domestic cats, wildcats on heat are more likely to mate with domestic cats. This leads to hybrid offspring very frequently. The latest estimated number of genetically pure wildcats left ranges between 35 to 'less than 400'.[16] But why is there so much discrepancy? The answer is that hybrid wildcat-domestic cats almost always very strongly resemble their wildcat parents. Since hybrids are not protected under law, this has caused a large amount of contention with gamekeepers needing to control numbers of feral cats but being in danger of shooting endangered Scottish wildcats. This is such a problem that a large amount of research has been directed at finding reliable 'pellage characteristics' to tell pest feral cats from protected wildcats.[17] Although the University of Oxford's own conservation team, the

---

[15] Francis, D. (1993), *My Highland Kellas Cats*, (Jonathan Cape Ltd. London). p.2. See especially Dr Andrew Kitchener's 'Investigating the Identity of the Kellas Cats' at the end of the book (pp.211-13).

[16] According to a Scottish Wildcat Association study, See: 'Scottish wildcat extinct within months' (http://www.bbc.co.uk/news/uk-scotland-highlands-islands-19569538), (13th September 2012); Scottish Natural Heritage disagrees see for example: 'FAQs about recent wildcat statement', (www.highlandtiger.com, no stable link available), (24th September 2012).

[17] Kilshaw, K., Drake, A. Macdonald, D.W. & Kitchener, A.C., 'The Scottish wildcat, a comparison of genetic and pelage characteristics', (commissioned by Scottish Natural Heritage, http://www.snh.gov.uk/publications-data-and-research/publications/search-the-catalogue/publication-detail/?id=1466), (2010)

WildCRU, have been working on developing a DNA test for the last few years, they have not yet been successful. If Kellas Cats were the explanation for the strange sightings over the years, we would expect to also see a large population of ordinary, non-melanistic wildcats in the same areas.

In a way, if only hybrid wildcats did resemble black panthers it would make both the continued existence of the wildcat and the explanation for many of the Beasts of Britain much simpler. The idea was an elegant solution for the mid-20th century and had some scientific backing, but unfortunately 'Kellas cats' are rare, and are also only slightly bigger than domestic cats. Although they may explain some sightings they cannot explain them all.

The Escapes and Releases theory

Option (iii) is by far the most likely of the four. The only objection that needs to be made is that Moiser forgot to mention that escapes could have happened long before the twentieth century. In Cervantes' *Don Quixote*, for example, a satirical romance from 1605-15, a lion which is being transported to the court of the King of Spain is released by Don Quixote the old knight in order than he can vanquish it.

> *The keeper, seeing that Don Quixote had taken up his position, and that it was impossible for him to avoid letting out the male without incurring the enmity of the fiery and daring knight, flung open the doors of the first cage, containing, as has been said, the lion, which was now seen to be of enormous size, and grim and hideous mien. The first thing he did was to turn round in the cage in which he lay, and protrude his claws, and stretch himself thoroughly; he next opened his mouth, and yawned very leisurely, and with near two palms' length of tongue that he had thrust forth, he licked the dust out of his eyes and washed his face; having done this, he put his head out of the cage and looked all round with eyes like glowing coals, a spectacle and demeanour to strike terror into temerity itself. Don Quixote merely observed him steadily, longing for him to leap from the cart and come to close quarters with him, when he hoped to hew him in pieces. So far did his unparalleled madness go; but the noble lion, more courteous than arrogant, not troubling himself*

> *about silly bravado, after having looked all round, as has been said, turned about and presented his hind-quarters to Don Quixote, and very coolly and tranquilly lay down again in the cage. (Don Quixote, 1605-15).* [18]

Now admittedly this is a fictional romance, and the episode is supposed to be funny, but it does illustrate that someone at the beginning of the seventeenth century was familiar with lions being transported across countries to the courts of kings. The latest research from Britain indicates that the Royal Menagerie was certainly established in the Tower of London in the time of Henry III (reigned 1216-1272), and might have been previously established at Woodstock Palace in the time of Henry I (reigned 1100-1135).[19] A lion skull has been radiocarbon dated to A.D. 1280-1385 and analysis suggests it probably originated in North Africa, and therefore must have been transported all the way across or around Europe.[20] These must have been expensive, rare and closely guarded in the medieval period, and in Britain only the Royal Menagerie was allowed to keep lions and leopards by royal decree, although this was ignored from the eighteenth century onwards.[21] All this together suggests it is possible, although unlikely that big cats could have escaped from menageries and established a breeding population any time from the twelfth century onwards, although the odds of this population evading discovery are very low.

At current, between 1,200 and 2,000 sightings are made of big cats each year, but the figure has been climbing to this point slowly over the last few decades.[22] Far from proving that the animals are around, and given that a century ago the figure was essentially zero, it is easy to assume that these sightings are just the latest craze, and that today's big cat enthusiasts are those who saw little green men in the

---

[18] Ormsby, J. (trans. 1885), *Don Quixote, Vol.2*, (Thomas Y. Crowell &Company, New York). p.115.
[19] Hahn, D. (2003), *The Tower Menagerie*, (ed. 2004, Pocket Books, London). Pp.7-13.
[20] O'Regan, H. Turner, A. Sabin, R. 'Medieval big cat remains from the Royal Menagerie at the Tower of London', pp.385-394 in: The International Journal of Osteoarchaeology, vol. 16, (2005); Barnett, R. Yamaguchi, N., Shapiro, B., Sabin, R. 'Ancient DNA analysis indicates the first English lions originated from North Africa' in *Contributions to Zoology, vol. 77*, (2008).
[21] *The Tower Menagerie*, pp.139-45.
[22] Minter, R. (2011), *Big Cats: Facing Britain's Wild Predators*, (Whittles Publishing, Dunbeath, Catithness). p.29-33

60s. However, this does *not* seem to be the case. Over the last century a small but significant number of the mystery cats purportedly stalking Britain have been caught, dead or alive. Big cat scats have been found, and at least three British animal hair samples have been tested as coming from big cats.[23]

The latest of these specimens was examined by academics this year, and a multidisciplinary investigation was begun. Strontium analysis from tooth extracts and DNA analysis was inconclusive, but skull analysis revealed it was probably a Canadian lynx (Lynx canadensis), possibly kept for most of its life in captivity before being shot in Devon in 1903. This specimen predates the 1970s when many exotic pets were released before and after the Dangerous Wild Animal Act of 1976, but based on the rest of the scientific analysis it does come from an exotic collection of some description.[24]

All such animals actually physically caught or killed have been explained by option (iii), except for the occasional dead animal remains planted as a hoax.[25] But when we consider the other theories, the only evidence that remains is eyewitness testimony and hasty photographs, along with occasional footprints and dead sheep. In fact, the evidence left over to support explanations (i) and (ii) is roughly equivalent to the evidence surviving for an alien visitation of earth. Option (iii) remains the only scenario we know to have certainly taken place within the last century.

Ultimately although there is substantial physical evidence for big cats in Britain, if a viable breeding population was established we would really expect even more. Throughout all of his books, Moiser, perhaps influenced by his training as a biologist, is primarily concerned with investigating physical phenomena (e.g. photographs, sightings, remains of sheep, footprints). He has made the understandable

---

[23] *Mystery Cats in Devon and Cornwall*, pp.10-11. *Cats: Facing Britain's Wild Predators*, p.94, 113-4, 180.

[24] Blake, M. Et alia, 'Multidisciplinary investigation of a 'British big cat'', in: *Historical Biology, vol. 25*, (2013) – article not yet published in paper format.

[25] See for example the Golitha Falls leopard skull which was almost certainly taken from a trophy-head or rug which spent most of its afterlife either in a warm warehouse or in the tropics: Moiser's *Mystery Cats in Devon and Cornwall*, p.19; Natural History Museum, 'The Beast of Bodmin Moor', (http://www.nhm.ac.uk/nature-online/life/mammals/beast-of-bodmin-moor/bm_i5.htm). (2013).

assumption that all of these physical pieces of evidence deserve a physical explanation. But there are two problems with this. First, the Beasts of Britain are far more a social phenomenon than they are a biological one. Although in a few scattered cases the animals in questions have been captured, in the majority of cases, the beasts have eluded even their most determined pursuers. Creatures like the Beast of Dartmoor probably have more in common with the Loch Ness monster than the lions of London Zoo. Even if there is, or was, a physical creature at the heart of the legend, the Beasts of Britain as we know them are more legends than flesh and blood.

The second problem with the physical evidence approach is that it confines its attention to the last fifty or so years of eye-witness sightings and media attention. Although during the last two decades of the twentieth century the stories were fairly homogenous, the further back we trace the legends the stranger (from a modern point of view) they become. Moiser has noted that the term 'Beast of ___' has only been in use since the 1980s, but, as we shall see, people were discussing monsters on the moors long before this.[26]

Ghosts and the Cultural Source Hypothesis

The brilliance of option (iv) as an explanation has not been fully realised. Variations of this theory come in all shapes and sizes, from the simple and superstitious idea that they are the ghosts of cats, to the convoluted idea of the thoughtform,[27] and even the pseudo-scientific theory that the cats represent images in our shared consciousness, and seeing them is a form of mass-hysteria.[28] Option

---

[26] *Mystery Cats in Devon and Cornwall*, p.3.

[27] 'In occult writings, an astral form created, deliberately or accidentally, by the power of human thought. According to a common magical teaching, any conception held in the mind for a long time or with sufficient energy takes shape on the astral plane as a thoughtform, and if reinforced with emotional or etheric energies, will gradually descend the planes to take shape on the physical plane.' (from Greer, J. (2003), *The New Encyclopedia of the Occult*, (Llewelyn Publications, St Paul, Minnesota)).

Also see Redfern, N. (2004), *Three Men Seeking Monsters: Six Weeks in Pursuit of Werewolves, Lake Monsters, Giant Cats, Ghostly Devil Dogs, and Ape-Men*, (Pocket Books, New York) for an in depth and highly entertaining exploration of the idea of the Beasts of Britain as thoughtforms.

[28] I call this pseudo-science because fear responses in humans are inherited socially not genetically, as proved by observations of infant humans and monkeys interacting with snakes. Humans have an associative bias towards learning to fear snakes, but not an innate fear. See: DeLoache, J. LoBue, V. 'The narrow fellow in the grass: human infants associate snakes and fear', pp.201-7, in: *Developmental Science, vol.12*, (2008)

(iv) does not demand that the physical evidence found has a physical cause, since a footprint might be for example a peculiar mark in the mud, given form by the unconscious mind. It also allows for the creatures to change over time, to persevere over centuries and to go for long periods of time undiscovered.

The most popular version of this theory can be read in Merrily Harpur's book, *Mystery Big Cats.* She points out that in order to explain all the sightings of big cats, one would need to conclude that every region of Britain has a breeding population of every species of big cat, some of which are not frequently found in the wild. All of these species would have to be incredibly discreet to evade all the hunters, military personnel and police forces that have been sent to capture them. She disposes of the other possible scenarios in turn, arguing: (i) More than one species would need to survive undetected to support all the findings, (ii) hybrid big cats have never been viable and (iii), there is no evidence that enough captives have ever been released to account for the current number of sightings, and most individuals which escaped from zoos and menageries were recaptured within a few days at most.[29]

After rejecting the usual explanations she considers several variations of Moiser's scenario (iv). These include that the sightings can be explained as thoughtforms or Tibetan Buddhist tulpas, embodiments of yin energy and the idea that there might be as many explaining theories as there are cat sightings. However the theory Harpur eventually finds the most satisfying is that the cat sightings represent 'daimons', or spiritual entities between spirits and gods. These creatures manifest differently depending on who sees them, and this explains why the big cat sightings have only started recently and why so little physical evidence has been found.[30]

This theory is inventive, and I do believe that Harpur was on the right track by discarding options (i)-(iii). However to me this explanation seems *too* neat and tidy, as if it was contrived specifically to address the weaknesses of the other theories. A more natural explanation

---

[29] Harpur, M. (2006), *Mystery Big Cats,* (Heart of Albion Press, Loughborough). Theory (i) is chapter 10, theory (ii) is chapter 9, theory (iii) is chapter 4.

[30] Theory (iv) is discussed in chapters 11-13 before the daimon theory is accepted, and this is used throughout chapters 13-20.

which explains (a) why sometimes a physical animal cannot be found behind a flurry of sightings (b) why the nature of the sightings have changed over time and (c) addresses all the evidence rather than just the physical is to examine the Beasts of Britain as favourite literary characters rather than animals, following the so called 'cultural source hypothesis'. Whilst some of Britain's Beasts certainly have physical form, they are all larger than life, and many potentially have more of a subjective than objective reality. The trouble is that when we examine the big cats as literary characters we very quickly start running into legends of dogs as well as cats, especially prior to about 1975 when the only beasts haunting Dartmoor were hounds.

Harpur did briefly consider the idea that modern big cat folklore has evolved from black dog folklore, citing the basic physical similarities of the monsters. She rejected the theory because to her mind on closer inspection the dogs and cats seemed to embody opposite concepts in the human psyche:

> 'Black Dogs are perceived as: rough, matt, close, engaged, habitual, staring, metaphorical, red eyed, and singular
>
> Anomalous Big Cats (ABCs) are perceived as: smooth, shiny, distant, indifferent, random, glancing, literal, green-eyed, and plural.'[31]

We will see many accounts of plural, distant and uninterested Monster Dogs over the course of this book which are far more 'cat' than they are 'dog' on Harpur's dichotomy-scale. Intriguingly though, Harpur herself seems to have realised that she drew the point too far. In her conclusion she states the following:

> 'Perhaps the most striking inference to be drawn from the behaviour of ABCs as compared to that of black dogs is that they are very much of this world. Apart from frightening or chasing other animals they have also been observed eating, drinking, crapping, spraying, raiding dustbins, stealing from

---

[31] *Mystery Big Cats*, p.53.

bird-tables, rooting in discarded chip-wrappers – activities no black dogs would be seen dead doing.'[32]

This gives us rather the opposite point of view, with distant dogs and habitual cats. I must bow to this charge, Britain's Hell Hounds, Wild Hunts and Phantom Dogs do not ever scavenge for food in the legends I have seen, nor do they even appear to bother cattle very much, although sometimes they frighten horses[33]. This certainly is a difference between the two sets of animals, but to my mind it is not one serious enough to preclude the possibility that accounts of British Big Cats evolved from accounts of phantom hounds.

Ultimately, arguments about the origin of big cats in Britain are only really relevant to those who already believe completely that there are big cats here. This means that ultimately Moiser's explanation is self-evident. The evidence of big cats in modern Britain can be explained by either (i) the continued existence of big cats, (iii) the release of big cats at some point intermediate or (ii and iv) something else peculiar. Admittedly the details of the theories are interesting, but the theories themselves can only ever be hypothetical.

Whatever their true origins, this book treats the Beasts of Britain as heroes in their own stories instead of animals to be outwitted and captured. Ultimately I hope that whether or not the reader believes in the physical existence of the modern Beasts, they will at least admit that the roots of the legends go very far back indeed, and enjoy reading some other stories which feature wild beasts roaming Britain long before it became the territory of the cat.

---

[32] *Mystery Big Cats*, p.62.
[33] Westwood, J. 'Friend or Foe? Norfolk Traditions of Shuck', pp.57-76, in: Trubshaw, B. (ed. 2005), *Explore Phantom Black Dogs*, (Heart of Albion Press, Loughborough).

The Beast of Exmoor in 1983

Introduction

In 1982 and 1983 a large number of sheep, both juveniles and adults were being killed in the area of Exmoor around South Molton. Now, every sheep farmer loses lambs in lambing season, and might occasionally also lose adult sheep to foxes, rarely to birds of prey, or certain natural dangers like falls and bogs. The element that separates out the case of the Beast of Exmoor on South Molton is the number of sheep involved. Over one hundred animals were eventually killed in the area, and one farmer alone Eric Ley, lost £2,000 of livestock.[34]

This eventually made national news, and the Royal Marines were called in to attempt to kill what was then dubbed the 'Beast of Exmoor'. There was a rush of sightings, including some by police and marines, which generated a great deal of excitement nationally about the creature. At one point the *Daily Express* newspaper put up a reward of £1,000 for a picture.

Even though the villain of this story is the Beast of Exmoor rather than the Beast of Dartmoor, it can still teach us a lot about how to approach such stories. In 1982-3 the subject of a mysterious animal terrorising the countryside was still relatively fresh, and the stories took Britain by storm. Since then, the stories have become legends among researchers of the anomalous in general and of big-cats in particular. The events on Exmoor at that time are still thought of as particularly 'hard to explain phenomena', and the sheer mass of sightings and the nation-wide impact of the story have been celebrated as hard evidence that there is something behind the mystery.

However, in its own way this story illustrates the very opposite. First, at the end of the hunt, a group of elite troops trained to shoot in rugged terrain, were unable to shoot the wild beast despite a

---

[34] Moiser, C. (2001) *Mystery Cats in Devon and Cornwall,* (Bossiney Books, Launceston, Cornwall). p.13.

concerted effort for months at a time. Nor was anyone else in the area able to produce the creature's body or any pictures, even though in 1983 the beast was the most frequently sighted it would be for years, and a financial fortune could be had by anyone capturing it.

Finally, the most interesting element for me is how the stories seem to change as time passes. I present the story as it is told in *The Daily Mirror*, at that time the second most purchased newspaper in Britain:

Extracts from the *Daily Mirror, 1983*

7*th* of May, 1983. p.9.

[From the end of an article about Gloucester puma attacks]

...

On Exmoor, marines hunting an animal which has killed 80 sheep now believe it is a puma.

The troops have seen the cat but were unable to shoot because a house was in the line of fire.

9th of May, 1983. p.3.

Moor beast kills again

By John Peacock,

The mystery Beast of Exmoor; which is believed to have killed more than 80 sheep and lambs, struck again at the weekend.

The animal, thought to be a puma, killed one lamb and savaged another at Drewstone Farm, South Molton, Devon.

Last night farmer Eric Ley, who had already lost £2,000 worth of livestock, criticised the Daily Express's £1,000 offer for a photograph of the beast.

Because of the offer, and the possibility of snap-happy civilians being hurt, the police withdrew a Royal Marine unit who had been hunting the beast.

31st of May 1983, p. 16.

We saw killer animal, say scared boys: Face to face with Beast of the Moor

Two schoolboys told yesterday of their terrifying encounter with the killer Beast of Exmoor.

Wayne Adams, 13, said; "It was about ten yards away and it stared at me with bulging, greeny eyes just like a lion.

"It was jet-black apart from white marlines down its chest and had a head like an Alsatian dog. But it was much too big to be a dog. I was dead scared and didn't know what to do."

Wayne's friend, 12-year-old Marcus White, said; "Its face was like an Alsatian's but it did not move like a dog."

As the boys stood terrified, the animal set off with a loping run.

The beast, which has slaughtered more than 80 sheep was prowling on a common when it was spotted by Wayne, of North Molton, Devon, and Marcus, of Exwick, Exeter.

Wayne's aunt, Mrs. Mary Adams, of Willingford Farm, Exford, where the boys were staying said: "When they realised the danger, they came home flat out."

The spot where the boys saw the beast was about five miles from where the last attack took place. Police are investigating

6th of June, 1983, p.5.

Net closes on moors beast

The Beast of Exmoor, savage killer of more than a 100 sheep, has been identified as a large wild dog.

Commando snipers brought in to hunt the animal have spotted it several times through their night sights, but have been unable to get a clean shot at it.

A spokesman said: "It has either been unsafe to shoot because of nearby houses or the thing has moved so damned fast and shown itself so little."

He said the animal was "completely wild and very cunning."

But the dozen men had closed in on its main hunting ground near South Molton, Devon.

7th of June 1983, p.13.

Face of the Beast

A Police chief showed farmers yesterday what the Beast of Exmoor looks like. Police Supt. Douglas Clary said it looks like a greyhound lurcher with a broad head like a bull mastiff's.

He showed one of each breed in Molland, Devon, and told farmers: "We need sightings reported to us immediately.

"Time is running out. The undergrowth is growing fast and soon the animal will be able to find all the cover it needs."

He added: "This is a very cunning animal which keeps close to the hedgerows and very rarely crosses open countryside, although it hunts and kills by night and day."

The beast, which is being hunted by Army snipers, has killed 81 sheep. It was originally thought to be a puma.

Jenny Hayes, 26, who saw the animal while out riding said "It was huge, definitely something out of the ordinary."

15th of June, 1983, p.15

'Beast' hunt shifts

Marines hunting the "Beast of Exmoor" have moved their base 15 miles to Dulverton, where the dog-like creature struck twice at the weekend. Eighty sheep and lambs *have been victims of the rogue killer in the South Molton area.*

Discussion

I have included above every newspaper article I could find by searching the *Daily Mirror's* online digital archive[35] between March 1st 1983 and December 31st 1983. Although I am sure there may be some articles which have not been fully digitalised or properly put through optical character recognition, this is a good selection of articles from the height of the Beast of Exmoor craze. Therefore it is very interesting that far from painting a coherent picture of the creature, the folklore almost seems to change from story to story. The animal is twice described as a 'puma', three times as various types of strange, wild dog and lastly ends up being called only the 'beast'. If we look at this in more detail a basic pattern emerges:

At first, in the beginning of May, the creature is believed to be a puma. There is a short lull in news, and then at the end of May, two schoolboys see an animal with an Alsatian's head. Even though the children were not convinced it was a dog, and even though they reported it had eyes like a lion, in early June the creature is suddenly also said to be a strange sort of dog by both marine commandos and the local police.

It might seem strange that even though the commandos at the beginning of May were hunting and even sighted a puma, they changed to believing that it was a dog by the middle of June. But there is a strange sort of predictability to the scenario, with each sighting following the last. The idea that the animal was a dog must have been gratefully received by those embarrassed by their long unfruitful search for the animal as this species-change gives them an excuse not to have found it. The fact that the police ask people to keep a special look out for this dog suggests that they believe it may even be passing as a household pet, thus explaining why they have not yet caught it.

---

[35] See UK Press Online database: (http://www.ukpressonline.co.uk)

Other researchers have dismissed this change as a story concocted by marines and police so they could retire gracefully from the field. Perhaps a more convincing explanation is that this is the magic of folklore in action, each story changes under close observation and alters itself to suit the most popular theory. Looking at legends of the moorland beasts like this, surely it is possible that not every sighting needs to reflect a real animal. Perhaps this very mutable shape was the reason that the early accounts tell of 'Beasts' rather than Mystery Big Cats or ABCs (Anomalous Big Cats) as the creatures tend to be described by researchers today.

Scholars have long been unable to trace legends of the Beast of Dartmoor past the mid-twentieth century, but given the natural fluid state of the legend, and especially some of the early confusion between feline and canine beasts, it does not seem too outrageous an idea that today's Mystery Big Cats may find their origins in yesterday's legends of the Monster Dogs of Dartmoor.

After this introduction we will be leaving the modern Beast of Exmoor far behind, and immersing ourselves in legends of Monster Dogs. In the Conclusion though we will be able to return to the question of whether stories of Monster Dogs could have inspired modern stories of Mystery Cats and the reader is invited to answer for themselves whether such comparisons are justified as we progress.

Format of this Book

This book goes through all the main pieces of folklore about the Monster Dogs of Dartmoor which can be traced to prior to 1930. These make up a range from 1830-1929, with the publication of *The Hound of the Baskervilles* in 1901 as a special watershed moment for the genre. We will go backwards through time, looking at each legend in turn. Each one is introduced with a summary of any salient features about the author's life and intentions with their story. Following this the legends are set out with as much context as possible with a commentary alongside exploring the texts in greater detail. Finally a discussion explores the special significance of the account and compares it with its successors.

After analysing the hounds of Dartmoor the focus is expanded to the rest of Britain, and a range of British texts from the seventeenth back to the twelfth century are presented in turn. Each is examined in exactly the same manner as the Dartmoor texts from the first half of the book. The aim is to set out the evolution of the legend into the form or forms in which it appears in the nineteenth and twentieth centuries, and in the conclusion we will show the similarities and differences we find between the Beasts of Dartmoor today and the Monster Dogs of Britain earlier on.

Cultural meme theory suggests that our culture can be broken down into small units, which repeat themselves over and over again. According to this theory, sightings of the Beast of Dartmoor are self-perpetuating. Each sighting provides fodder for the next sighting, with only slow evolution over time.[36]

The legends of Monster Dogs in Britain grow steadily over time, and observing the evolution of these legends is much like looking at a family tree. All the family members of this tree share certain resemblances but it is also clear where certain features entered into

---

[36] See: Harpur, M. (2006), *Mystery Big Cats,* (Heart of Albion Press, Loughborough). Pp.194-5.

the tree, and where certain features were bred out of existence (see the stemma diagram on the next page). It is hoped that this approach will vindicate the idea that the monsters of Britain can be best approached from a folkloric point of view rather than a biological one – the Beast of Dartmoor can be more profitably chased through literature than across the moors.

27

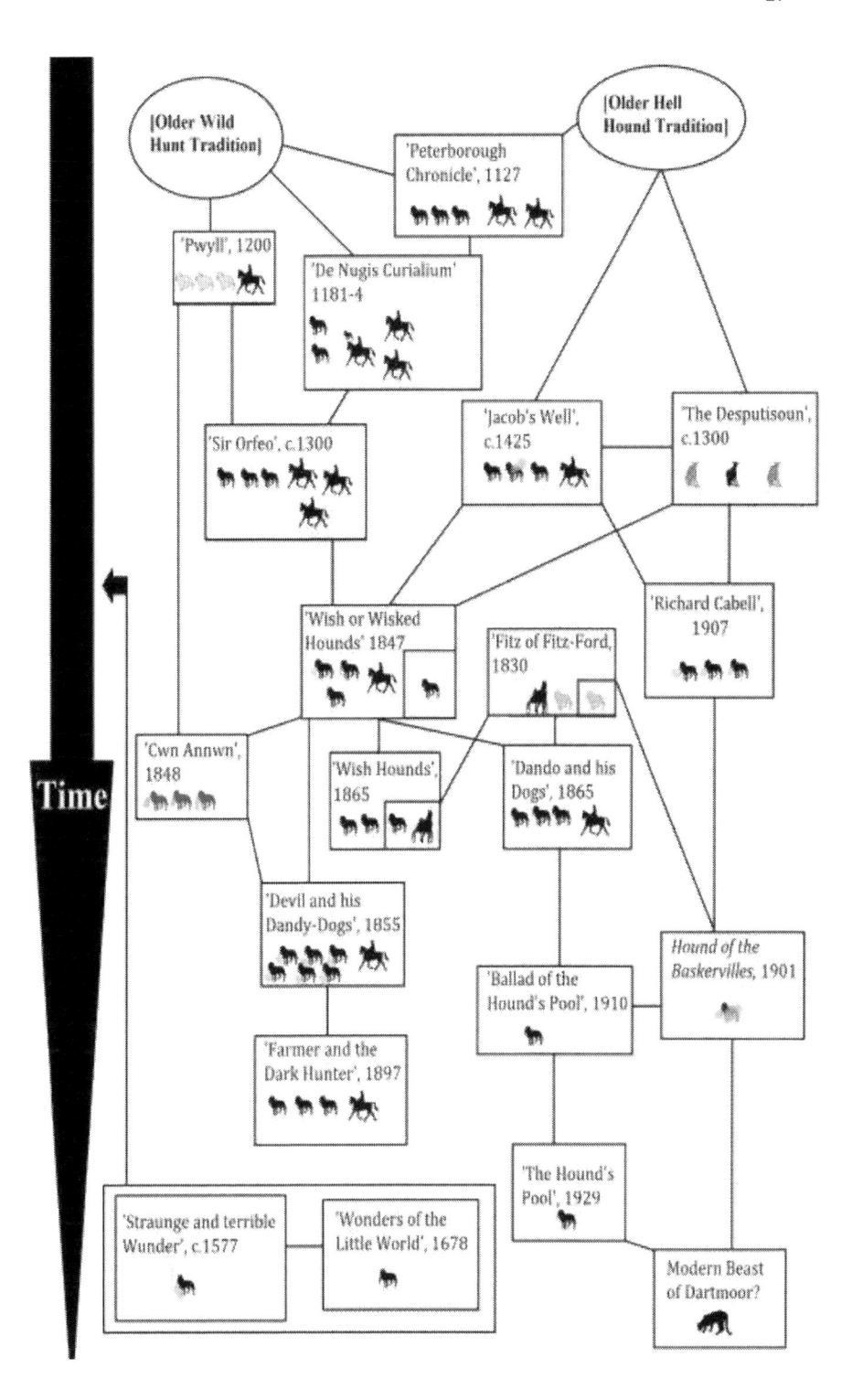

[Older Wild Hunt Tradition]

[Older Hell Hound Tradition]

'Peterborough Chronicle', 1127

'Pwyll', 1200

'De Nugis Curialium' 1181-4

'Sir Orfeo', c.1300

'Jacob's Well', c.1425

'The Desputisoun', c.1300

'Wish or Wisked Hounds' 1847

'Fitz of Fitz-Ford', 1830

'Richard Cabell', 1907

'Cwn Annwn', 1848

'Wish Hounds', 1865

'Dando and his Dogs', 1865

'Devil and his Dandy-Dogs', 1855

'Ballad of the Hound's Pool', 1910

Hound of the Baskervilles, 1901

'Farmer and the Dark Hunter', 1897

'Straunge and terrible Wunder', c.1577

'Wonders of the Little World', 1678

'The Hound's Pool', 1929

Modern Beast of Dartmoor?

Time

Beasts of Dartmoor 1929-1830

'The Hound's Pool', by Eden Phillpotts, 1929

Introduction

Eden Phillpotts was an author living in Devon at the beginning of the 20th century. He is sometimes called 'the Thomas Hardy of Devon' because most of his books are set in Devon, and even use South Western dialectal spelling and vocabulary in direct speech. The most famous of these are the historical romance 'Dartmoor Novels' of which there are eighteen. These give a nostalgic idea of life on rural Dartmoor of the not too distant past (perhaps the nineteenth century). Although Phillpotts was born in South Africa, his stories demonstrate a fair local knowledge of Devon in general and Dartmoor in particular. In 1920 Phillpotts wrote a guidebook to the region where he was one of the first to attest to the legend of 'Arthur as a chough' (almost all references before this refer to Arthur as a raven)[37]. At the least, it is clear that Phillpotts' books are based on a real knowledge of the area.

For our purposes it is Phillpotts' incursions into other genres which are the most interesting, but his enthusiasm for Devon and local area knowledge continues to be relevant in all of his stories. He wrote some science fiction, but also, more importantly, a large amount of horror. One of his short stories in the horror genre is about a ghostly hound sighted by a pool on Dartmoor by those foolish enough to go walking after dark. Considering Phillpotts description of this story as folklore, and his significant local knowledge, it can probably be regarded as a reliable, albeit romantic rendition of an authentic legend.

The story's main topic is an 'ancient tale' of a ghostly hound, and how that old legend affected the real lives of a group of young people who lived on the moor:

---

[37] See: Phillpotts, E. (1920*), A West Country Pilgrimage*, (Leonard Parsons, London). p.100; For Arthur as a chough see: Ramsay, L., 'Was Arthur once a Raven? The Legend of 'Arthur as a Chough" pp.19-27 in: *Old Cornwall, vol. xiv, no.7*, (2012)

Text and Commentary

1.

By day the place was inviting enough and a child wouldn't have feared to be there. Dean Burn came down from its cradle far away in the hills and threaded Dean Woods with ripple and flash and song. The beck lifted its voice in stickles and shouted over the mossy apron of many a little waterfall; and then under the dark of the woods it would go calm, nestle in a backwater here and there, then run on again. And of all fine spots on a sunny day the Hound's Pool was finest, for here Dean Burn had scooped a hole among the roots of forest trees and lay snug from the scythe of the east wind, so that the first white violet was always to be found upon the bank and the earliest primrose also. In winter time, when the boughs above were naked, the sun would glint upon the water; and sometimes all would be so still that you could hear a vole swimming; and then again, after a Dartmoor freshet, the stream would come down in spate, cherry-red, and roll big waters for such a little river. And then Hound's Pool would be like to rise over its banks and drown the woodman's path that ran beside it and throw up sedges and dead grasses upon the lowermost boughs of the overhanging thicket to show where it could reach sometimes.

'Twas haunted, and old folk--John Meadows among 'em--stoutly maintained that nothing short of Doomsday would lay the spectrum, because they knew the ancient tale of Weaver Knowles, and believed in it also; but the legend had gone out of fashion, as old stories will, and it came as a new and strange thing to the rising generation. 'Tis any odds the young men and maidens would never have believed in it; but by chance it happed to be a young man who revived the story, and as he'd seen with his own eyes, he couldn't doubt. William Parsloe he was, under-keeper at Dean, and he told what he'd seen to John Meadows, the head-keeper; but it weren't till he heard old John on the subject that he knew as he'd beheld something out of another world than his own.

The first section of the story introduces and situates the folklore. Dean Burn and Dean Woods (just south of King's Wood) are at the south east of Dartmoor, west of Buckfast and Buckfastleigh which is mentioned later on. The Hound's Pool is in the centre of the wood and can still be visited today.

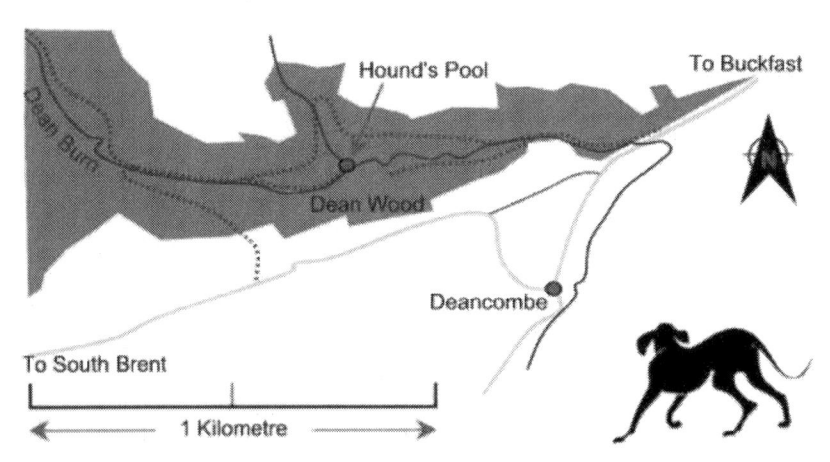

Map ©Tim Sandles, 2009, *LegendaryDartmoor.co.uk*, Used with permission.

The legend of Weaver Knowles is a famous one around Dartmoor[38], and I include a variant version in the Discussion. Phillpott's version differs only in a few minor details.

> 2.
>
> *The two men met where a right of way ran through the preserves--a sore trial to the keepers and the owners also, but sacred under the law--and Harry Wade, the returned native, as had just come back to his birthplace, was walking along with Parsloe at the time.*
>
> *The keepers were a good bit fretted and on their mettle just then, because there was a lot of poaching afoot and*

---

[38] For more information and a modern version of the legend, see: Sandles, T. 'The Deancombe Weaver' (http://www.legendarydartmoor.co.uk/old_weaver_of_deancombe.htm), (2009)

> pheasants going, and a dead bird or two picked up, as had escaped the malefactors, but died after and been found. So when Parsloe stopped Mr. Meadows and said as he'd got something to report, the old man hoped he might have a line to help against the enemy. One or two law-abiding men, Wade among 'em, had been aiding the keepers by night, and the police had also lent a hand; but as yet nobody was laid by the heels, nor even suspected. So it looked like stranger men from down Plymouth way; and the subject was getting on John Meadows' nerves, because his master, a great sportsman who poured out a lot of money on his pheasants, didn't like it and was grumbling a good bit.

The second section contains a very important detail which is easy to overlook the first time you read the story. 'there was a lot of poaching afoot and pheasants going... but as yet nobody was laid by the heels'. The position of this detail, situated right before the introduction of the hound might suggest that at the time, as now, the presence of Darmoor's Beast was often imagined to be indicated by the loss of livestock, although nowadays it is sheep rather than pheasants which are the key. At the end of the story it is revealed that the poacher is actually one of the main characters, but before this is revealed the reader might well assume that the hound was responsible.

The idea of a physical hound, able to take livestock does not fit in with earlier impressions of the Phantom Dog of Dartmoor as a ghostly creature, but it does fit in well with later impressions of the Beast as some large exotic predator which might even be captured. Perhaps it was an innovation of the time.

> 3.
>
> Then William Parsloe told his tale:
>
> 'I was along the Woodman's Path last night working up to the covers,' he said, 'and beside Hound's Pool I fell in with a hugeous great dog. 'Twas a moony night and I couldn't be mistook. 'Twas no common dog I knowed, but black as sin and near so large as a calf. He didn't make no noise, but come like a blot of ink down to the pool and put his nose down to drink, and in another moment I'd

have shot the creature, but he scented me, and then he saw me, as I made to lift my gun, and was off like a streak of lightning.'

John Meadows stared and then he showed a good bit of satisfaction.

'Ah!' he said. 'I'm glad as it is one of the younger people seed it, and not me, or some other old man; because now 'twill be believed. Hound's Pool, you say?'

Parsloe nodded and Harry Wade asked a question. He was a tall, handsome chap tanned by the foreign sun where he'd lived and worked too.

'What of it, master?' he said.

[...]

The third section finally comes to describe the beast in detail. It is a pure-black unnaturally large dog, and strangely moves soundlessly and as fast as lightning. The imposing physicality of the creature's uncanny size, shape, speed and cautiousness are all also reminiscent of modern descriptions of the creature rather than of a disappearing ghost. The dog's drinking from the pool will become more significant when we look at alternate versions later.

At the end of extract four I have omitted a small part of the text for the sake of clarity and brevity.

4.

'For my part, knowing all I know, I never feared the Hound's Pool,' he said, 'though a wisht place in the dimpsey and after dark as we know. But when a lad I drew many a sizeable trout out of it--afore your time, John, when it weren't poaching to fish there as it be now. Not that I ever see the Hound; but I've known them that have, and if I don't grasp the truth of the tale, who should, for my grandfather acksually knowed the son of old Weaver Knowles, and he heard it from the man's own lips, and I heard it from grandfather when he was eighty-nine year old and I was ten.'

'Then we shall have gospel truth for certain,' said Harry Wade, with his eyes on Millicent Meadows.

'Oh, yes,' answered Silas, 'because my grandfather could call home the taking of Canada and many such like far-off things, so that shows you the sort of memory he'd gotten. But nowadays the learning of the past be flouted a good bit and what our fathers have told us don't carry no weight at all. Holy spells and ghostesses and--'

'You get on to Hound Pool, Silas,' said John Meadows, 'because Parsloe will have to go to his work in ten minutes.'

'The solemn truth be easily told,' declared Mr. Belchamber. 'Back along in dim history there was a weaver by name of Knowles who lived to Dean Combe. Him and his son did very well together and he was a widower with no care but for his work. Old Weaver, he stuck to his yarn and was a silent and lonely fashion of man by all accounts. Work was his god, and 'twas said he sat at his loom eighteen hours out of every twenty-four. Then, coming home one evening, the man's son heard the loom was still and went in and found old Knowles fallen forward on the top of his work, dead. So they buried him at Buckfastleigh.

'Then young Knowles, coming home to his empty house after the funeral, suddenly heard the music of the loom and thought his ears had played him false. But the loom hummed on and he crept up over to see who was weaving. In a pretty good rage he was, no doubt, to think of such a thing; but then his blood turned from hot to cold very quick, I warn 'e, for there was his father sitting on the old seat and working weft through warp as suent and clever as if he was alive!

'Well, young Knowles he glared upon his dead parent and felt the hair rising on his niddick and the sweat running down his face; but he kept his nerve pretty clever and crept away and ran for all his might to the village and went to see Parson. They believed more in those days than what they do now, and Parson, whatever he may have thought, knew young Knowles for a truth-teller and obeyed his petition to come at once. But the good man *stopped in the churchyard and gathered up a handful of sacred ground; and then he went along to the dead weaver's house.*

'Sure enough the loom was a-working busy as ever; but it couldn't drown Parson's voice, for he preached from one of they old three-decker pulpits, like a ship o' war, and his noise, when the holy man was in full blast, would rise over a thunderstorm.

"Knowles! Knowles!' he cried out; 'Come down this instant. This is no place for you!'

'And then, hollow as the wind in a winter hedge, the ghost made answer.

"I will obey so soon as I have worked out my quill, your reverence,' replied the spirit of Weaver Knowles, and Parson didn't raise no objection to that, but bade the dead man's son kneel down; and he done so; and the priest also knelt and lifted his voice in prayer for five minutes.

'Then the loom stopped and old Knowles came forth and glided downstairs; and not a step creaked under him, for young Knowles specially noted that wonder when he told my grandfather the adventure.

'At sight of Old Weaver, Parson took his churchyard dust and boldly threw it in the face of the vision, and afore you could cross your heart the shadow had turned into a gert black dog--so dark as night. The poor beast whimpered and yowled something cruel, but Parson was short and stern with it, well knowing you can't have half measures with spirits, no more than you can with living men if you will to conquer 'em. So he takes a high line with the weaver, as one to be obeyed.

"Follow me, Knowles,' he said to the creature. 'Follow me in the name of the Father, Son, and Ghost'; which the forlorn dog did do willy-nilly; and he led it down the Burn, to Hound's Pool, and there bade it halt. Then the man of God took a nutshell--just a filbert with a hole in it bored by a squirrel--and he gave it boldly into the dog's mouth.

"Henceforth,' he said, 'you shall labour here to empty the pool, using nought but this nutshell to do so; and when *you have done your work, but no sooner, then you shall go back whence you came.'*

'And the Hound will be on the job till the end of the world afore he gets peace, no doubt, and them with ears to hear, may oft listen to a sound in the water like the rattling of a loom to this day; but 'tis no more than that poor Devil-dog of a Knowles at his endless task.'

Millicent poured the old man another cup of tea and Parsloe went to work and Wade applauded the tale-teller.

'A very fine yarn, uncle,' he said, 'and I'm glad to know the rights of it; and if the Hound brings luck, I hope I'll see him.'

'More would see him if faith was there,' answered old Belchamber. 'But where do you find faith in these days? For all I can see the childer taught in school don't believe in nothing on earth but themselves. In fact, you may say a bald head be a figure of scorn to 'em, same as it was in the prophet's time.'

[...]

As I said there are various discrepancies between this version and others you might hear, but they are all small. The most important of these is that Phillpotts makes it clear that seeing the hound is good luck. This is not indicated by any other version of the story, and it might represent an embellishment of Phillpotts'. More minor variations concern the reaction of Knowles' son to hearing the sound. Here he is angry (presumably) that anyone would dare to take up his father's loom, whereas in most other versions of the story he immediately knew it was a ghost and was afraid. The parson also uses graveyard dirt to affect Knowles rather than a Holy Rood (cross) or any other fixtures of the priest's trade.

I have left a larger gap at the end of this section as the story is quite long in full, so we now skip forwards in the story to a little later when an old lady of the area is sick:

5.

Mrs. Meadows was a lot worse when they came home and they got her to bed and put a hot brick in flannel to her feet; but she'd had the like attacks before and John weren't feared for her till the dead of night; and then she went off her head and he touched her and found she was living fire. So he had to call up his girl and explain that, for all he could tell, death might be knocking at the door.

Such things we say, little knowing we be prophets; but in truth a fearful peril threatened the Meadows folk that night, though 'twas Millicent and not her mother was like to be in highest danger.

"Tis doctor,' said John, 'and I can't leave her, for she may die in my arms, so you must go; and best to run as never you run before. Go straight through Dean Wood and don't draw breath till you've got to the man.'

She was up and 'rayed in less than no time and away quick-footed through the forest; and so swift had been her actions that she hoped to cheat her own fear of the darkness and get through Dean Woods afore she had time to quail. But you can't hoodwink Nature that way, and not long afore the trees had swallowed her up Millicent felt nameless dread pulling at her heart and all her senses tingling with terror. She kept her mind on her mother, however, and sped on with her face set before her, though a thousand instincts cried to her to look behind for the nameless things that might be following after.

'Twas a frosty night with a winter moon high in the sky, and Millicent, who knew the Woodman's Path blindfold, much wished it had been darker, for the moonlight was strong enough to show queer faces in every tree-hole and turn the shadows from the trees into monsters upon her path at every yard. She prayed as she went along.

'My duty--my duty,' she said. 'God help me to do my duty and save mother!'

Then she knew she was coming close to the Hound's Pool and hesitated for fear, and wondered if she might track into the woods and escape the ordeal. But that wasn't possible without a lot of time wasted, and so she lifted up another petition to her Maker and went on. She'd travelled a mile by now and there was another mile to go. And then she came alongside the Pool and held her hands to her breast and kept her eyes away from the water, where it spread death-still with the moon looking up very peaceful out of it. But a moment later and poor Millicent got the fearfullest shock of her life, for right ahead, suddenly without a sound of warning, stark and huge with the moonlight on his great open mouth, appeared the Hound. From nowhere he'd come, but there he stood within ten yards of her, barring the way. And she heard him growl and saw him come forward to meet her.

One scream she gave, though not so loud as a screech owl, and then she tottered, swayed, and lost her senses. If she'd fallen to the left no harm had overtook her; but to the right she fell and dropped unconscious, face forward into Dean Burn.

The waters ran shallow there, above the Pool, yet, shallow or deep, she dropped with her head under the river and knew it not.

The fifth extract describes Millicent's own meeting with the hound. Interestingly it is revealed later that both this sighting, and William Parsloe's earlier one was not of a ghost, but a real dog, owned by a smuggler. This is so interesting because it suggests a tendency to rationalise the Hound into a creature of flesh and blood already in force during the 1920s. Nowadays very few enthusiasts indeed would be happy with what I called 'explanation iv' in the introduction, that is, the idea that the Beasts of Britain do not have a physical existence. Indeed this story treats the idea of the Monster Dog of Dartmoor being a ghost as unbelievable, since every modern sighting of the creature is explained. Phillpotts perfectly captures the tension between the scepticism of the young and the belief of the old. In 'The Hound's Pool' this tension actually becomes the difference between semi-modern ideas of a Beast of Dartmoor, and older ideas of a ghostly Hound.

6.

Many a day passed afore the mystery of her escape from death got to Millicent's ears; but for the moment all she could mind was that presently her senses returned to her and she found herself with her back against a tree and her face and bosom wet with water. Slowly her wits worked and she looked around, but found herself a hundred yards away from the Pool. Then she called home what had befallen her and rose to her feet; and presently her blood flowed again and she felt she was safe and the peril over-got. 'Twas clear the Hound had done her no hurt and she felt only puzzled to know why for she was so wet and why, when she went fainty beside the Pool, she'd come to again a hundred yards away from it. But that great mystery she put by for another time and thanked God for saving her and cleared the woods and sped to doctor with her bad news.

And he rose up and let her in and, hearing the case was grave, soon prepared to start. And while he dressed, Millicent made shift to dry herself by the heat of a dying fire. Then he put his horse in the trap and very quick they drove away up to the gamekeeper's house. But no word of her amazing adventure did the woman let drop in doctor's ear; and the strange thing was that peace had come upon her now and fear was departed from her heart.

Milly Meadows had got the influenza very bad and, guessing what he'd find, the physician had brought his cautcheries along with him, so he ministered a soothing drug and directed her treatment and spoke hopeful words about it. He was up again next day and found all going very orderly, and foretold that, if the mischief could be kept out of Milly's lungs, she'd recover in due course. So the mind of her husband and her daughter grew at peace when Milly's body cooled down; and then the girl told her father of what had befell her by Hound's Pool, and he was terrible interested and full of wonder.

Section six does not tell us anything new about the hound, but is worth including for the sake of completion.

7.

In fact, naught would do but they went there together the morning after, and there--in the chill light of a January day, Millicent pointed out where she stood when the vision come to her and presently the very tree under which she had returned to life.

But John, being skilled in all woodland craft, took a pretty close look round and soon smelled out signs and wonders hid from common sight. He'd been much pleased with the tale at first, for though sorrowful that his girl had suffered so much, he hadn't got enough mind himself to measure the agony she'd been through; and, whether or no, since the Hound brought good luck, he counted on some bright outcome for Millicent presently, if it was only that her mother should be saved alive. But when he got to his woodcraft, John Meadows weren't so pleased by any means, because he found another story told. Where the girl had fainted and dropped in the water on seeing the Hound was clear to mark; but more than that John discovered, for all round about was the slot of a big dog with a great pad and claws; and, as if that weren't enough, the keeper found something else also.

He stared then and stood back and scratched the hair on his nape.

'Beggar my shoes!' said John. 'This weren't no Devil-dog, but a living creature! The Hound be a spirit and don't leave no mark where he runs; but the dog that made these tracks weighs a hundred and fifty pound if he weighs an ounce; and look you here. What be this?'

Well, Millicent looked and there weren't no shadow of doubt as to what her father had found, for pressed in the mire and gravel at river edge was the prints of a tidy large boot.

William Parsloe came along at the moment; but he knew nought, though he put two and two together very clever.

"Tis like this,' he said; 'you ran into the poachers, Millicent, though what the blackguards was up to with a hugeous dog I couldn't tell you. And now I'll lay my life that what I saw back along was the same creature and he whipped away and warned his masters.'

'But me?' asked the girl. 'Why for if I fainted and fell into the river, didn't I drown there for you or father to find next day?'

'Yes,' added John. 'How came that to be, Bill?'

'I see it so clear as need be,' explained Parsloe, who had a quick mind. 'You fell in the water and the dog gave tongue. The blackguards came along and, not wishful to add murder to their crimes, haled you out. Then they carried you away from the water, loosened your neckerchief and finding you alive, left you to recover.'

'Dear God!' said Millicent, shivering all down her spine, 'd'you mean to tell me an unknown poaching man carried me in his arms a hundred yards, William?'

'I mean that,' answered Parsloe, 'and if we had the chap's boot, we should know who 'twas.'

So they parted, and John he went home very angry indeed at such triumphant malefactors, and though Millicent tried her bestest to be angry also, such is the weakness of human nature that she couldn't work up no great flood of rage. And when she was alone in her bed that night, for it was her father's turn to watch over her mother, she felt that unknown sinner's arms around her again and his wicked hands at her neckerchief, and couldn't help wondering what it would have been like if she'd come to and found herself in that awful position.

[...]

Section seven, apart from the frankly amusing idea of someone finding it offensive and risqué that anyone dared to pick them up and save them from drowning, seems to convey a mixture of old and new folklore.

Most obviously, the idea that the hound brings good luck is again repeated, and as I have said, that seems to be a modern innovation on the legend. However, after this we find the characters knowing 'this weren't no Devil dog' by the fact that it left footprints. This is very definitely a throwback to the more classical idea of a phantom dog, but it also contradicts some other elements of the story which given the beast a more physical form. I shall discuss this in more detail after the text is finished.

At the end of the text I have again omitted some more, this time mainly love scenes between the two main characters.

> 8.
>
> Not for a week, however, till he felt safe in his promised state, did Harry ever open out his dark secrets to her; but then, for her ears only, out it came.
>
> 'You mind that fatal night?' he asked; and they were beside the Pool again, for she loved it now, because 'twas there he begged her to marry him.
>
> 'Ess fay and I do, but I don't hate the Pool no more--not after you told me you loved me there,' said Millicent.
>
> "Twas I that saved you,' he confessed. 'At a loose end and for a bit of a lark--just sport, you understand, not wickedness--I done a bit of poaching and picked off a good few birds, I fear.'
>
> She looked at him round-eyed.
>
> 'You wretch!' she cried; but his arms were close about her, and she was powerless.
>
> 'Oh, yes. And my great dog it was as I kept hid on a chain by day. And when he frightened you into the water that night, I was behind him and had you out again and in my arms in half a second. And then I carried you away from the river, and when I held you in my arms I knew you'd be my wife or nobody would.'
>
> 'Thank the watching Lord 'twas you!' she gasped.
>
> 'I waited till I see you come to and knew you'd be all right then; but I followed you, to see what you was up to, and didn't go home till I saw you drive away with the doctor. My dog was my joy till that night--a great mongrel I picked up when I was to Plymouth and kept close of a day. Clever as Satan at finding fallen birds in the dark, though unfortunately he didn't find 'em all. But after the

happenings I took him back to Plymouth again on the quiet, and he won't frighten nobody no more.'

Then 'twas her turn and she dressed him down properly and gave him all the law and the prophets, and made him promise on his oath that he'd never do no more crimes, or kill fur or feather that didn't belong by rights to him.

And he swore and kept his oath most steadfast.

'I've catched the finest creature as ever harboured in Dean Woods,' he said, 'and her word be my law for evermore.'

But nobody else heard the truth that Wade was the unknown sinner, for Millicent felt as her father would have been cruel vexed about it.

They was wed in the summer and Wade found open-air work to his taste not a mile from their home. But often, good lovers still, they'll go to Hound's Pool for memory's sake and sit and hear Weaver Knowles working unseen about his task.[39]

Section eight finishes off the text and is very much reminiscent of the *Hound of the Baskervilles* beast in its details. If the reader can get past the very outdated romance, there are some features of considerable interest. The hound which everyone has seen is dismissed as a fake, purchased from far off Plymouth (just outside of Dartmoor). The missing pheasants are also explained as having been taken by Harry, even though at the beginning of the text, as I have said, the story suggests that the hound might have been responsible.

Discussion

For our purposes, Phillpotts' most impressive achievement with 'The Hound's Pool' is her reconciliation of the classical folklore of a phantom hand to a more modern, scientific worldview where a

---

[39] Phillpotts, E. (1929.), *The Torch and Other Tales*, (Macmillan Co., New York). pp.126-140. Available for free from Project Gutenberg: (http://www.gutenberg.org/ebooks/15737).

phantom hound must be explained as either a physical being or a trick. At the start of the story we believe that somebody has seen a ghostly hound, which makes the older characters very happy to have some evidence for their folklore at last. However as the story unfolds we find there were actually two hounds being described from the start.

The dog described by the folklore is a large, black, perhaps silent phantom figure. It brings luck to those who see it, and is the ghost of a weaver called Knowles who is attempting to empty out Hound's Pool with a thimble. A slightly older version of the folklore was the subject of a poem in 1910 by Charles John Perry-Keene:

> **The Ballad of the Hound's Pool**
> *Deep in the churchyard Knowles was laid-*
> *The Weaver of Dean Coombe;*
> *But short time that weaver stayed*
> *Within the silent tomb!*
>
> *None ever looked old Knowles to see*
> *Until the crack of doom;*
> *But there is Astral body he*
> *Sat working at his loom!*
>
> *The wondering neighbours roundly swear*
> *That through the livelong night*
> *His wheel and shuttle they can hear --*
> *For no ghost needs a light!*
>
> *And as beneath his narrow stair*
> *They terror-stricken stood,*
> *All horrid rose each listener's hair*
> *All curdled grew his blood!*
>
> *Then up there spake old Abraham Steer.*
> *Says he, 'My lads, 'tis plain*
> *We'd best get our old Parson here*
> *To lay old Knowles again.'*
>
> *They hurried off to Dean Church Town.*
> *'Oh, Parson dear, come quick --*
> *Old Knowles you buried won't stay down;*
> *He's back--or else old Nick!'*

The Parson fetched the Holy Rood,
And calmly to them said,
'With this I fear not flesh and blood,
With this I'll face the dead.'

Then slow and stately up the hill
Aloft the cross he bore,
First of that dumb procession, till
He stopped at Knowles's door.

Then loud he cried, 'Thou miser soul,
Who mad'st this earth thy home,
With sordid riches for they goal,
Come down! I bid thee come!'

'No marvel that thou can'st not sleep,
Though laid in holy ground;
But back to thy poor lodge dost creep,
Where all thy heaven is found.'

Then straightly that lean ghost came down,
As pale as pale could be;
The Parson with his sternest frown
Said, 'Knowles, you follow me?'

All up the stream did Parson lead,
All up between the wood,
Past Clitters and past Biddy Mead,
Till at the pool he stood.

There, 'mid the roar of waters white
Which echoing rocks resound,
He turned old Knowles' trembling sprite
Into a coal-black hound.

'Thou who did'st toil for earthly dross,
I give thee toil,' he said,
'That thou may'st learn how great thy loss,
Though earthly toil has sped.'

'Take thou this nutshell, bale the pool,

*And when thy task is o'er,
A human form shall veil thy soul
And thou have peace once more.'*

*Should you my reader, fondly ask
If this old tale be true--
Go list the hound still at his task;
I'll show the pool to you!*

*And if you're not devoid of sense,
And keep an open mind,
Here's circumstantial evidence
Of most convincing kind.*

*For here's the pool! and here's the wood!
And here's old Knowles' door!
And here's the place where Parson stood! -
What can a man have more?*[40]

This poem has been mistakenly attributed to Robert Herrick, an English poet of the early seventeenth century. If true this would make the poem one of the very earliest references to any Dartmoor legend, and definitely the definitive version of the legend of Weaver Knowles, who only died in the mid sixteenth century. However the attribution is almost certainly false. Robert Herrick has been extensively researched but I cannot find any reference to this poem in any of the three definitive versions of the *Collected Works of Robert Herrick* which have since been written. Perry-Keene first publishes this poem in his 1910 book without attribution, and I suspect the poem is original to him. Its language too is far more strongly indicative of the early twentieth century than the seventeenth.

However at the same time, the folklore behind the poem is not original to Perry-Keene. We will find it referenced again more than 60 years earlier in an Athenaeum essay of 1847.

Returning to Phillpotts' version of the story, by the ending we know this creature has never been seen by anyone in the story, and the very

---

[40] Perry-Keen, C.J. (1910*), Songs of the Dean Bourn*, (Bowering and CO., Plymouth)

defensiveness of the older characters about it suggests to the reader that it is probably fictional. This suggests a scepticism about the folklore which we do not find in older versions of the story.

The idea of commanding or challenging a supernatural entity to do an impossible task like empty the sea or build a bridge across the sea made of sand is a very common one in folklore, and we will see it again in the Legend of Lady Howard. In neighbouring Cornwall a legend of a giant called Bolster was killed by a challenge from St. Agnes to fill a bottomless pit with his blood. The early origin of this legend may be in a piece of Norse mythology which is attested from the fourteenth century in the 'Younger Edda', although the stories are almost certainly older. The legend of 'Thor and Loki in Jotunheim' sees Thor being challenged to drink to empty a horn of liquid. He fails to do so, much to his own amazement, but it is later revealed that this horn had its tip in the ocean, and although Thor failed to empty it he did significantly lower its level.

Contrary to the ghost of the Hound of Dean Coombe, the hound seen by young people is supernaturally large, pure black, fast as lightning and has a strong physical presence. It is first seen drinking from Hound's Pool. Although it is fake, not the real ghostly hound it is the only one of the two which actually physically exists.

The reason this is so interesting is because the phantom hound described by old Silas and John Meadows seems very reminiscent of the older Hounds which we find in earlier folklore, and especially that of Lady Howard in *Fitz of Fitz-Ford*. However, the modern hound is also reminiscent, this time of more modern folklore. The idea that the hound is a very large smuggler's dog might almost be one accepted by modern beast researchers[41], although the modern folklore is now very much more tied up with stories of escaped big cats.

---

[41] Trevor Beer advocates a similar theory in his 1984 book: *The Beast of Exmoor Fact or Legend?* (Countryside Productions, Barnstaple). pp.38-9.

'Richard Cabell of Brooke', by Sabine Baring-Gould, 1907

Introduction

Sabine Baring-Gould (1834-1924) was a popular folklorist, antiquarian and song-writer at the beginning of the twentieth century, and he remains respected today. By trade he was a clergyman, but he was a prolific author and wrote hymns, including most famously 'Onward Christian Soldiers' folklore accounts and popular novels which he sold to raise money for local causes. He tended to learn languages easily, and he started the still highly respected Lives of the Saints which translates from Latin the biographies of 3600 saints.

He lived most of his life in Horbury Brig, Yorkshire where he was curate and involved in a mission to help the local area. However in 1872 he inherited his family's Devon estate, and in 1881 moved into Lew House or Lewtrenchard Manor to be the local parson. Since this was his family estate he had close ties to the area, and personally oversaw the restoration of house and church there[42].

Despite his achievements as a folklorist, it was only in his years as local squire and parson that he wrote much about Devon folklore. His version of the Beast of Dartmoor tradition is very short, and was written only as a marginal point of curiosity in his Little Guide to Devonshire. There, under the section on Buckfastleigh we find the following text written about the Holy Trinity Church:

Text and Commentary

> There are two features of interest in the churchyard. Outside the S. porch is the enclosed tomb of Richard

---

[42] Colloms, B. 'Gould, Sabine Baring-, Church of England clergyman, author, and folksong collector' in: *The Oxford Dictionary of National Biography*, (2004, online ed. 2005) (http://www.oxforddnb.com/view/article/30587)

> *Cabell of Brooke, who died in 1677. He was the last male of his line, and died with such an evil reputation that he was placed under a heavy stone, and a sort of penthouse was built over that with iron gratings to it to prevent his coming up and haunting the neighbourhood. When he died (the story goes), fiends and black dogs breathing fire raced over Dartmoor and surrounded Brooke, howling.*[43]

Although this legend is the shortest that we will examine, it does contain a fair amount of information about the beasts themselves. We have a whole pack of 'black dogs breathing fire', together with fiends (presumably demons from Hell).

This is obviously very different from the image of the single hound which brings good luck in 'The Hound's Pool'. We will discuss the differences in more detail later, but part of the change is to do with the age of the text. By 1927 monster-dogs seem to have lost their power to terrify, but in 1907 the danger was still very real.

Later versions of the legend interpret the hounds' intention as seeking to take Cabell's soul to Hell. Although that is not clear in Baring-Gould's version of the legend, it would be very compatible with the combination of black dogs and fiends present, and especially with Richard Cabel having such 'an evil reputation'. It would also give the hounds the attribute of 'hunters of the dead'. This attribute is also seen in texts like the short story 'Cwn Annwn' (The Hounds of Annwn) from 1848 and in a folklore article in *the Athenaeum* magazine from 1847, but it not seen otherwise after the mid-nineteenth century.

Discussion

The 1907 version of the Cabell legend, although very short does give a good, traditional version of the hounds. They are black and howling and breathe fire, which agrees well with many contemporary accounts.

---

[43] Baring-Gould, S. (1907), *The Little Guide to Devonshire,* (Methuen &Co. Ltd., London. Tenth Edition, 'revised edition' by Hicks, R.H., 1941). p.86.

The number of hounds present is probably a clue to the age of the folklore. As I have said, the folklore about Cabell is attested from 1847 onwards, but the majority of hound legends in particular and beast legends in general from Dartmoor after 1901 have single rather than plural hounds. This suggests that the folklore belongs more to the nineteenth century than it does to the twentieth, even though Baring-Gould published it in 1907.

Modern folklorists often argue that stories of the Wild Hunt or packs of Hell Hounds are entirely different to stories of the individual black hounds. That is true in the modern period where they are entirely different folkloric phenomena, and it was also true around the turn on the twentieth century, c.1900. Stories like this one of Richard Cabell have a lot more in common with other multiple hound stories like those of the Wish Hounds and the Dandy Dogs than they do to stories like the 'Hound's Pool' which we have already seen. The reason I have included both types of story in this book is first to note the comparative popularity of the two types of story at various points in history and also to point out that the two types of story appear to stem from a single tradition, which we shall see when we have gone back a few more centuries.

The turn of the twentieth century saw some big changes for South Western hound folklore, thanks partially to the influence of Arthur Conan Doyle which we will read more about in the next chapter. Ultimately though, we can probably take 1907, the year that Baring Gould's *Guidebook* was published, as the watershed moment for the three biggest changes in the folklore of the hounds: (i) After 1907, the idea of the hound being ghostly is ridiculed, and no-one is ready to right a story about such a creature. (ii) The majority of the legends which are invented or adapted about Monster Dogs after this point use single hounds like in *The Hound of the Baskervilles* before it, (iii) 1907 is the last year when the idea of the hound being otherworldly at all is accepted.

The Hound of the Baskervilles, by Arthur Conan Doyle, 1901

Introduction

The Hound of the Baskervilles is probably the best known Dartmoor tale ever written, and is perhaps one of the only stories set in Dartmoor well known to those living outside of the area. Its author, Arthur Conan Doyle, is best known for creating the fictional detective Sherlock Holmes, and *The Hound of the Baskervilles* stands out as one of the few stories starring Holmes which is full novel rather than a short story.

Sir Arthur Conan Doyle was a very different person to Eden Phillpotts and their stories reflect this. Conan Doyle spent most of his childhood in Scotland, and although he visited the area to give his story a definite setting and knew the landscape well enough to describe it vividly, the moors remained a highly romantic area to him. Conan Doyle's Dartmoor is wreathed in mist and covered in 'mires' (surely more romantic than 'bogs') which swallow up people instantly. The area is covered in craggy tors with rare plants and butterflies whilst dangerous escaped prisoners make their home in the trackless wilderness with huge hounds. A five mile radius of moorland contains only four educated gentlemen and ladies of note, whilst all the other humans around are superstitious locals and servants. Early on in the story, Sherlock Holmes himself rejects the idea that anything supernatural is occurring. However, the narrator of the story, John Watson, is not nearly so rational and the romantic arena of the action eventually convinces most of the characters that the idea of a family cursed to be haunted by a phantom hound is not too incredible.

Undoubtedly some of these ideas are justifiable, whilst others just reflect the classist notions of the time, but all of the notions together reflect the author's opinions and biases about the countryside. Conan Doyle certainly does not have the informed knowledge of the area that Eden Phillpotts does. Not too long after writing *Hound of the Baskervilles* Conan Doyle became a keen Spiritualist (a person who communes with the dead through mediums and séances), and the author's romanticism sets him apart from Eden Phillpotts. But at the same time, as we shall see there are also very definite similarities between the two stories.

Text and Commentary

1.

I looked over his shoulder at the yellow paper and the faded script. At the head was written: 'Baskerville Hall,' and below in large, scrawling figures: '1742.'

'It appears to be a statement of some sort.'

'Yes, it is a statement of a certain legend which runs in the Baskerville family.'

'But I understand that it is something more modern and practical upon which you wish to consult me?'

'Most modern. A most practical, pressing matter, which must be decided within twenty-four hours. But the manuscript is short and is intimately connected with the affair. With your permission I will read it to you.

' Holmes leaned back in his chair, placed his finger-tips together, and closed his eyes, with an air of resignation. Dr. Mortimer turned the manuscript to the light and read in a high, cracking voice the following curious, old-world narrative:

'Of the origin of the Hound of the Baskervilles there have been many statements, yet as I come in a direct line from Hugo Baskerville, and as I had the story from my father, who also had it from his, I have set it down with all belief that it occurred even as is here set forth. And I would have you believe, my sons, that the same Justice which punishes sin may also most graciously forgive it, and that no ban is so heavy but that by prayer and repentance it may be removed. Learn then from this story not to fear the fruits of the past, but rather to be circumspect in the future, that those foul passions whereby our family has

suffered so grievously may not again be loosed to our undoing.

'Know then that in the time of the Great Rebellion (the history of which by the learned Lord Clarendon I most earnestly commend to your attention) this Manor of Baskerville was held by Hugo of that name, nor can it be gainsaid that he was a most wild, profane, and godless man. This, in truth, his neighbours might have pardoned, seeing that saints have never flourished in those parts, but there was in him a certain wanton and cruel humour which made his name a by-word through the West. It chanced that this Hugo came to love (if, indeed, so dark a passion may be known under so bright a name) the daughter of a yeoman who held lands near the Baskerville estate. But the young maiden, being discreet and of good repute, would ever avoid him, for she feared his evil name. So it came to pass that one Michaelmas this Hugo, with five or six of his idle and wicked companions, stole down upon the farm and carried off the maiden, her father and brothers being from home, as he well knew. When they had brought her to the Hall the maiden was placed in an upper chamber, while Hugo and his friends sat down to a long carouse, as was their nightly custom. Now, the poor lass upstairs was like to have her wits turned at the singing and shouting and terrible oaths which came up to her from below, for they say that the words used by Hugo Baskerville, when he was in wine, were such as might blast the man who said them. At last in the stress of her fear she did that which might have daunted the bravest or most active man, for by the aid of the growth of ivy which covered (and still covers) the south wall she came down from under the eaves, and so homeward across the moor, there being three leagues betwixt the Hall and her father's farm.

'It chanced that some little time later Hugo left his guests to carry food and drink—with other worse things, perchance—to his captive, and so found the cage empty and the bird escaped. Then, as it would seem, he became as one that hath a Devil, for, rushing down the stairs into the dining-hall, he sprang upon the great table, flagons and trenchers flying before him, and he cried aloud before

all the company that he would that very night render his body and soul to the Powers of Evil if he might but overtake the wench. And while the revellers stood aghast at the fury of the man, one more wicked or, it may be, more drunken than the rest, cried out that they should put the hounds upon her. Whereat Hugo ran from the house, crying to his grooms that they should saddle his mare and unkennel the pack, and giving the hounds a kerchief of the maid's, he swung them to the line, and so off full cry in the moonlight over the moor.

'*Now, for some space the revellers stood agape, unable to understand all that had been done in such haste. But anon their bemused wits awoke to the nature of the deed which was like to be done upon the moorlands. Everything was now in an uproar, some calling for their pistols, some for their horses, and some for another flask of wine. But at length some sense came back to their crazed minds, and the whole of them, thirteen in number, took horse and started in pursuit. The moon shone clear above them, and they rode swiftly abreast, taking that course which the maid must needs have taken if she were to reach her own home.*

'*They had gone a mile or two when they passed one of the night shepherds upon the moorlands, and they cried to him to know if he had seen the hunt. And the man, as the story goes, was so crazed with fear that he could scarce speak, but at last he said that he had indeed seen the unhappy maiden, with the hounds upon her track. 'But I have seen more than that,' said he, 'for Hugo Baskerville passed me upon his black mare, and there ran mute behind him such a hound of Hell as God forbid should ever be at my heels.' So the drunken squires cursed the shepherd and rode onward. But soon their skins turned cold, for there came a galloping across the moor, and the black mare, dabbled with white froth, went past with trailing bridle and empty saddle. Then the revellers rode close together, for a great fear was on them, but they still followed over the moor, though each, had he been alone, would have been right glad to have turned his horse's head. Riding slowly in this fashion they came at last upon the hounds. These, though known for their valour and their breed, were whimpering in a cluster at the head of a deep dip or goyal, as we call it, upon the moor, some slinking away and some, with starting hackles and staring eyes, gazing down the narrow valley before them.*

'The company had come to a halt, more sober men, as you may guess, than when they started. The most of them would by no means advance, but three of them, the boldest, or it may be the most drunken, rode forward down the goyal. Now, it opened into a broad space in which stood two of those great stones, still to be seen there, which were set by certain forgotten peoples in the days of old. The moon was shining bright upon the clearing, and there in the centre lay the unhappy maid where she had fallen, dead of fear and of fatigue. But it was not the sight of her body, nor yet was it that of the body of Hugo Baskerville lying near her, which raised the hair upon the heads of these three dare-Devil roysterers, but it was that, standing over Hugo, and plucking at his throat, there stood a foul thing, a great, black beast, shaped like a hound, yet larger than any hound that ever mortal eye has rested upon. And even as they looked the thing tore the throat out of Hugo Baskerville, on which, as it turned its blazing eyes and dripping jaws upon them, the three shrieked with fear and rode for dear life, still screaming, across the moor. One, it is said, died that very night of what he had seen, and the other twain were but broken men for the rest of their days.

'Such is the tale, my sons, of the coming of the hound which is said to have plagued the family so sorely ever since. If I have set it down it is because that which is clearly known hath less terror than that which is but hinted at and guessed. Nor can it be denied that many of the family have been unhappy in their deaths, which have been sudden, bloody, and mysterious. Yet may we shelter ourselves in the infinite goodness of Providence, which would not forever punish the innocent beyond that third or fourth generation which is threatened in Holy Writ. To that Providence, my sons, I hereby commend you, and I counsel you by way of caution to forbear from crossing the moor in those dark hours when the powers of evil are exalted.

> *'[This from Hugo Baskerville to his sons Rodger and John, with instructions that they say nothing thereof to their sister Elizabeth.]'*
>
> ...

Just like in Eden Phillpotts' short story, the first we hear of the Hound in Conan Doyle's novel is an old legend about the creature. Also just like in Phillpotts story we get the impression that we need not accept the old tale at face value. Before it is read, Holmes begins by questioning the importance of the legend at all, and although he then listens indulgently his attitude still has 'an air of resignation'.

The 'document' itself is written to confirm the reader's suspicion. It contains a number of archaic features intended to lend it an air of great age but also of out-of-fashion superstition. 'Justice' is capitalised as an embodiment of God and the idea of sins as something inherited is also stressed. The term 'my sons' is reminiscent of a Biblical or at least Christian setting. The next sentence starts with an outdated command 'Learn to...' and continues with outdated dramatic expressions like 'fruits of the past' when we would say 'past mistakes; 'that' instead of 'so that'; 'foul passions' for 'out of control tempers'; and 'loosed to our undoing' for 'make the same mistake again'.

But it is important to notice that throughout this document, the way that the description is given is more important that the description itself. Most of the archaic modes of expression and style, the romanticism and what we might today call 'melodrama' which I described earlier would have been just as obvious to readers in Conan Doyle's time as they are to us today. Before we even come to hear about the hound we are therefore highly sceptical about it. With the exception of 'the young maiden' who is not named, none of the characters in the story are described sympathetically or sensitively and therefore the reader is inclined to be disdainful of the people in the tale. The archaic sounding narrator seems to fully believe the events he describes which makes us suspect his gullibility. For readers of *The Hound of the Baskervilles*, this legend is another clue to the case, and the source of the legend is not trustworthy. Clearly for Arthur Conan Doyle, just like Eden Phillpotts the legend of the hound does not have a place in the modern world of rational explanations.

The hound's role in the 'document' is first foreshadowed when Hugo Baskerville promises his body and soul to the Devil if he can overtake his maiden. Later Hugo's pursuers are told by a watching shepherd that Hugo is being pursued by a Hell-hound, and the pack of hounds tracking him becomes too nervous to continue forwards. As a grand crescendo to the story the witnesses find the hound itself eating Hugo. The creature was 'a foul thing, a great, black beast, shaped like a hound, yet larger than any hound that ever mortal eye has rested upon' with 'blazing eyes and dripping jaws' and it drives the witnesses mad.

> 2.
>
> *The idea of some ghastly presence constantly haunted him, and on more than one occasion he has asked me whether I had on my medical journeys at night ever seen any strange creature or heard the baying of a hound. The latter question he put to me several times, and always with a voice which vibrated with excitement.*
>
> *'I can well remember driving up to his house in the evening some three weeks before the fatal event. He chanced to be at his hall door. I had descended from my gig and was standing in front of him, when I saw his eyes fix themselves over my shoulder and stare past me with an expression of the most dreadful horror. I whisked round and had just time to catch a glimpse of something which I took to be a large black calf passing at the head of the drive. So excited and alarmed was he that I was compelled to go down to the spot where the animal had been and look around for it. It was gone, however, and the incident appeared to make the worst impression upon his mind.*
>
> ...

It is clear in *The Hound of the Baskervilles* that seeing the hound is considered to be terribly unlucky, and perhaps even a sign of encroaching death. The hound kills Hugo Baskerville, drives his companions mad, and years later a ghostly hound obsesses and frightens Sir Charles Baskerville to death. This is very different to Eden Phillpotts' hound which was a good omen and lucky to those who saw it. It may however be a more authentic version of the legend.[44] Even in modern times, the bestselling Harry Potter books have characterised the sign of a black dog or 'grim' as 'the worst omen of death', and this version of the legend has always been more popular.[45]

3.

'I could not call you in, Mr. Holmes, without disclosing these facts to the world, and I have already given my reasons for not wishing to do so. Besides, besides—'

'Why do you hesitate?'

'There is a realm in which the most acute and most experienced of detectives is helpless.'

'You mean that the thing is supernatural?'

'I did not positively say so.'

'No, but you evidently think it.'

'Since the tragedy, Mr. Holmes, there have come to my ears several incidents which are hard to reconcile with the settled order of Nature.'

'For example?'

'I find that before the terrible event occurred several people had seen a creature upon the moor which corresponds with this Baskerville demon, and which could not possibly be any animal known to science. They all agreed that it was a huge creature, luminous, ghastly, and spectral. I have cross-examined these men, one of them a hard-headed countryman, one a farrier, and one a moorland farmer, who all tell the same story of this dreadful apparition, exactly corresponding to the Hell-hound of the legend. I assure you that there is a reign of terror in the district, and that it is a hardy man who will cross the moor at night.'

---

[44] Hunt, R. (1903), *Popular Romances of the West of England*, New Edition, (Chatto &Windus, London). p.471.
[45] Rowling, J.K. (2001 ed.) *Harry Potter and the Prisoner of Azkaban*, (Scholastic Edition, New York). p.107.

'And you, a trained man of science, believe it to be supernatural?'

'I do not know what to believe.'

Holmes shrugged his shoulders. 'I have hitherto confined my investigations to this world,' said he. 'In a modest way I have combated evil, but to take on the Father of Evil himself would, perhaps, be too ambitious a task. Yet you must admit that the footmark is material.'

'The original hound was material enough to tug a man's throat out, and yet he was diabolical as well.'

'I see that you have quite gone over to the supernaturalists.'

...

Section three brings up once again the tension between superstition and rationalism which we saw briefly in section one, and which also characterised Phillpotts' 'The Hound's Pool'. Despite what I said earlier about Conan Doyle's spiritualism, and that his idea of Dartmoor is more romantic than Phillpotts', it is nevertheless the case that his hero, Sherlock Holmes utterly refuses to take the idea of a phantom hound seriously whenever it is discussed. Like Phillpotts twenty years later, Conan Doyle seems to believe that something more is needed that a local superstition before the hound can be taken seriously by readers.

4.

This small clump of buildings here is the hamlet of Grimpen, where our friend Dr. Mortimer has his headquarters. Within a radius of five miles there are, as you see, only a very few scattered dwellings. Here is Lafter Hall, which was mentioned in the narrative. There is a house indicated here which may be the residence of the naturalist—Stapleton, if I remember right, was his name. Here are two moorland farmhouses, High Tor and Foulmire. Then fourteen miles away the great convict prison of Princetown. Between and around these scattered points extends the desolate, lifeless moor.

...

Our fourth extract introduces the physical geography and setting for the story when the characters finally leave London and head to Dartmoor. Jim Hargen has analysed the book's physical descriptions in detail and has attempted to locate the story past Ashburton, along the miners road on the East Dart River. He believes that Grimpen is probably based on Postbridge, a town in the centre of the moor and that the famous mire in the story may be based on Fox Tor Mire nearby.[46] Weller, the author of the standard edition has argued that Hexworthy is a more probable site based on the inn and relative location.[47] Both arguments are convincing, but I am not sure how correct they can possibly be. Jim Hargen suggests that the author was entirely authentic and sympathetic to the facts of local geography with his descriptions, but I would argue that Conan Doyle's Dartmoor was actually a much more mist-covered and dream-like place than the stark, wet and frequently unpleasant reality. The fact that Conan Doyle, unlike Phillpotts, invented place names on Dartmoor suggests that he did not intend to set his story anywhere concrete although certain places may have inspired him. This is of course completely contrary to his policy in London where he describes real places like Baker Street.

5.

Twice I have with my own ears heard the sound which resembled the distant baying of a hound. It is incredible, impossible, that it should really be outside the ordinary laws of nature. A spectral hound which leaves material footmarks and fills the air with its howling is surely not to be thought of. Stapleton may fall in with such a superstition, and Mortimer also, but if I have one quality upon earth it is common sense, and nothing will persuade me to believe in such a thing. To do so would be to descend to the level of these poor peasants, who are not content with a mere fiend dog but must needs describe

---

[46] Hargan, J. 'The Dartmoor of the Baskervilles', *Exclusively Dartmoor*, (http://www.exclusivelydartmoor.co.uk/arthur-Conan Doyle-c467.html), (1997)
[47] Weller, P. (2001), *The Hound of the Baskervilles: Hunting the Dartmoor Legend*, (Devon Books, Tiverton). P.73

> him with Hell-fire shooting from his mouth and eyes. Holmes would not listen to such fancies, and I am his agent. But facts are facts, and I have twice heard this crying upon the moor. Suppose that there were really some huge hound loose upon it; that would go far to explain everything. But where could such a hound lie concealed, where did it get its food, where did it come from, how was it that no one saw it by day? It must be confessed that the natural explanation offers almost as many difficulties as the other.
>
> ...

Conan Doyle here briefly suggests again that the rational explanation is the only acceptable one, and is opposed to the idea of accepting the superstitious myth which he has Watson describe as belonging to peasants. At the same time he discounts the practical version of the myth with practical considerations. Where does the beast hide? Where does it come from? Why is it not seen by day and what does it eat? It is amusing that these questions remain those debated most fiercely by enthusiasts of the Beast of Dartmoor today.

The real significance of this extract is that Conan Doyle felt the physical explanation for the hound to be so obvious that he needed to insert a red herring at all. The whole point of the passage is to leave readers uncertain of the cause of the hound phenomena. Is the creature phantasmal or physical? If even solid John Watson is not certain, the reader too might feel a few shivers of uncertainty. The necessity of this passage suggests that contemporary readers would be expected to be naturally far more inclined to a rational explanation, much like today.

6.

> A sound of quick steps broke the silence of the moor. Crouching among the stones we stared intently at the silver-tipped bank in front of us. The steps grew louder, and through the fog, as through a curtain, there stepped the man whom we were awaiting. He looked round him in surprise as he emerged into the clear, starlit night. Then he came swiftly along the path, passed close to where we lay, and went on up the long slope behind us. As he

walked he glanced continually over either shoulder, like a man who is ill at ease.

'Hist!' cried Holmes, and I heard the sharp click of a cocking pistol. 'Look out! It's coming!'

There was a thin, crisp, continuous patter from somewhere in the heart of that crawling bank. The cloud was within fifty yards of where we lay, and we glared at it, all three, uncertain what horror was about to break from the heart of it. I was at Holmes's elbow, and I glanced for an instant at his face. It was pale and exultant, his eyes shining brightly in the moonlight. But suddenly they started forward in a rigid, fixed stare, and his lips parted in amazement. At the same instant Lestrade gave a yell of terror and threw himself face downward upon the ground. I sprang to my feet, my inert hand grasping my pistol, my mind paralyzed by the dreadful shape which had sprung out upon us from the shadows of the fog. A hound it was, an enormous coal-black hound, but not such a hound as mortal eyes have ever seen. Fire burst from its open mouth, its eyes glowed with a smouldering glare, its muzzle and hackles and dewlap were outlined in flickering flame. Never in the delirious dream of a disordered brain could anything more savage, more appalling, more Hellish be conceived than that dark form and savage face which broke upon us out of the wall of fog.

With long bounds the huge black creature was leaping down the track, following hard upon the footsteps of our friend. So paralyzed were we by the apparition that we allowed him to pass before we had recovered our nerve. Then Holmes and I both fired together, and the creature gave a hideous howl, which showed that one at least had hit him. He did not pause, however, but bounded onward. Far away on the path we saw Sir Henry looking back, his face white in the moonlight, his hands raised in horror, glaring helplessly at the frightful thing which was hunting him down. But that cry of pain from the hound had blown all our fears to the winds. If he was vulnerable he was mortal, and if we could wound him we could kill him. Never have I seen a man run as Holmes ran that night. I am reckoned fleet of foot, but he outpaced me as much as I outpaced the little professional. In front of us as we flew up the track we heard scream after scream from Sir Henry and the deep roar of the hound. I was in time to see the beast spring upon its victim, hurl him to the ground, and worry at his throat. But the next instant Holmes had emptied five barrels of his revolver into the creature's flank. With a last howl of agony and a vicious snap in the air, it rolled upon its back, four feet pawing furiously, and then fell limp upon its side. I stooped, panting, and pressed my pistol to the dreadful, shimmering head, but it was useless to press the trigger. The giant hound was dead.

...

In mere size and strength it was a terrible creature which was lying stretched before us. It was not a pure bloodhound and it was not a pure mastiff; but it appeared to be a combination of the two—gaunt, savage, and as large as a small lioness. Even now in the stillness of death, the huge jaws seemed to be dripping with a bluish flame and the small, deep-set, cruel eyes were ringed with fire. I placed my hand upon the glowing muzzle, and as I held them up my own fingers smouldered and gleamed in the darkness.

'Phosphorus,' I said.

'A cunning preparation of it,' said Holmes, sniffing at the dead animal. 'There is no smell which might have interfered with his power of scent.

The mystery of the fifth extract is preserved throughout the beginning of the sixth. All of Conan Doyle's characters, including even the usually aloof Sherlock Holmes, are taken aback by their first glimpse of the hound. The dog appeared coal-black, monstrously huge and with fringes of glowing flame colour upon it. It is only after Holmes and Watson fire upon it and the hound is injured that they know that it is not actually a phantom Hell hound.

In fact, as we find out, the hound was specifically intended to resemble a Hell hound in order to deceive and terrify the main character. The plot was carried out by a younger brother in order to eliminate competition for an inheritance.[48] The belief in the existence of a phantom dog is once again shown to be a foolish superstition, and something which brings trouble to the main character, and once again Sherlock Holmes' rational approach is vindicated.

Discussion

Since *The Hound of the Baskervilles* is a Sherlock Holmes story, it has attracted a great deal of attention over the years, from both contemporary and modern readers and critics Because of the books popularity, many researchers have been attracted to trace the source of Arthur Conan Doyle's hound over the years, with varying success. The trouble with this is that Conan Doyle was an author of fiction, not a collector of folklore, and his story is as original as any story set on quasi-supernatural Dartmoor can be. Philip Weller, the author of the standard edition of the text has described the problem as:

> 'What should constantly be borne in mind, though, is that A[rthur] C[onan] D[oyle] merely acknowledged the inspiration provided by this legend. Far too many scholars have assumed that it provided the basis for the story of The Hound [of the Baskervilles] or for the hound legend recorded in that story.'[49]

Weller goes on to trace possible source legends for the story himself, including several legends which were current on Dartmoor, and elsewhere in Britain at the time. He found very little evidence that there were any 'solitary hound' stories circulating on Dartmoor before Conan Doyle's story, and favoured the explanation that either the Black Shuck of Norfolk or possibly the Hound of Vaughan was a greater influence on the hound of Sherlock Holmes.[50]

It does not really affect our study significantly where Conan Doyle drew his main inspiration from, whether it was a Dartmoor hound

---

[48] *The Hound of the Baskervilles* is a full length novel and I am unable to reproduce it in full here, but I strongly recommend reading the entire story which sees Sherlock Holmes at his best. The book is in the public domain and thus available for free online.

[49] Weller, P. (2001), *The Hound of the Baskervilles: Hunting the Dartmoor Legend*, (Devon Books, Tiverton). P.41

[50] See. Pp.43-50.

story, a Norfolk or Midlands hound story, or his own imagination. Whatever influenced him, he himself went on to influence later accounts of the Beast of Dartmoor. Weller is not correct to say that this story represents the first attested single hound legend on Dartmoor, as we shall see but it was the popularity of *The Hound of the Baskervilles* which reversed centuries of tradition about packs of ghostly hounds. The modern Beasts of Dartmoor are almost always alone and physical rather than ghostly and in packs. However, the tradition of Dartmoor legends was probably already headed in this direction. We shall see later the highly influential legend of Lady Howard in *Fitz of Fitz-Ford* attests a single hound far before Sherlock Holmes, and other legends like that of 'Richard Cabell of Brooke' which we have already seen are almost certainly also older than Arthur Conan Doyle's conception too.

In addition, although Weller's examples of Black Shuck legends do fit in well with Conan Doyle's beast, it may be that he cherry-picked his choice of stories. The earliest and most authoritative version of the Black Shuck legend I am aware of which explicitly names its monster is found in the Notes and Queries journal of 1850:

> *'Shuck the Dog-fiend. – This phantom I have heard many persons in East Norfolk, and even Cambridgeshire, describe as having seen as a black shaggy dog, with fiery eyes, and of immense size, and who visits churchyards at midnight. One witness nearly fainted away at seeing it, and on bringing his neighbours to see the place where he saw it, he found a large spot as if gunpowder had been exploded there. A lane in the parish of Overstrand is called, after him, Shuck's Lane. The name appears to be corruption of "shag," as shucky is the Norfolk dialect for "shaggy." Is not this a vestage of the German "Dog-fiend?"*[51]

This monster is a good match for Conan Doyle's hound, but it is not a perfect match. Sherlock's Monster Hound did not leave gunpowder burnt marks on the ground, and although it was shaggy it did not frequent graveyards and even seemed to spurn settled areas. Some of the earlier legends we will find set around Dartmoor match Conan

---

[51] Taylor, E.S., 'Shuck the Dog-fiend' p.468 in: *Notes and Queries, vol.1, no.29.*, (1850)

Doyle's version much better. One legend, 'The Ghost of the Black-Dog' in *Nummits and Crummits* from 1900 seems an especially close match. I have not had time to edit the story separately but it features a man who is killed by a single ghostly dog, 'neither mastiff or bloodhound' breathing sulphurous fire.[52] Ultimately Weller both understates the evidence for a Dartmoor influence on *Hound of the Baskervilles*, and overstates the evidence for a Black Shuck influence.

There are other modern legends of hounds in Britain, we find the Gwyllgi of Wales, the Gytrash of Northumbria (famously described in Jane Eyre), and the Bargest of Yorkshire but since this book's focus is on The Beast of Dartmoor and its potential sources I will not examine all these in detail.

Returning to Dartmoor though, even apart from physical descriptions there is at least one characteristic of *The Hound of the Baskervilles* which earlier Dartmoor hounds do not possess. In *The Hound of the Baskervilles,* just like in 'The Hound's Pool' the story begins when the beast is seen on Dartmoor. In both cases, the creature is initially explained according to local legend and superstition, but in both cases more shrewd and rational characters refuse to accept this explanation. In both cases they are also ultimately correct in doing so. This scepticism is something new to the 20th century, and not seen in the earlier material.

As I previously said in my commentary on 'The Hound's Pool', both these stories reflect a more pragmatic and modern approach to the folklore than we will find in earlier versions of the legend. And yet there is also a significant difference between the two stories in how they approach the legend. To Eden Phillpotts in 1929 the story is a quaint legend told by old people. The hound brings luck to those who see it and even seems to save the main character early in the story. But to Arthur Conan Doyle in 1901 the hound was still a terrifying beast. It brought death to those who saw it, and even attempted to kill one man. Even though the legend of *The Hound of the Baskervilles* was unfounded, it remained horrific rather than fantastical. Arthur Conan Doyle may not have believed in the creature but he was still frightened by it.

---

[52] Hewett, S. (1900), *Nummits and Crummits*, (Thomas Burleigh, London). pp.39-41.

The most probable explanation for the discrepancy, as I have suggested, is the relative time at which the authors were writing. Over the course of 28 years it is possible the legend became less imposing and believed. There are at least two other explanations however. Although both of the stories belonged to more or less the same genre (mystery-horror), the two authors had very different experiences in life. Eden Phillpotts had a local's knowledge of Dartmoor and its legends whereas Arthur Conan Doyle was approaching from the outside. What to Conan Doyle might have seemed terrifying and romantic might have seemed fairly mundane and ordinary to Phillpotts. It is said that scary ghost stories are less popular in war time than in peace time, and World War I occurred between the two writer's books. However the reactions of the characters to the beast are much more interesting. It seems unlikely that Phillpotts could have made up the idea that the hound was a lucky thing to see, just as it seems unlikely that Conan Doyle could have made up the hound's Devilish connotations. The reactions of the local characters to hearing about the hound are most likely to be based in real life.

Looking back to the beginning of Conan Doyle's story though, the 'document', which I presented as extract one of *The Hound of the Baskervilles* might suggest to readers that the legend of the hound is of great antiquity. As I have said, the 'document' itself, with its anachronistic, archaic features was purposefully written to give the impression of great age, whereas the truth is that Arthur Conan Doyle invented much of his geography, physical features and folklore of Dartmoor. There are however earlier versions of the hound folklore than the twentieth century, and they do resemble Conan Doyle's terrifying hound more than Phillpott's fantastic one. Arthur Conan Doyle's story was his own fabrication, but it does reflect older stories nevertheless.

'The Farmer and the Black Hunter', recorded by M.J. Walhouse, 1897

Introduction

Not much is known about M.J. Walhouse, except from the work which he left behind. Walhouse left a small collection of Asian folkloric materials in the Pitt Rivers Museum, (a museum of ethnology managed by the University of Oxford). He was also a a very active member of the Folklore Society, and its records suggest he had a house in St. John's Wood, London.[53]

Walhouse contributed three articles and two notes to the Folklore Journal, two in 1893, one in 1894 and two in 1897. Three of these are on matters of Asian folklore, and in one of his articles he describes visiting Asia himself shooting game in India. Another article describes him living on Jamaica and the note we are interested in describes a local Devon newspaper, suggesting he may have been living there for a time, perhaps on a hunting holiday. From these traces we might deduce he was a wealthy man who in the 1890s was very interested in folklore.

Since his account is short, and he seems to be summarising what he has read from a newspaper, we can move straight on to looking at his text:

Text and Commentary

> *The same story, but with a more ghastly ending, is told, if we may trust an account which appeared in a Devonshire newspaper one day last spring, on the Dartmoor, where the foaming river Plym rushes through a ravine under the tall cliffs of the Dewerstone. This wild spot is haunted by the Black Huntsman, who with his "Wish-hounds" careens over the waste at night.*

---

[53] See: 'List of Officers and Members' in: *Folklore, vol. 8.* (1897) P.xii,

> *A story is told of this phantom that a farmer, riding across the moor by night, encountered the Black Hunter, and being flushed with ale, shouted to him "Give us a share of your game!"*
>
> *The Huntsman thereupon threw him something that he supposed might be a fawn, which he caught and carried in his arms till he reached his home, one of the old moorland farms. There arrived, he shouted, and a man came out with a lantern.*
>
> *"Bad news, master," said the man; "you've had a loss since you went out this morning."*
>
> *"But I have gained something," answered the farmer, and getting down brought what he had carried to the lantern, and beheld---his own dead child! During the day his only little one had died.*[54]

Walhouse's account of what he calls the Wish-hounds is short but very interesting. Usually we imagine local newspapers to have a local readership but the name 'Wish-Hounds' and their connection to Dewerstone is something we will encounter again in the nineteenth century accounts.

For now it is sufficient to explain that before *The Hound of the Baskervilles*, most Dartmoor Monster Dogs run in packs, and the most common name for this pack is the 'Wish-Hounds'. But in this story the hounds are barely mentioned at all, and the attention of the story is instead on the Black Huntsman, a phantom who rides careening over the waste (moors?) at night, leading the hunt.

This is the first time we have come across a lead huntsman at all, but it is the norm in the nineteenth century, and there always tends to be something uncanny about the way the character is described in the story.

The most interesting element of the story for our purposes is the shocking reveal that the present of the Dark Huntsman is not a present at all but a cruel jest at the main character's expense. For a more

---

[54] Walhouse, M.J. 'Folklore parallels and Coincidences' in: *Folklore, vol. 8.* (1897). p.196.

thorough explanation as to why this is we need to compare the story with other texts.

Discussion

Considering that the Monster Dogs of Dartmoor are certainly supposed to resemble a hunting pack, it is interesting that they are very rarely in pursuit of animals. Rather, as we saw in the 'Richard Cabell of Brooke' story, their more frequent targets seem to be the souls of humans, and this is especially true of children. A short poem has from 1865 illustrates this point. It was written by Edward Capern, who introduces himself as a 'rural postman of Bidford, Devon', who was inspired to write poems by what he saw around him. I present the entire poem here, together with the author's explanation for it at the end.

> **The "Yeth" Hounds**
> *The reds are in the eastern sky*
> *I wot they are for wind or rain:*
> *For the sun has got a coppery eye;*
> *And list the thunder of the main!*
>
> *"How loud the tumbling billows roar!*
> *God save the wight upon the sea--*
> *For that ground swell is evermore*
> *A merry signal unto me.*
>
> *"I hear the storm shriek o'er the land.*
> *And see the furies ride the clouds*
> *Above the wreck upon the strand,*
> *With drown'd men dripping in the shrouds.*
>
> *"O for a wild and starless nighty*
> *And a curtain o'er the white moon's face,*
> *For the moor-fiend hunts an infant sprite,*
> *At cock-crow, over Parkham chase!*
>
> *"Hark to the cracking of the whip!*
> *A merry band are we, I ween;*
> *List to the 'Yeth' hounds' yip! yip! yip!*
> *Ha, ha! 'tis thus we ride unseen."*
>
> *A lady weeps within her hall.*

*And fairer than the snow is she;
Alas! alas! so black a pall
Should shroud her little dead babyé.*

*A lady weeps within her hall,
"My little lost one," crieth she,
"No holy priest came at the call
To shrive my soul and christen thee!*

*"O, I had roses on my cheek,
And I had summer in mine eyes,
But roses fade when winds are bleak,
And joy is never fed on sighs.*

*"I was a moon with one bright star,
A dove with one wee doveling dear,
Away the light has wander'd far,
I mourn my doveling with a tear."*

*The mother's hair is trailing down.
And hides the coffin like a pall,
"My lovely babe can wear no crown,"
She wails within the silent hall.*

*She wails within her silent hall.
And fairer than the snow is she,
"Alas! alas! so black a pall
Should shroud thee, little dead babyé!*

*"Thou mad'st thy heaven of my breast.
And I found mine within thine eyes,
Woe! woe for thee, thou canst not rest.
Bereft of me and Paradise!*

*"And ever, when the nights are dark,
A phantom-hunter on his steed,
They say, will chase thy spirit - hark! -
O whither do those horsemen speed?"*

*"Good lady, prithee do not fear,
Thy Lord is waiting at the door;"
Poor heart, she open'd it to hear*

> The "yeth"-hounds yipping on the moor."
>
> *[The author adds the following account at the end of his poem] The above ballad illustrates a superstition still lingering in the rural districts of North Devon. I knew an old matron who was a firm believer in the existence of the moor-fiend and his hounds, and that every unbaptized infant that died became the prey of the "Yeth" hunter.*[55]

Although the above poem calls the monster creatures Yeth hounds rather than Wish hounds, it perfectly illustrates how the Monster Dogs of Devon sometimes hunted children.

The text makes an especially interesting comparison because if we imagine the black hunter of the 'Farmer and the Black Hunter' story was actually hunting humans, some elements of that story take on a new significance. The farmer's drunken shout at the hunters was not only rude it was also foolhardy and invited disaster, especially since he had a young son. The farmer was mocking a supernatural being, and to some extent the death of his only son becomes a punishment for his words. This is again a common motif, and we will see a large amount of stories, both others from the nineteenth century and some from earlier in which people are punished for their careless words. 'Dando and his Dogs', one of the very next texts we will look at is one such, but we might also consider 'De Nugis Curialium' to be a prototype, and by the time we examine that text we will have gone back seven hundred years.

Although I have pointed out some highly significant details, Walhouse's story is of course very different to both *The Hound of the Baskervilles* and the 'Hound of the Pool'. I have already explained why this is in my Discussion of 'Richard Cabell of Brooke', but to explain again briefly, at this point in time stories about packs of hounds were evolving fairly independently from stories about individual hounds on Dartmoor. Modern folkloric researchers will normally consider them completely different types of folklore, but as we go back further in time we will start to see the two types of story influencing each other more and more.

---

[55] Capern, E. (1865), *Wayside Warbles,* (Sampson Low, Son, and Marston, London). pp.204-7

For now readers need only remember the following: Packs of Hounds (a) hunt humans (b) may be accompanied by a lead huntsman and (c) may come from Hell, whereas single hounds (a) haunt areas or people and (b) more often represent ghosts. This distinction is not wholly accurate, and we will be able to distinguish the different genres much more finely in the Interlude and Conclusion.

Popular Romances of the West of England by Robert Hunt, 1865

Introduction

Robert Hunt (1807-1887) was a Victorian folklore collector, and the author of the famous *Popular Romances of the West of England*. He was born in Plymouth, Devon but moved to Penzance in Cornwall when he was eight or nine and then to London when he was twelve to take an apprenticeship.

When he was a young man in 1829 he returned to Cornwall, visiting old sites, collecting stories and writing poetry, and he spent most of his life in the South West after this. He made his living from engineering and mining but he also had keen interests in photography and geology. Today he is probably best remembered for his *Popular Romances*, and this was the only folkloric work he seems to have attempted. They were initially published in 1865 and were based on the stories he collected in 1829. However the book proved such a success that subsequent editions were published, adding additional material collected nearer the time.[56]

Hunt should be celebrated as an early pioneer of folklore in general, and Dartmoor's folklore in particular. He was ahead of his time in recording legends in dialect as this policy was not common until modern folkloric studies took off. That is not to say his book is perfect. For our purposes his focus on Cornwall over the rest of the South West is problematic, but more importantly the book often mixes authentic collected folklore with discussion and interpretation of that folklore. This is usually easy to distinguish, but at times it can be difficult to be sure where Hunt's recorded information ends and his speculation starts.

---

[56] Pearson, A. 'Hunt, Robert', in: *The Oxford Dictionary of National Biography*, (Oxford University Press, 2004) www.oxforddnb.com/view/article/14203

Legends of Dartmoor's hounds are found from the very first 'series' (edition) onwards, meaning that the folklore existed certainly before the book was published in 1865, and possibly even when Hunt did most of his research in 1829. Other folklore was added later, but we can trace two main legends of Dartmoor Hounds in existence already in the first edition. There we find most especially the Wish Hounds and Yeth Hounds, which were the staples of Dartmoor hound legend of the time, but also the legend of Dando and his dogs. This legend is tied to Cornwall rather than Devon, but I have included it since, according to Hunt, 'the Wish hounds of Dartmoor are but other versions of the same legend'.[57] The author also sketches out comparative legends about Cheney's Hounds, and the Bargest, but of these, the first is a very basic story belonging to Devonshire, and the second is an account of a bear-ghost in Yorkshire, never connected to Dartmoor until Hunt's comparison.

It will be useful to provide some historical background to the story of Dando's Hounds before we start. St Germans is in western Cornwall and was early on established as the cathedral seat of the region by King Athelstan, the grandson of King Alfred the Great. It fell into ruin and lost its status as a cathedral in 1050.

The church was rebuilt in late Norman times, and it acted as a friar's priory from the Norman period up to the reformation. The canons there were initially known for refusing the vow of poverty, and this story might have influenced the creation of the 'jolly friar' seen in Dando and his dogs. The church remains a Grade 1 listed building today but, in 2010, its ownership was transferred to the Churches Conservation Trust, meaning that it is now rarely ever used as a place of worship[58].

---

[57] Hunt, R. (1865), *Popular Romances of the West of England*, First Edition, (Chatto &Windus, London). Pp.251.
[58] Wall, L. 'St Germans' in: *Great English Churches*, (http://greatenglishchurches.co.uk/html/st_germans.html), (2009).

Text and Commentary
The Wish Hounds

> The Abbot's Way on Dartmoor, an ancient road which extends into Cornwall, is said to be the favourite coursing ground of 'the wish or wisked hounds of Dartmoor,' called also the 'yell-hounds,' and the 'yeth-hounds.' The valley of the Dewerstone is also the place of their midnight meetings. Once I was told at Jump, that Sir Francis Drake drove a hearse into Plymouth at night with headless horses, and that he was followed by a pack of 'yelling hounds' without heads. If dogs hear the cry of the wish hounds they all die. May it not be that 'wish' is connected with the west-country word 'whist,' meaning more than ordinary melancholy, a sorrow which has something weird surrounding it?

Hunt's record of this legend is very brief, but it is interesting for its originality. From a modern point of view, looking backwards, here in the nineteenth century for the first time we have plural hounds rather than a story of a single hound. This is obviously very different from the single large Hound in Sherlock Holmes and a world away from today's 'Beast of Dartmoor', but I will argue that it is an older version of the same vein of folklore. Today in Britain hunting with hounds is illegal unless the huntsman is using the hounds only to flush out game. Back in the times of hare, fox, otter, deer and wolf hunting though, hounds always hunted in packs. The Wish[/t] and Yeth hounds of Dartmoor are usually described as hunting packs rather than on their own, and the shift in folkloric taste which made Darmoor's beast a solitary hunter can probably be dated to the publication of the bestselling *Hound of the Baskervilles* (1901). There are many legends of single hounds from before this time, but stories of packs of hounds definitely predominate over them until 1901.

Hunt's source for his information about Wish Hounds is probably the story of the 'Wish or Wisked Hounds' in *the Athenaeum*, which we will return to later on, but also mentions Dewerstone, which we previously saw in the 1897 folklore.

Other than the number, the Wish or Yeth Hounds are a staple of Dartmoor, and guide books will still talk about them today. In this version of the legend, the Wish Hounds lack heads, so they cannot have fiery or smoky breath, or glowing teeth and eyes. However, the cry these hounds make, even without their heads, kills those dogs which hear it, and this is certainly a staple of later (and earlier) accounts about them. The headless nature of the hounds may well be an extension of the horseman who rides with them, as headless horsemen have been common ghosts for hundreds of years. I have not been able to find another reference to St Francis Drake leading a pack of Wish Hounds, but he may well be the strangest character ever to lead a wild hunt!

The second half of the account has Hunt further discussing the etymology of the wish hounds. I have only recorded the very beginning of this discussion but the author goes on to discard the idea that the hounds might have been named after 'Wyse' as an Old English name for Woden. Hunt's etymology is probably correct, but since the word 'whist' in this sense is a modern term, the etymology Hunt provides suggests that the hounds themselves may not be of ancient origin. I shall explain the reason for this further in the Discussion.

Dando and his Dogs

In the neighbourhood of the lovely village of St Germans formerly lived a priest, connected with the old priory church of this parish, whose life does not appear to have been quite consistent with his vows.

He lived the life of the traditional 'jolly friar.' He ate and drank of the best the land could give him, or money buy; and it is said that his indulgences extended far beyond the ordinary limits of good living. The priest Dando was, notwithstanding all his vices, a man liked by the people. He was good-natured, and therefore blind to many of their sins. Indeed, he threw a cloak over his own iniquities, which was inscribed 'charity,' and he freely forgave all those who came to his confessional.

As a man increases in years he becomes more deeply dyed with the polluted waters through which he may have waded. It rarely happens that an old sinner is ever a repentant one, until the decay of nature has reduced him to a state of second childhood. As long as health allows him to enjoy the sensualities of life, he continues to gratify his passions, regardless of the cost. He becomes more selfish, and his own gratification is the rule of his existence. So it has ever been, and so was it with Dando.

The sinful priest was a capital huntsman, and scoured the country far and near in pursuit of game, which was in those days abundant and varied over this well-wooded district. Dando, in the eagerness of the chase, paid no regard to any kind of property. Many a corn-field has been trampled down, and many a cottage garden destroyed by the horses and dogs which this impetuous hunter would lead unthinkingly over them. Curses deep, though not loud, would follow the old man, as even those who suffered by his excesses were still in fear of his priestly power.

Any man may sell his soul to the Devil without going through the stereotyped process of signing a deed with his blood. Give up your soul to Satan's darling sins, and he will help you for a season, until he has his chains carefully wound around you, when the links are suddenly closed, and lie seizes his victim, who has no power to resist

Dando worshipped the sensual gods which he had created, and his external worship of the God of truth became every year, more and more, a hypocritical lie. The Devil looked carefully after his prize. Of course, to catch a dignitary of the church was a thing to cause rejoicings amongst the lost; and Dando was carefully lured to the undoing of his soul.

Health and wealth were secured to him, and by and by the measure of his sins was full, and he was left the victim to self-indulgences — a doomed man. With increasing years, and the immunities he enjoyed, Dando became more reckless. Wine and wassail, a board groaning with dishes which stimulated the sated appetite, and the company of both sexes of dissolute habits, exhausted his nights. His days were devoted to the pursuits of the field; and to maintain the required excitement, ardent drinks were supplied him by his wicked companions. It mattered not to Dando, — provided the day was an auspicious one, if the scent would lie on the ground, — even on the

Sabbath, horses and hounds were ordered out, and the priest would be seen in full cry.

One Sabbath morning, Dando and his riotous rout were hunting over the Earth estate; game was plenty, and sport first-rate. Exhausted with a long and eager run, Dando called for drink. He had already exhausted the flasks of the attendant hunters.

'Drink' I say; give me drink,' he cried.

'Whence can we get it?' asked one of the gang.

'Go to Hell for it, if you can't get it on Earth,' said the priest, with a bitter laugh at his own joke on the Earth estate.

At the moment, a dashing hunter, who had mingled with the throng unobserved, came forward, and presented a richly-mounted flask to Dando, saying, —

'Here is some choice liquor distilled in the establishment you speak of. It will warm and revive you, I'll warrant.'

'Drink deep; friend, drink.'

Dando drank deep; the flask appeared to cling to his lips. The strange hunter looked on with a rejoicing yet malignant expression; — a wicked smile playing over an otherwise tranquil face.

By and by Dando fetched a deep sigh, and removed the flask, exclaiming, 'By Hell! that was a drink indeed. Do the gods drink such nectar?'

'Devils do,' said the hunter.

'An they do, I wish I were one,' said Dando, who now rocked to and fro in a state of thorough intoxication, 'methinks the drink is very like ---' The impious expression died upon his lips.

Looking round with a half-idiotic stare, Dando saw that his new friend had appropriated several head of game. Notwithstanding his stupid intoxication, his selfishness asserted its power, and he seized the game, exclaiming, in a guttural, half-smothered voice, 'None of these are thine.'

'What I catch I keep,' said the hunter.

'By all the Devils they're mine,' stammered Dando.

The hunter quietly bowed.

Dando's wrath burst at once into a burning flame, uncontrolled by reason. He rolled himself off his horse, and rushed, staggering as he went, at the steed of his unknown friend, uttering most frightful oaths and curses.

The strange hunter's horse was a splendid creature, black as night, and its eyes gleamed like the brightest stars, with unnatural lustre. The horse was turned adroitly aside, and Dando fell to the earth with much force. The fall appeared to add to his fury, and he roared with rage. Aided by his attendants, he was speedily on his legs, and again at the side of the hunter, who shook with laughter, shaking the game in derision, and quietly uttering, 'They're mine.'

'I'll go to Hell after them, but I'll get them from thee,' shouted Dando.

'So thou shalt,' said the hunter; and seizing Dando by the collar, he lifted him from the ground, and placed him, as though he were a child, before him on the horse.

With a dash — the horse passed down the hill, its hoofs striking fire at every tread, and the dogs, barking furiously, followed impetuously. These strange riders reached the banks of the Lynher, and with a terrific leap, the horse and its riders, followed by the hounds, went out far in its waters, disappearing at length in a blaze of fire, which caused the stream to boil for a moment, and then the waters flowed on as tranquilly as ever over the doomed priest. All this happened in the sight of the assembled peasantry. Dando never more was seen, and his fearful death was received as a warning by many, who gave gifts to the church. One amongst them carved a chair for the bishop, and on it he represented Dando and his dogs, that the memory of his wickedness might be always renewed.' There, in St German's church, stands to this day the chair, and all who doubt the truth of this tradition may view the story carved in enduring oak.

If they please, they can sit in the chair until their faith is so far quickened that they become true believers. On Sunday mornings early, the dogs of the priest have been often heard as if in eager pursuit of game. Cheney's hounds and the Wish hounds of Dartmoor are but other versions of the same legend.' [59]

The main legend recorded by Hunt is that of 'Dando and his Dogs', but, as I said in the introduction, this legend is not actually set in Dartmoor. I have included it anyway based on Hunt's assurance that this story is very similar to the origin legend for the Wish Hounds of Dartmoor.

The 'chair' mentioned by Hunt in 1865 lasted until the 21st century, although I am informed it is no longer to be found in the church. It is actually a misericord, a lean-on-rest used to help those who must stand for long periods of time, and a remnant from when the church was a monastery before the reformation in the sixteenth century. I display it below:

Photograph © Lionel Wall, (2009), *GreatEnglishChurches.co.uk*, Used with permission.

Even ascribing a conservative sixteenth century date, if this misericord was originally intended to depict Dando and his dogs as the nineteenth

---

[59] Hunt, R. (1865), *Popular Romances of the West of England, First Edition,* (Chatto &Windus, London). Pp.150-1; 247-51.

century legend records, then this would be one of the very earliest legends about hounds in Britain. Unfortunately though, at the moment there is no evidence that this hunter was originally supposed to be interpreted as Dando. Hunting scenes are fairly common on church carvings and this hunter could have been interpreted as Dando only late in his career.

It would be easy to suggest that the non-supernatural and phantom nature of the hounds is a late feature, since both Arthur Conan-Doyle and Edith Phillpotts had ordinary hounds in their stories. However at the end of the story it is stated that Dando's hounds continue to make ghostly sounds to this day. Presumably they were also seen, since in other folklore of the Dandy-Dogs, their ghostly forms rather than sound is emphasised. The story as we have it therefore represents an origin myth for a pack of phantom hounds, not an example of real hounds in legend.

The Devil's involvement in the story does not help us to establish its age. The hounds are said to be infernal rather than earthly in many early stories, but not all of them. Only the early medieval stories are completely free of this theme, and since none of those are set on Dartmoor they are not perfect parallels anyway.

The bishop who is briefly mentioned as the receiver of the "chair" is interesting since, as I have said, St Germans was once a cathedral and the seat of a bishop. However it has not been the bishop's seat for almost a thousand years, since before the Norman Conquest of 1066. Misericords were only first produced in Britain in the thirteenth century, and since the misericord was supposed to have been created at the time of the event, there is no chance that the story actually occurred as described before the Norman Conquest. Further, since it is very unlikely that the comments about the bishop and the 'merry friar' were coincidental to St Germans once being the seat of the Bishop of Cornwall, and later a priory, it is probable that the author of the story inserted this deliberately anachronistic feature to try and fool us into believing the story is older than it actually is. This clearly makes the story even more difficult to date.

Dando is a rare surname, but looking through the Cornish Parish Records, I have found records of a Robert Dando who married Annie Auger in 1900 as well as several other Dandos and Dandows going back to the beginning of the nineteenth century[60]. If we include also people called Dandy or Dandye (after the 'Dandy Dogs', which we will hear more about in the next chapter) we find many more results, so that there are some possible candidates for the historic figure of Dando the hunting priest. The names of clergy who lived in the area 1840-1535 are being indexed by the Clergy of the Church of England Database[61], but unfortunately I have not managed to find any clergy with surnames starting with Dand- living within Cornwall in this period. Considering that the surname was fairly common this may reflect the incomplete nature of the database rather than anything about the existence of a real Dando, especially since he is also attested in an earlier legend (as we shall see in the next chapter)

Returning to the text, it is unfortunate that Hunt does not spell out the 'other versions of the same legend' which are actually relevant to Dartmoor, as now no origin legend survives for the Wish Hounds of the county. Assuming that the story Hunt heard was fairly identical – a man becomes sinful and corrupted by greed and hunting and is carried away by the Devil, it is interesting to note that this would make the hounds spectral rather than at all physical. I will return to this point later.

A final feature really worth pointing out is style taken on by Hunt when telling this story, defined by simple sentences and descriptive, narrative voice. If the word choice and sentence structure seem familiar, it is because they have become clichés of written storytelling. Children's fairytales in particular will often use this soothing style as a sort of mark of the genre. In the same way, the motif of a fallen saint being doomed to Hell, and the motif of a huntsman confronting Death or the Devil are also fairly generic. This does not mean that the story is not authentic, but its striking literary form does mean that if there is an ancient legend at the heart of the 'Dando and his Dogs' story it may be impossible to separate it from the trappings and the literary spin which it has acquired.

---

[60] Some of St Germans' Parish Records can be viewed online: (http://www.cornwall-opc-database.org/).
[61] Also available online, see: http://www.theclergydatabase.org.uk.

Discussion

From Hunt's *Popular Romances of the West of England*, written in 1865, we have extracted early descriptions of two main groups of hounds. The Wish Hounds are probably the best known pack of hounds on Dartmoor, and although we do not find many details about them in the 1865 account about them, earlier legends do give us more information. One of the only details we do get about the hounds in this text is that they are headless, a feature which is not seen in either earlier or later versions of the folklore, and is probably peculiar to Hunt's version.

In the commentary on the Wish Hounds legend I argued that the etymology Hunt suggests, although probably correct, actually suggests that the term 'wish hounds' is not very old. The reason for that is complicated so I wanted to explain further in the discussion:

The Oxford English Dictionary has a very large corpus of the earliest references to words in English literature. There the word 'wistful' (having or showing a feeling of vague or regretful longing) is attested commonly in the English language from the beginning of the eighteenth century. But, the first part of that word, 'whist', originally meant 'a silence' or 'please hush!' The word 'wistful' only acquired its nostalgic tone because it sounded like 'wishful'. The word 'wisht' in the sense of 'wistful' is only attested from the beginning of the nineteenth century, shortly before the wish hounds first appear in literature. It seems almost certainly to have been a back-formation from 'wistful', meaning that the term 'wish hounds' cannot be much older than the early nineteenth century. [62] Although we will look at Monster Dog legends which are earlier than this, the Wish Hounds themselves probably originate in the nineteenth century

There is no reason to suggest that the legend of Dando is any older than the legends of the Wish Hounds, especially since the tale of Dando cannot seem to decide if it is set when St. Germans was a cathedral, when St. Germans was a monastery or when the St. Germans misericord was being created. Hunt's claims for the age of his folklore seem to be inserted to lend an air of legitimacy to the material

---

[62] O.E.D., 'Wistful', 'Wistly', 'Whist', 'Wisht', 'Wish-Hounds', in: *The Oxford English Dictionary*, (http://www.oed.com), (Online edition 2012).

which it does not need or deserve, just like Conan Doyle's insertion of the ancient 'document'.

Attempts to overcompensate by setting the folklore in the ancient past might make us believe that the folklore was modern in Hunt's time, but this is not the case. Dartmoor's hound legends can reliably be traced still further back, as we will shortly discover. The phantasmal, otherworldly and collective depiction of the hounds in Hunt's legends compare well with this folklore as we shall see.

'The Devil and his Dandy-Dogs' by Thomas Quiller Couch, 1855

Introduction

Dr Thomas Quiller Couch (c.1827-1884) was a medical doctor, but also a life-long folklore researcher in his native county of Cornwall. According to the 1851 census he was born and lived in Lansallos, although in his writings he claims to have spent most of his childhood in Polperros, in the neighbouring parish of Talland. Either way, he is known to have moved to the then thriving county-town of Cornwall, Bodmin, to practice medicine as the local GP after he became a doctor.[63]

He recorded the legend of 'The Devil and his Dandy Dogs' when he was 28, before he got married and had his first child in 1863. This child was the more famous Sir Arthur Thomas Quiller-Couch (all his children used the hyphenated form of the name). After having children, the father, Dr. Thomas Quiller Couch retained his interest in folklore, although he struggled to support his family financially while his five children were growing up. At the end of his life he was still collecting material on the ancient wells and springs of Cornwall which were believed by locals to have miraculous powers.[64]

Dr. Quiller Couch's work on the Monster Dog folklore uses the term 'Dandy-Dogs' for the phantom hounds, which is clearly a reference back to Dando's legend which we read in the last chapter. However in this story the hounds are said to be ubiquitous all around the country, and the huntsman who leads the hounds is the Devil rather than Dando himself. It is even possible that the legend we found in Hunt's account of 1865 was invented to explain the term 'dandy-dog',

---

[63] Brittain, F. (1947), *A Biographical Study of Q.*, (Cambridge University Press), Pp.1-4; The 1851 census is viewable online at http://freecen.rootsweb.com, search for "Thomas Q Couch" who was then 24 and a student in medicine.

[64] Quiller-Couch, M and Quiller-Couch, L. (1894), *Ancient and Holy Wells of Cornwall*, (Chas J. Clark, London). See Preface.

although since Hunt was collecting folklore from 1829 onwards, and considering the level of detail in the story this seems unlikely.

Text and Commentary

> 1.
>
> ... 'The Devil and his Dandy-Dogs' frequent our bleak and dismal moors on tempestuous nights, and are more rarely heard and seen in the cultivated districts by the coast, where they assume a less frightful character. They are most commonly seen by those who are out at night on wicked errands, and woe betide the wretch who crosses their path. A very interesting legend is told here, though it has reference to the wild moorland district far inland:
>
> A poor herdsman was journeying homeward across the moors one windy night, when he heard at a distance among the Tors the baying of hounds, which he soon recognised as the dismal chorus of the Dandy-Dogs.

The first part of 'The Devil and his Dandy-Dogs' situates the story. In Hunt's 1865 version of the legend, the Dandy-Dogs were said to haunt St Germans in the west of Cornwall. Now though, the hounds are placed explicitly on the moors. Quiller Couch also does not mention the misericord in St Germans parish church, suggesting that the hounds are not specific to that area at all, lowering the chances that the misericord was carved to describe the legend.

The moor which Dr Quiller Couch's story is set in has 'tors', and this might make us think immediately of Dartmoor. However Cornwall does have its own moorland with tors, and this story is most probably set on Bodmin Moor, since Quiller Couch lived in Bodmin for most of his life. It is interesting to note though that Bodmin Moor is almost as far from St Germans, the setting of the last story, as Dartmoor itself.

> 2.
>
> It was three or four miles to his house; and very much alarmed, he hurried onward as fast as the treacherous nature of the soil and the uncertainty of the path would

> *allow; but, alas! the melancholy yelping of the hounds, and the dismal holloa of the hunter came nearer and nearer. After a considerable run, they had so gained upon him, that on looking back, — oh horror! --he could distinctly see hunter and dogs. The former was terrible to look at, and had the usual complement of saucer-eyes, horns, and tail, accorded by common consent to the legendary devil. He was black, of course, and carried in his hand a long hunting-pole. The dogs, a numerous pack, blackened the small patch of moor that was visible; each snorting fire, and uttering a yelp of an indescribably frightful tone.*
>
> *No cottage, rock, or tree was near to give the herdsman shelter, and nothing apparently remained to him but to abandon himself to their fate, when a happy thought suddenly flashed upon him, and suggested a resource. Just as they were about to rush upon him, he fell on his knees in prayer. There was strange power in the holy words he uttered: for immediately, as if resistance had been offered, the Hell-hounds stood at bay, howling more dismally than ever, and the hunter shouted, 'Bo Shrove' which (says my informant) means in the old language, 'the boy prays,' at which they all drew off on some other pursuit and disappeared.*
>
> *This ghastly apparition loses much of its terrible character as we approach more thickly populated areas, and our stories are very tame after this legend of the Moors...*[65]

In the second half, we once again find a huntsman described along with a pack of hounds. This time the figure is unmistakeably the Devil, with the Devil's 'usual complement of features'. The hounds are also finally warded off by a prayer, which would hardly have worked against the more ambiguously aligned hounds of the later nineteenth and twentieth centuries. The Devil's horns and tail are persevered in legend to the current day, and very wide, round 'saucer' eyes are still seen in modern Exorcist movies. One final aspect of the Devil,

---

[65] Couch, T.Q. 'The Folklore of a Cornish Village', spread *through Notes and Queries, ser 1, vol.11*, (1855), p.458

thankfully now gone from modern depictions is Quiller Couch's idea of the Devil as 'black, of course'.

The language the Devil speaks is ambiguous. Modern versions of the legend call the language Cornish, but this is unlikely to be accurate. In Cornish about the closest we can come to 'bo shrove' is '[ma'n] flogh a pysi' (the child prays), which is phonologically not very close at all. Actually though, we need not take the passage to be Cornish at all. In English, 'Shrove', as in 'Shrove Tuesday' was originally the past tense of 'shrive' meaning 'to confess sins'. If we take 'bo' as just a dialectal shortening of boy, the sentence might have originally been 'bo shrive', ([the] boy confesses). In this case, the Devil might have been coming to take the poor herdsman to Hell for his sins until he confessed to God and was therefore absolved. Perhaps though, the most likely scenario is that Quiller Couch chose an archaic sounding word 'shrove' which he knew had something to do with religious observation, and made up 'bo'.

Returning to the hounds, Quiller Couch's dogs continue to breathe fire, just like most of Dartmoor's hounds until the 'Hound of the Pool' almost two centuries later. The strange sound that the hounds make is also reminiscent of the howling of the Wish Hounds in *Popular Romances* which kills any dogs that hear it. The dogs' saucer eyes are probably due mainly to the influence of the popular 'Tinder Box' story by Hans Christian Anderson, which was first translated into English in 1847 and included three dogs with 'eyes big as saucers', although as we shall see large, glowing eyes are frequently seen in earlier hounds too.

One final feature which is uncertain in this text is the colour of the dogs. The twentieth century hounds tended to be black, but Hunt's depiction of Dando's Hounds is not specific about colour. The hounds in the text darken the ground where they run, but this is more probably due to their large number than anything else.

Discussion

Quiller Couch's 'The Devil and his Dandy-Dogs' from the year 1855 brings two new overt innovations to the hound legends of the West Country. First, the hounds in this legend have multiplied in number from the wish hound pack of Hunt's 1865 story. This is probably an independent embellishment of Quiller-Couch or his immediate source, since most other sources have more ordinary-sized packs, or do not comment on the number of hounds seen. The second innovation in Quiller Couch's account is that the master of the hounds is explicitly stated to be the Devil. This is much more common, and something we shall see more frequently as we go further back to periods where faith in the power of God and the Devil was universal.

The prayer of the poor herdsman is interesting, not only because it is a feature seen in other earlier stories but also for what it tells us about the nature of the hounds. The hounds of 'The Devil and his Dandy-Dogs' are not physical but spiritual, they represent mainly a spiritual rather than physical peril, and they can be fought by spiritual but not physical means. This seems to be a natural development from the hounds being phantasmal rather than physical and led by the Devil rather than any neutral agency.

Comparing the Dandy-Dogs of Quiller Couch and the later version of the legend by Hunt, there are also several marked differences. The term 'Dandy-Dogs' is used generically by Quiller Couch and the legend is general rather than confined to St Germans. This adds credence to Hunt's claim that all packs of Phantom Hounds share similar origin stories, even though he only gave 'Dando and his Dogs'.

One final interesting development is that 1855 is the first time we hear of a hound with 'saucer eyes' which have since become a vital part of the genre, and are still seen by witnesses today.

In other respects the Dandy-Dogs are the quintessential phantom pack of hounds. They even breathe fire like in almost every other version of the legend, and yelp in a horrible way, although this time their barking and howling does not seem to be actually harmful.

'Cwn Annwn' by James Motley, 1848

Introduction

Much like Robert Hunt, James Motley (1822-59) made his living as a geologist and miner with a strong interest in natural history. Although he spent his early life in Leeds, and attended the University of Cambridge for a while, when he was 18 he moved to South Wales and began a career as a mining engineer. Botany was a passion of his, and he made important discoveries of new species of plants and flowers. At least 80 plants have been named after him, most notably those he discovered when he went to Borneo to appraise the coal there in 1848.[66]

For our purposes he is significant because he wrote several 'traditional' poems in English when he was still living in Wales which he published as the *Tales of the Cymry*. 'Cymry' is the Welsh word for the people of Wales, and Motley's poems all have as their basis the folklore and supernatural beliefs of the Welsh, although all of the poems and Motley's commentaries have a strong classical (Latin and Greek) influence as well. Despite this, one of his poems called 'Cwn Annwn' is of special interest to us. The hounds in it are strongly influenced by those from Dartmoor, and when explaining his influences Motley quoted nearly the entirety of the influential nineteenth century article about the 'Wish or Wisked Hounds' which we shall look at in the next chapter. The extent to which this story is of Dartmoor's hounds relocated to Wales, and the extent to which it is about native Welsh hounds is debatable, but has many features in common with our other stories as we shall see.

All Motley's poems in *Tales of the Cymry* are of the Celtic heroic epic genre begun by James Macpherson's 'Ossian' the century before. Epic poems in this genre are long with narrative verses and a simple rhyme scheme which does not detract from the content of the poems.

---

[66] For a full biography see: Walker, A.R. 'James Motley (1822-1859): The life story of a collector and naturalist', pp.20-37, in: *Minerva, vol. 13,* (2005)

Sometimes such poetry can be difficult for modern readers to understand, as the verse can become very figurative (especially metaphorical or allegorical), and descriptive rather than action based. Luckily, Motley's poetry is more straightforward than many of his contemporaries, and the part of the story we are interested in is fairly accessible.

Other than form, the Celtic heroic epic genre is also characterised by its subject matter. Poems in the genre are usually set in a 'Celtic' heroic past, which may bear little or no resemblance to any real historical time or place. Motley's poetry does not disappoint in this respect. The plot of the poem we are interested in follows a young, beautiful Celtic maiden. The setting is the romantic, lush and purple Welsh mountain fastness of Tor Curig. There the maiden's people, led by the chieftain Madoc are under siege by the Normans. The maiden managed to run through the siege lines in order to seek the aid of Idris, the old druid, but she is being chased by a cruel Norman knight.

Even ignoring the over-romanticising of the Normans as heartless philistines and the Welsh as poor and helpless, the story is not historically accurate at all. After the druids of Britain rebelled around 60 A.D., druids were unlikely to be tolerated under Roman rule (from the first to the fifth century A.D.), and were even less likely to be tolerated after the Christianisation of Britain in the fifth century. The Normans only ever had short periods of control over Wales, sometimes being entirely thrown out, sometimes forcing the Welsh princes to pay homage for some time. By the time Wales was finally fully incorporated into the kingdom under in the late thirteenth century, England was ruled by Plantaganets rather than Normans. The Welsh were not bandits, and those who could afford armies had castles to flee to rather than mountain camps. Further, rich prisoners of war especially were often treated very well. The rules of chivalry were not always followed, but when they were women and children certainly would not have been attacked by invested knights, although they are likely to have been robbed. Although there are some accounts of medieval people being chased by sleuth-hounds, bloodhounds have recently been proved unable to hunt people across moorland.[67] A siege

---

[67] Weller, P. (2001), *The Hound of the Baskervilles: Hunting the Dartmoor Legend*, (Devon Books, Tiverton). P.26.

under the chivalric rules of combat may even have allowed non-combatants to leave whenever they liked, although the Anglo-Welsh wars were probably more barbaric than this chivalric ideal.

Often the authors of 'Celtic' heroic epics claim to be translating their poetry rather than writing it. Despite his misleading title, Motley does not make such a claim, although his stories are strongly based on pieces of folklore which he claims to have translated. The first of his poems is called 'Cwn Annwn' (the Hounds of Annwfn)[68]. I have already described the beginning of the plot as following an evil Norman knight hunting a young Celtic woman. The knight had been hunting the maiden using bloodhounds, However, the part of the poem we are interested in follows what happens when Idris finds the young woman. He decides to take revenge against the Norman knight, and summons hounds of his own, as we shall see in the passages following. I shall give the relevant part of the poem first, followed by an extract from Motley's commentary.

Text and Commentary

1.
And now the furious blasts yet fiercer blew,
And yet more madly yelling, wilder grew,
And o'er the shrouded heaven in frantic race
The huddling heavy thunder clouds they chase;
The big cold rain comes hissing to the ground,
And in the turf the dancing hailstorms bound.
But o'er the tempest's awful voice they hear
Echoing afar, loud screams of maddened fear,
And as the maiden listening stood aghast,
A long fierce howl was borne upon the blast

---

[68] Readers of *Aliens in Celtic History and Legend* may remember Annwn or Annwfn (the medieval spelling) as the underground otherworld of Welsh mythology, which was accessed via a floating, submergible fortress made of glass. The place also produced familiar-seeming items like bottles which would keep drink hot for long periods of time and chariots which drove themselves. By the nineteenth century, the term is entirely literary, although we might not be surprised to find that the hounds of Annwn in this poem are preceded by a storm, which was an important literary device even in the medieval period.

The first verse of our extract introduces the hounds. They are preceded by a storm, which has been a common topos of otherworldly characters in Welsh literature since the medieval period at least. After the storm, the next sign of their arrival is a 'long fierce howl'. The howling of the hound is a motif important in *The Hound of the Baskervilles* as well as other earlier texts which we shall see as we progress.

> 2.
> *When Idris heard the long-expected cry,*
> *With exultation flashed his sparkling eye,*
> *'Ha, ha, right well my trusty spirits know*
> *To wreck dire vengeance on their Cambria's foe,*
> *The quarry's raised, the hounds are on his trail.'*
> *And as he spoke, a thin mist filled the vale,*
> *And a broad vivid flash, that scorching came*
> *O'er their seared eyeballs like a liquid flame,*
> *For one short, fearful moment glanced, to shew*
> *A huge red hound upon the mountain's brow*
> *Then a faint cloud of pale unearthly light*
> *Came slowly stealing through the lowering night,*
> *And shewed the woods and black rocks frowning grim*
> *In faint dusk hues, all indistinct and dim*
> *Through the blue mist, from which in ceaseless flash*
> *With blinding glare the forked lightnings dash.*

The allegiance of the hounds in this part of the poem is very interesting. Idris calls them 'trusty spirits', strongly suggesting they are in league with the druid. They are summoned by his magic, but only seem to hunt the Norman knight. The storm which comes along with the hounds does not touch the druid or the Welsh maiden and the hounds are clearly chasing the knight to avenge the wrong done to her. After dawn, later on, when the hounds disappear it is revealed that even the knight's horse was spared; only the knight himself was taken. This suggests that the hounds are somehow a moral force in the world, but to explain how this works we need some background information.

It is a cliché of the Celtic heroic epic that the protagonists are 'Celtic' and they usually fight romantic but hopelessly for their independence from the 'Saxon' or 'Norman' English. Part of the baggage of Celtic characters in this genre is a spiritual quality and closeness to the Otherworld. Characters might have the second sight or go to meet fairies. At the least they are likely to be in touch and in harmony with nature. This cliché has gone on to be part of what we might imagine to be 'Celtic' today, but it is also part of what we imagine to be 'native', whether 'Aboriginal Australian', 'First American' or even just 'tribal'. Most of these characteristics are inherited from Classical (Latin and Greek) scholars discussing the barbarian others.

This is interesting for our purposes because the hounds are allied with these 'Celtic' figures. This suggests that in some ways the hounds are a force for 'good'. At the very least they are not evil or sent from Hell. They may be supernatural but their allegiance is still to nature.

But there is a discrepancy in the description of these creatures. They are red, with red glowing fangs, and red blazing eyes. They are explicitly said to have 'demon heads' and they breathe smoke. All of these aspects suggest that they have come from Hell, and this impression is strengthened when we hear that their introduction is a sudden scorching flash 'like a liquid flame'. They are even overtly called 'Hounds of Hell' at one point.

This discrepancy is interesting because it mirrors something we found in the later stories. In 'The Hound's Pool', the characters were said to be lucky to see a hound, but in *The Hound of the Baskervilles*, the creature was a Hellish monster that was not friendly to anyone. We shall continue to see this discrepancy as we go back in time, and it seems that the hounds were paradoxically seen as both from the Otherworld and from the Underworld.

> 3.
> *And now a ghastly form, in armour drest,*
> *With blood-besprinkled mail and cloven crest,*
> *And shattered shield and helm, and swordless sheath,*
> *And sobs of toil, and laboring panting breath,*
> *In furious haste dashed wildly down the dell,*
> *With terror-stricken looks and fearful yell,*
> *And on his brow the starting sweat-drops stood,*
> *'Mongst half-dried gouts of black and curdling blood;*
> *And as he went, all heedless of his way,*

> *Which 'mongst huge stones and tangled bushes lay*
> *All reckless where his fear-urged footsteps went,*
> *His glassy starting eyes behind were bent*
> *On his pursuers dread, that yelling came*
> *In close hot chase upon their ghastly game,*
> *Twelve blood-red hounds, whose tangy shaggy hides*
> *Hung loose upon their gaunt and bony sides*
> *Dripping with gore, 'neath brows of thick dark hair*
> *Their small red angry eye-balls fiercely glare,*
> *And as they raised their demon heads on high,*
> *And the hills rang with their exulting cry,*
> *From their black jaws dark clouds of vapour flowed*
> *And their huge fangs like heated iron glowed.*

Even physically the hounds themselves are different in a number of ways from the hounds we see in the later literature. Their blood red colour may be an innovation of Motley's since we do not find it described in any other source. On the other hand, the hounds are in a pack, breathing smoke and have glowing fangs like in the later sources, but, as we will find later on, they are actually ghostly in form rather than physical.

> *4.*
> *Still on, on, on, in madly furious race*
> *Through the deep vale swept past the fearful chase,*
> *Dashed through the Ogmore's terror-stricken tide*
> *And slowly toiled up steep Gaer's fern-clad side,*
> *Till o'er the distant mountain's brow at last,*
> *The gaunt Hell hounds and ghastly quarry past;*
> *Still by the fainter yells the maid could trace*
> *For many a mile the progress of the chase,*
> *Till the hounds' howl of joy and victim's wails*
> *Were lost afar among the winding vales.*
> *'Idris,' the trembling maiden shuddering said,*
> *'Yon are the hounds of Hell, that hunt the dead.'*
> *'Yes, but my child, e'en by that dubious light*
> *Knowest not the fell Cŵn Annwn's game to-night?'*
> *''Twas the dark chief of that fierce Norman horde*
> *Who broke our midnight dreams with fire and sword.'*
>
> *5.*

The first faint light of morning glimmering wide
Rose in grey gleams upon Tor Curig's side,
And the young joyous sun, with glowing breath
Deepened to crimson all the purple heath,
And the bright drops of dew his glittering rays
Flashed scattering back in imitative blaze;
But the red mountain blushed with deeper hue
Than the gay ruby light the sunshine threw,
For on the trampled war-town turf there stood,
Many a dark pool of curdling Norman blood;
And brighter than the flashing dew drops, glance
The scattered silver casque and broken lance,
Though broad foul stains the dewy metal bore
Of brown damp rust, and clots of blackening gore

6.
The loose rein ringing on his barded breast,
The wild wind ruffling his unbraided crest,
All masterless the warhorse calmly grazed,
Save when his mailed head he listening raised,
And gazed, till to his loud unanswered neigh
The mountain echoes slowly died away.
And his strong trusty helm all rudely riven,
The long keen arrow through his breastplate driven,
His steel-clad limbs in that young joyous ray
Cold, shining, there the Norman chieftain lay;
His lance's broken truncheon tightly strained,
The stiffened gauntlet's iron grasp retained,
And from the battered visor dimly glare
His glassy eyes in fierce but soulless stare,
While the black beaten turf and miry steel,
The earth-fixed spur that armed his outstretched heel,
Told but too well with what convulsive strife
His strong limbs wrestled for the ebbing life. [69]

I have put the final three stanzas together since they do not produce much extra information, but I thought the reader might wish to read the entirety of the ending.

---

[69] Motley, J. (1847), *Tales of the Cymry*, (Longmans, London) pp.35-9; 60-2

We can at least deduce though that whether the hounds are from Hell or from the land of magic, they do have a supernatural task. When the Welsh maiden first sees the hounds she exclaims:

> 'Yon are the hounds of Hell, that hunt the dead'.

This has the ring of authentic folklore about it, and is reminiscent of other stories we shall read as we progress. It is also clear that the Norman knight is already dead when the druid and maiden see him. His battered and riven armour could not have been caused by hounds and the cause of his death seems to have been 'the long keen arrow through his breastplate driven'. An earlier dramatic exclamation by Idris suggests that the knight was killed by Madoc, the leader of the Welsh, with the help of the druid's magic:

> 'If the dread powers by which our sires of yore
> Could make these mountains tremble to their core,
> And call black tempests to the calm blue heaven,
> Can yet to spells of later days be given,
> The Norman Chief 'neath Madoc's blade shall yield
> His streaming life-blood to the purple field.' [70]

If it is the case that Madoc killed the Norman chieftain, then the Cwn Annwn are 'hunting the dead' just like the maiden suggested, and are responsible for hounding the knight into Hell.

Discussion

The most original thing about the hounds found in 'Cwn Annwn' is that James Motley's hounds are very definitely supernatural creatures. Further, they hunt in packs rather than in solitary, they come either from the Otherworld or the Underworld, and their prey are the ghosts of mortals. These are not features which we have seen frequently in later references, but they are also not innovations of Motley's, since we start to find them more commonly as we go further backwards in time.

---

[70] P.25.

At the same time, Motley tells us that 'the dread of them [the hounds is now gone quite out of the country', and although he does apparently find one old man in Glamorgan who still believes in the hounds, it is unclear whether in 1848 people were any more credulous than they were in 1901 or 1929 when they required a rational explanation for the creature. At the least though, in Motley's story he was able to get away with describing the hounds as incorporeal ghosts rather than physical creatures. The reason the story had more currency in the mid nineteenth century than the early twentieth is not clear, but it may be simply that more people believed in ghosts.

There is some discrepancy in the story regarding whether the hounds are good or evil creatures. Motley explains this away by seeing them as 'personifications of the Druids, who of course devoted to eternal punishment all who were not of their own persuasion'. Although they avenge wrongs done on mortals, physically they appear red with glowing red eyes and fangs, and breathe smoke. They terrify the spirits that they hunt and seem very blood-thirsty, and are even explicitly said at one point to come from Hell.

Motley's hounds do have some attributes which we might call Welsh. Their red colour, and druidic nature from Annwn are very Welsh features, and we will find the prototypes for these features in the earliest Welsh hound legend – 'Pwyll', which we will see later in this book.

Like Hunt's hounds in 1865, Motley's hounds are ghostly, hunt in packs and come from another world. However Motley's hounds are unique in two ways. Their red colour I have already described may be simply another version of the flaming coat, perhaps best known from the 'phospherus paint' of *The Hound of the Baskervilles*. On the other hand it might instead be a peculiarly Welsh feature, since it echoes some Welsh folklore of the Hounds of Annwn known from the medieval period. However, their explicit hunting of the dead is definitely a feature we find in earlier Dartmoor legends and this is one of the last examples.

'The Wish or Wisked Hounds of Dartmoor', in *The Athenaeum*, 1847

Introduction

The Athenaeum was a London based learned magazine, published once a week and which contained articles on a broad range of 'current-affairs' subjects which learned gentlemen and ladies might like to know about like medicine, social science, environmental science, and especially literature, art and theatre. It was printed from 1828 to 1923[71].

Our interest in the publication is for a single article on the folklore of Dartmoor which was published in the magazine in 1847. The author of the article signs himself only as R.J.K. but considering those initials and the dating, this is most likely to be Richard John King. King wrote extensively on Dartmoor and its history and folklore. He edited the 'Folk-lore' section of The Report and Transactions of the Devonshire Association from 1875 and wrote a history of The Forest of Dartmoor and its Borders[72], together with a multitude of Guidebooks to the counties of England and their cathedrals.

One of the central themes of 'The Wish or Wisked Hounds of Dartmoor' is that much modern folklore has its roots in Celtic or Germanic paganism. This is not such an usual belief to find among folklorists even today, but it is definitely one which was espoused by Richard John King, even whilst he was still an undergraduate at Exeter College, Oxford.

> On our own Dartmoor, the deep baying of the heath hounds with fiery tails and flaming eyes is not only heard in the wild hollows and rocky glens, but they occasionally enter houses in the dead of night for the sake of devouring sleeping children. Such a 'companye' always

---

[71] *The Athenaeum Projects*, http://athenaeum.soi.city.ac.uk/athall.html, (2001)
[72] (1856, John Russell Smith, London)

> accompanied the [medieval] Fairies in their visits to 'middle earth'.[73]

If Richard John King was not the writer of the following text, he probably knew the writer and even the short quotation I have given above proves that he would have agreed with the author's approach.

Text and Commentary
'The Wish or Wisked Hounds of Dartmoor.

> 1.
>
> In passing over that wild moorish district through which the river Aune or Avon runs in its earlier course, you come upon a long narrow tract of the brightest greensward, winding onward between the heather. It is such a path as is called in Scotland a 'blind road;' scarcely seen when you are actually on it, but easily traced in its course over the distant hills, from the strong contrast of its close short turf with the fern and heather of the surrounding moors.
>
> This is the 'Abbot's Way' – an ancient hill road, which the abbots of the 'poor-house of St. Mary's of Buckfast,' are said to have used in their journeys to and from the great Benedictine monastery at Tavistock. A portion of its course was anciently marked out by rude stone crosses; --'signa' says a charter of the Abbey, 'Christiano digna:' and four hundred years ago, you might perhaps have seen one of the hooded brethren resting beneath the shelter of the cross, in his way over the moors to the wooded valley where the towers of his ancient church rose up by the river side. The Abbot's Way is now traversed by far different visitors. It is the especial haunt

---

[73] King, R.J. 'On The Supernatural Beings of the Middle Ages' in: Two Lectures Read Before the Essay Society of Exeter College, Oxford, (Privately Printed, Oxford, 1840). p.22
The University of Oxford to this day maintains a collegiate system so that every student is placed in one of forty or so colleges. Each college has its own library, common room, kitchen and lecturing, although advanced lectures are usually carried out on a university-wide level. Together with St Edmund Hall, Exeter College is one of the two traditionally standard colleges for students from the south west of England.

> of the Wish, or Wisked Hounds;--the wildest and most remarkable of the supernatural beings which still linger within the bounds of the old forest of the Dartmoors.
>
> The Wish Hounds, as they are called, (a name probably connected with the Anglo-Saxon 'wicca', a witch,) are under the immediate guidance of that mysterious being, whose nature 'well may I guess, but dare not tell.' In the pauses of the storm, and mingling with the hoarse voices of the rapidly- swelling mountain waters, the broken cry of dogs, the shouting of the hunters, the loud blast of their horns, and the sounds of 'hoofs thick beating on the hollow hill' are borne onward upon the winds of the forest; and when the dark curtain of mist rolls slowly up over the hill side, they may sometimes be seen to sweep across the moors, rough, swarthy, and of huge size, with fiery sparks shooting from their eyes and nostrils. It is not safe to leave the door of the house ajar, for in this case they have the power of entering, and have been known to devour sleeping children in the absence of the household. For this reason, it is still the custom in some of the wilder parts of Devonshire to place a crust of bread beneath the pillow of the cradle: a custom which perhaps had its origin in the very ancient custom or reserving a certain portion of the consecrated bread of the Eucharist,--which, carried by its communicant to his own home, might there be partaken of daily, and was supposed to preserve the house from all evil.

If the first extract from *the Athenaeum* sounds familiar, it is because Hunt previously told the story of the 'Wish or Wisked Hounds' who lurked around the Abbot's Way and who might have something to do with Odin. Unfortunately all these similarities seem more than coincidental, and indeed Hunt goes on to quote this article as his source of information about the Dartmoor Hounds.

I have already discussed the etymology of the term 'Wish Hound', and suggested that Hunt was right, twenty years later, in rendering it 'Wisht Hound' rather than 'Wicca Hound'. Ignoring the incorrect etymology though, for the first time in 1847 we get the sense that the Beasts of Dartmoor were a real threat to those living in the area, and a danger which was carefully guarded against. The author explains that people should close their doors and keep crusts of bread under their pillows. The author's wording here 'for in this case they have the power of entering, and have been known to devour sleeping children' is very similar to that in the essay of seven years earlier written by Richard John King 'enter houses in the dead of night for the sake of devouring sleeping children'.

2.

Certain spots on Dartmoor are more commonly haunted by the Wish hounds than others: and on its borders there are many long narrow lanes, closely overgrown with thorn and hazel, through which they pass in long procession on particular nights,--of which St. John's Eve is always one. A person, who was passing at night over the moors above Withecombe, heard them sweep through the valley below him with a great cry and shouting; and when he reached the highest point of the hill, he saw them pass by, with the 'Master' behind,--a dark gigantic figure, carrying a long hunting pole at his back, and with a horn slung round his neck. When they reached the ancient earthwork off Hembury Fort,-- which rises on a high wooded hill above the Dart,--the Master blew a great blast upon his horn, and the whole company sank into the earth.

Their appearance, however, is by no means without danger to the beholder: and even the sound of their distant cry amongst the hills is a forewarning of evil to those who hear it. Not long since, a number of men, with dogs and ferrets, proceeded (on the Sabbath day), to trespass on a large rabbit-warren, near the source of the water of Avon: but when they got to a wild hollow in the hillside, the dogs 'heard the Wish Hounds' and at once set up a dismal howling. They were cheered on by their masters,--but nothing could prevent them from running homewards as fast as they could: "and at the end of a fortnight,' said the warrener, 'the dogs were all dead'.

The Spectre Hounds of Dartmoor are immediately connected with the famous hunt of Odin,--the Wilde Jager of the German forests. The Einheriar, or Spirits of the Slain, were believed to pass, at close of day, in one great army, through the golden gates of Valhalla, led by their

> might chief, Odin 'the powerful, the severe.' Their time was passed in the chase, or in the fiercest and most sanguinary combats –during which many fell on both sides; but all came to life again when the hour of the great mead feast arrived. It was the battle of the Einheriar that the Northern peasant thought he saw, when high above his head he heard the faint hurtling of the Aurora--
>
> 'And knew by the streamers that shot so bright
> That spirits were riding the Northern Light.'
>
> ...

We get a few interesting descriptive features coming through in the second section. The 'Master' of the hunt is described first as 'a dark gigantic figure, carrying a long hunting pole at his back, and with a horn slung round his neck'. This figure is not the Devil which we saw in 'The Devil and his Dandy-Dogs' but nor is it a human ghost like Dando. The figure of the 'Master of the Hounds' is a shadowy, supernatural huntsman. Clearly the author believes the Dartmoor Huntsman to be connected to Odin and the master of the Wild Hunt which may well be correct as we shall see.

The fact that the hunt is following an ancient path, and the fact that they sink into the ground when they reach their destination at Hembury Hillfort shows clearly that the hunt is not entirely natural, and may have ties with the underworld and the lands of the dead.

The danger of hearing the howls of the pack is also very interesting. After this point although the howling, screaming or yelping is a central part of the folklore, and is often mentioned as fierce or terrifying it does not seem to be dangerous. However before this point the idea that the howling could kill was fairly common.

> 3.
>
> With the extinction of heathenism, however, many changes took place in the old belief. In the north of Devon the spectral pack are called 'Yeth hounds', or 'Yell hounds;' and are supposed to be the unembodied or transmigrated souls of unbaptized children, which, having no resting-place, wander about the woods at night,

> *making a wailing noise. There is another legend, evidently of Christian origin, which represents them in incessant pursuit of a lost spirit. In the northern quarter of the moor, the Wish hounds, in pursuit of the spirit of a man who had been well known in the country, entered a cottage, the door of which had been incautiously left open, and ran round the kitchen, but quietly, without their usual cry. The Sunday after, the same man appeared in church, and the person whose house the dogs had entered, made bold by the consecrated place in which they were, ventured to ask why he had been with the Wish hounds.*
>
> *'Why should not my spirit wander,' he replied, 'as well as another man's'. Another version represents the Hounds as following the spirit of a beautiful woman changed into the form of a hare; and the reader will find a similar legend, with some remarkable additions, in the 'Disquisitiones Magicae' of the Jesuit Delrio. (Lib, vi. c.2)*

Section three introduces some more really interesting pieces of folklore. The author begins by confirming that the term 'Yeth Hounds' was known even in 1848, and the idea that the hounds may be the souls of un-baptised children is mentioned. Un-baptised children have been said to turn into many creatures over the years from birds to spirits, but it is interesting that other texts like the 1897 Folklore journal piece have the hounds actually hunting children. Perhaps one of these motifs was created by someone misunderstanding or re-interpreting the other.

The idea that the hounds chase women as hares seems more reminiscent of classical mythology than any particular folklore. However the idea that they chase lost spirits, especially the spirits of the dead was repeated in later times by James Motley who has his 'Cwn Annwn' chasing the soul of the already vanquished leader of the Normans, and also perhaps indirectly of the Hounds which surrounded Cabell's tomb after his death.

> 4.
>
> *Besides the Wish Hounds, some of the wild valleys on the borders of the moor are frequented by a solitary apparition in the shape of a black, shaggy dog. The glen*

below the Dewerstone Rock, and a deep, wooded valley in the parish of Dean Prior, are both so haunted. This is rather the Celtic form of the superstition than the Northern:--which dwells more on the dark 'Master' than on the dogs themselves. It is similar, too to the Welsh 'Cwn Annwn' or 'Dogs of Hell;' which, although they occasionally hunted in packs were more frequently seen alone. They have been particularly described by a Mr. Jones, of the Tranch who conceives them to be the same kind of doogs against which David prayeth in Ps.xxii.20-- 'Deliver my soul from the power of the dog' From his 'Relation of Apparitions of Spirits in the Country of Monmouth,' the following curious narration has been extracted:--

'As R.A. was going to Laugharn town one evening on some business, it being late, her mother dissuaded her from going, telling her that it was late, and that she would be benighted: likely she might be terrified by an apparition, which was both seen and heard by many, and by her father among others, at a place called 'Pant-y-madog.' which was a pit by the side of a the lane leading Laugharn, filled with water and not quite dry in the summer. However, she seemed not to be afraid, therefore went to Laugharn. On coming back before night, (though it was rather dark) she passed by the place, but not without thinking of the apparition. But being a little beyond this pit, in a field where there was a little rill of water, and just going to pass it, having one foot stretched over it, and looking before her, she saw something like a great dog (one of the dogs of Hell) coming towards her; being within four or five yards of her, it stopped, sat down, and set up such a scream so horrible, so loud and so strong, that she thought the earth moved under her, with which she fainted and fell down. She did not awake, and go to the next house, which was but the length of one field from the place, until about midnight, having one foot wet in the rill of water which she was going to pass when she saw the apparition.[74]

---

[74] K--, R.J. (full surname not given but possibly 'King'), 'The Wish or Wisked Hounds of Dartmoor', in: *Athenaeum, no. 1013*, folklore section, (1847), pp.334-5 in full year volume.

The fourth and final extract is the most interesting of all for our purposes. We can safely ignore R.J.K.'s assertion that seeing a single hound is a more 'Celtic' version of the folklore, since we shall see as we progress that both Celtic and Norse language versions of the text have both huntsmen and hounds. James Motley, the author of the 'Cwn Annwn' which we looked at previously, quotes this article slavishly. However, even though he was trying to make his hounds as Welsh as possible he still made them multiple rather than singular.

On the other hand, the author's testimony about a single 'black, shaggy dog', almost 70 years before Arthur Conan Doyle wrote the *Hound of the Baskervilles* proves that this folklore was not invented in the twentieth century. R.J.K. even talks about one story that we know. The ghost which haunts 'Dean Prior' is certainly the 'Weaver of Dean Combe', and the very oldest still extant version of this legend.

The final paragraph of this story is also reminiscent of the 'The Hound's Pool' which we saw earlier. That story also described a woman who was so scared by a hound whilst travelling at alone at night that she fell into a small pool of water. When the protagonist of that story woke up she found she too was wet, but pushed-on to the next house anyway and dried-off there.

Discussion

R.J.K. describes the wish or yeth hounds as 'rough, swarthy, of huge size' with 'fiery sparks' shooting from the eyes and nostrils. They accompany parties of mounted hunters on horses, and these hunters shout and play horns as they go. The howling of the dogs kills other dogs and even makes humans faint with terror. This is actually the earliest example of hounds howling as they travel, in earlier texts this howling is left out and replaced with the barking of dogs and the playing of horns.

The leader of the pack and the master of the hounds is definitely a supernatural figure, but just like in 'Cwn Annwn' it is not certain whether he is the Devil or just a ghost or god of hunting. On the one hand, these hounds hunt and eat children and the dead, but can be fended off by bread. Just like R.J.K. says, the origin of this tradition may well have been the keeping of part of the Eucharist bread, which was a common tradition in centuries past. A fiery figure which eats children and is warded off by a Christian relic might seem to be demonic in nature.

On the other hand, it is not Eucharist bread which wards off the figures in the modern version of the story, but ordinary bread. The Master of the Hunt in R.J.K.'s story does not have any overtly Devil-like characteristics like in 'The Devil and his Dandy-Hounds'. In folklore fairies are often warded off by the name of 'Jesus Christ' or the sign of a cross, and the Devil is certainly not the only supernatural character who ever works evil. The idea of the pack following old roads like the Abbot's Way is more reminiscent of ghost stories than stories of demons, especially since the road is associated with Christianity. Ultimately, just like in 'Cwn Annwn' the hounds in 'The Wish or Wisked Hounds of Dartmoor' seem to be of an ambiguous nature, somewhere between Otherworldly and Underworldly.

This folklore covers a lot of new ground, but there are still only a few things which we are seeing for the first time in 1847. This is the earliest use of the terms 'Wish Hound' or 'Yeth Hound'. The packs are half way between otherworldly and underworldly and for the first time we see their cry doing actual quantitative damage to other creatures. The hounds hunt the dead just like the Cwn Annwn, and are said to be the spirits of un-baptised children. The Hound of Dean Prior and the Hound of Dewerstone, two single hounds are also mentioned along with the Wish Hounds, demonstrating that *The Hound of the Baskervilles* was not the first Dartmoor legend to have a single hound.

Fitz of Fitz-Ford, by Anna Eliza Bray, 1830

Introduction

One of the very earliest attested legends of a black hound around Dartmoor which I have heard about is in the legend of the ghost of Lady Howard. This ghost is said variously to either ride in her carriage from Fitzford to Okehampton preceded by a hound, or to turn into that hound herself. As we shall see, both legends are attested very early on, but the latter is especially interesting since it mirrors the penitence of Weaver Knowles from the later traditions we have already seen.[75]

Okehampton, the destination of the ghostly procession, is the most major settlement on the northern portion of Dartmoor. Buses run there from around Devon and 'Okehampton Camp' has in recent years become the main headquarters for the army on the moors. Okehampton is also one of the most easily accessible villages on the border of the High Moor, and the camp is the most usual starting place for those on arranged hikes like Ten Tors.

The earliest record of this ghost is found in *Fitz of Fitz-Ford*, a kind of prototype historical novel written by Anna Eliza Bray in 1830. Bray (1790-1883) was a lifelong collector of folklore and writer who acquired an interest in the stories of Devon after marrying her second husband, the Rev. Edward Atkyns Bray of Tavistock in 1822. She was responsible for producing the *Description of the Part of Devonshire Bordering on the Tamar and the Tavy*, released in three volumes in 1836. She also wrote more than one novel based on local legends and events, one of which was Fitz of Fitz-ford, which told the story of the ghost of Lady Howard[76].

---

[75] I first heard of Lady Howard's ghost in Mark Norman's unpublished conference paper in 'The Black Dog in the West Country', and my thanks are due to him for first pointing this folklore out to me.

[76] Schneller, B.E. 'Bray, Anna Eliza (1790-1883)' in: *Oxford Dictionary of National Biography, 2004* (Oxford University Press, www.oxforddnb.com/view/article/3291).

Lady Mary Howard (see above: 1596-1671), was herself a real historical figure, and her story has been the object of much research. She was the only child of the deeply disturbed and paranoid John Fitz, who committed suicide after killing his best friend whilst still a young man. This made Lady Mary a 'ward of the court', an orphan whose hand in marriage and inheritance could be bought from the royal court by wealthy suitor's families, if she was not wanted by any relatives.

Mary Fitz was bought by the family of the Earl of Northumberland, and given in marriage as a child to Sir Allan Percy.

Sir Allan Percy died of 'a severe chill' before Mary Fitz grew up, and responsibility for marrying off the poor child thus returned to the Court of Wards and Liveries. By this time her good looks (see picture opposite) and the very good income she would inherit from her estates upon turning 21 were remarked by many, and there were rivals for her hand. It is easy to understand why, before she could be sold again she ran off with a young man called Thomas Darcy, son of Lord Darcy of Chiche. Since the man was of good birth, and his father was high in favour in court, no complaints were raised. Unfortunately Thomas Darcy lived only a few months after marrying lady Howard, and she was once again returned to her wardship.

She was married for the third time at 16 to Sir Charles Howard, son of the Earl of Suffolk in 1612, and this husband lasted by far the longest. He lived with her ten years, and their marriage seems to have been fairly equitable since Sir Charles left her a small dower. After six years as a relatively young, single woman she married Sir Richard Grenville in 1628, and her marriage with him was not nearly so civil. He was a poor man while she was a rich heiress, so before she married she made arrangements to prevent him from controlling all of her finances. This led to bitter quarrels, and they were separated (but not divorced) at most a few years into the marriage. Together, her battles to keep her finances intact, her interactions with her children and estranged husband make quite a colourful and inspirational life story, perhaps explaining why Anna Eliza Bray found the subject suitable material for her book.[77]

The only problem is that the real historical character died more than a century and a half before Bray's biography, which is the earliest authenticable account of Lady Howard's ghost. It is impossible to be sure how soon after Lady Howard's death the story of her ghost and the hound was written. Lady Howard's story could well have inspired legends of ghosts by itself, but the journey of the ghost has so little to do with the life of the woman that we may suspect that the story was

---

[77] See: Radford, G. 'Lady Howard of Fitzford', in: *Reports and Transactions of the Devonshire Association, vol. 22,* (1890), pp.67-110.

invented long after her death by those who knew her only by reputation. Indeed there is reason to be sceptical: The invention of the coach which Lady Howard is supposed to ride in was not even popularised until sometime in the middle of the eighteenth century, so the folklore cannot have been invented until almost a century after her death.[78]

Text and Commentary

1.

It was a summer evening when, in company with Mr. Bray, I first visited this ancient gateway. And as we passed along he related to me the various anecdotes, respecting the place of his birth that I have mentioned above. But he more particularly drew my attention to Fitz-ford, as he told me tradition had peopled even the solitary gateway, now in ruins, with the restless spirits of the invisible world; that strange forms were said to be there seen; and that one of these was of a truly German character: since a Lady Howard, famed in her life-time for some great offence, was now nightly doomed, as a penance, to follow her hound which was compelled to run from Fitz-ford to Oakhampton Park between midnight and cock-crowing, and to return with a single blade of grass in its mouth; a punishment from which neither the mistress nor the hound could be released till every blade was consumed. I laughed at this wild tradition. And Mr. Bray then told me that there were other and more probable traditions, supported by the evidence of history, connected with this gateway at Fitz-ford, which in early life had much interested his imagination.[79]

The first extract comes from Bray's introduction to her story, and describes how she first came to hear of the folklore of the ghost of Lady Howard. This is the very earliest reference we have to the legend. It gives the 'woman following hound' rather than 'woman as

---

[78] See the above article, p.68.
[79] Bray, A.E. (1830), *Fitz of Fitz-Ford, vol. 1*, (Smith, Elder and Co., London). pp.10-11

hound' version of the folklore, but is otherwise pretty much the same version of the story still told today. Interestingly though it is not the same as the tale recorded in Bray's own book later on, as we can see if we turn to the main description of the hound there:

> 2.
>
> *We should here notice, however, that the first intimation of its approach, even before the noise of the wheels announced it, was conveyed to John Fitz by the sight of a well-known bloodhound bounding by his horse, which he recognised as the constant attendant of Lady Howard, and to which she had given the significant name of Redfang.*
>
> *Redfang was of that race of bloodhounds now almost extinct in England, but which at the period of our tale were to be found in the country residence of every nobleman, baron, or person of distinction throughout the kingdom.*
>
> *Redfang was of a breed extraordinary even in these usual distinctions of his kind; and Lady Howard, proud of every distinction claimed by her house, would frequently speak of her favourite by the name of the Redfang Howard. He had limbs of a giant mould, his countenance was fierce and stern, with a dark spot above each eye, long black ears, and a heavy jowl; a grisled back, and a body of a deep sand colour, almost approaching to red, completed the striking appearance of the noble hound, the favourite of his mistress and the terror of all deer-stalkers, mendicants, and intruders upon the person or property of Lady Howard.*[80]

Bray has clearly adapted her source quite far from the original folklore. The phantom dog here becomes one that accompanied Lady Howard during her life time rather than only after her death, although as we shall see, there is no evidence that the real Lady Howard had such a hound. Physically it is possible that the fictional hound was based on descriptions of the real ghostly hound. The dog here is a huge, fierce,

---

[80] Bray, A.E. (1830), *Fitz of Fitz-Ford, vol. 3*, (Smith, Elder and Co., London). pp..128-9

sandy-red bloodhound and with a grizzled back, black eyes and a savage disposition, which sounds not unlike a modern ghost. Although it is not explicitly said that this hound accompanied Lady Howard as a ghost after death in the text, this was confirmed by Bray six years later:

3.

All I knew of her was, that she bore the reputation of having been hard-hearted in her lifetime; that for some crime she had committed (nobody knew what), she was said to be doomed to run in the shape of a hound from the gateway of Fitz-ford to Okehampton Park, between the hours of midnight until cock-crowing, and to return with a single blade of grass in her month whence she had started; and this she was to do till every blade was picked, when the world would be at an end. Dr, Jago, the clergyman of Milton Abbot, however, told me, that occasionally she was said to ride in a coach of bones up the West-street, Tavistock, towards the Moor; and an old man of this place told a friend of mine the same story, only adding that "he had seen her scores of times!"

A lady also, who was once a resident here, and whom I met in company, assured me that, happening many years before to pass the old gateway at Fitz- ford, as the church-clock struck twelve, in returning from a party, she had herself seen the hound start! Now, I verily believe the lady told truth; for my husband's father, many years ago, rented Fitz-ford — it was the residence of his hind or bailiff, and there the late Mr. Bray used to keep a pack of hounds; it is, therefore, nothing improbable, that one of them might have slipped the kennel, and ran out as the church-clock struck twelve, and so personated, in the eyes of imagination, the terrific spectre of the old tale. My husband can remember that, when a boy, it was a common saying with the gentry at a party — "Come, it is growing late, let us begone, or we shall meet Lady Howard, as she starts from Fitz-ford."

The above anecdotes were all I knew about her, when I determined to make her take a part in my story; but the hound, the gateway, and the coach of bones, were all fine

> hints for imagination to work upon. I walked down to Fitz-ford with Mr. Bray, and reconnoitred the spot; and there, such is the bewitching power of locality, all seemed to rush at once into my mind. The plot was formed with ease; and I went home determined to connect the adventure of Fitz and Slanning, under the gateway, with Lady Howard; to give her a real hound, or bloodhound, instead of turning her into one; and then the coach of bones, and her riding in it after death, might be made a legend, in consequence of a great crime, which by an evil passion she had been led to determine on committing whilst riding in her own coach, in all her pride, to the house of the person she had it in view to betray to ruin here on earth. This rude sketch of a plot was soon worked into shape, and committed to paper.
>
> Mr. Bray named the hound Redfang, as a significant appellative for a dog whose instinct was to become the agency in assisting to bring about the catastrophe. I had never seen a bloodhound, and I wished to be correct in describing one. Here fortune favoured me again; for the younger Lewis, the animal painter, in a few days arrived at our house. I ventured to tell him my wishes, and he very good-naturedly made me a most spirited sketch of a blood-hound; for he had painted one from life, I think he said, in Scotland. From that drawing I described Redfang, and Mr. Lewis's account of the habits and instinct of the animal was of great service. [81]

In this later commentary on the original legend and her book from 1836 Bray gives both the 'Lady Howard in her carriage' and the 'Lady Howard as a dog' versions of the legend. Although the latter version of the folklore was not included in the earliest description of the Lady Howard folklore in Extract 1 (from 1830), the six years between the two sources do not seem sufficient for the creation and naturalisation of a piece of folklore, so the 'Lady Howard as Hound' legend is probably just as old as the 'Lady Howard with Hound' version.

---

[81] Bray, A.E. (1836), *A Description of the part of Devonshire bordering on the Tamar and the Tavy, vol. 2*, (John Murray, London). pp.319-321.

Bray herself actually suggests an origin for the 'new' legend here, which is the idea that one of her father-in-law's hunting hounds may have escaped from the kennel and startled his bailiff. As tempting as this thegory is, it seems to be pure speculation on Bray's part and therefore inadmissible for our purposes. Finally Bray also describes the hound once more and confirms that the physical hound does take the place of the phantom one in her story. She then goes on to state that she described it based on an illustration made for her by an artist called Lewis. If this is wholly the case then perhaps it was not based on physical descriptions of the ghost at all.

> *"There is," says Mary Colling, in another letter, "scarcely an old man or woman in Tavistock but can tell some story or other about your Lady Howard. Some have seen her in the shape of a calf; others as a wool-sack full of eyes, rolling away from Fitz-ford. But most have seen her as a greyhound, and very often in the coach of bones, as described by you in Fitz of Fitz-ford. This story is frequently told of her: Two servant girls, whose sweethearts came one Sunday evening to see them, being informed they intended to get up early the following morning to washing, offered to come to the house, at the hour named, for company. The servants were very glad of this, as the house was so haunted, according to report. The young men, anxious to fulfil their promise, determined to get up early. One heard Tavistock chimes play at twelve o'clock and concluded it was four. He arose, awoke his companion, and they went together to Fitz-ford. When they came there, the doors being open and the fires all lighted, they thought that the servants were gone up stairs to prepare the clothes, &c. They agreed upon playing a trick, and got under the stairs in order to frighten the maids. Soon after they heard footsteps, and, peeping out cautiously, they saw two very large black dogs, with eyes as big as saucers, and fiery tongues, which hung out of their mouths. The young men thought at all events they had best remain quiet, which they did till cock-crowing ; when directly the dogs vanished, the fire went out, and the doors instantly closed. Soon after the servants came down stairs, and on*

> *hearing this story became so alarmed that they determined to quit Fitz-ford. But on recollecting they were each the first-born of their parents, they felt they were safe; as it is said that no witch, ghost, or pixy can injure the first-born child. They became, therefore, reconciled to the place."* [82]

This last extract was written a few years later again and purports to be an exact quotation from a piece of fan-mail, sent to Bray by a "Mary Colling". Mary Colling is described by Bray as 'a most intelligent and exact registrar of all the old tales, traditions, and characters of any note in her native town [Tavistock], and a large proportion of Bray's book on Devonshire is indebted to the folklore recounted by Colling. If Mary Colling existed, as seems likely, and if this is truly a quote from her book, then it becomes a very important alternative early version of the folklore of Lady Howard.

It is very interesting that according to Colling's folklore, the breed of dog denoted is the greyhound rather than the bloodhound. A bloodhound has better folkloric resonance, agreeing with many tales from 'De Nugis Curialium' (examined in a later chapter) onwards. The dogs of this folklore are large, black, with fiery tongues and saucer-eyes. It is fascinating to see this example of 'saucer eyes' in use before the first translation of Hans-Christian Anderson's 'Tinderbox' into English. This suggests that the term was already being used in English before 'The Tinder-Box' was published, although this is difficult to prove from a single use of the term.

It is also interesting that there are two dogs in this version of the legend. Perhaps this was an early attempt to reconcile the two versions of the folklore, but whatever the reason it makes the text seem rather more like a story of a pack of Wish Hounds than a single Phantom Hound.

---

[82] Bray, A.E. (1838), *Traditions, Legends, Superstitions and Sketches of Devonshire*, (John Murray, London). pp.299-300.

Discussion

Ultimately, although the legend of Lady Howard in *Fitz of Fitz-Ford* does not seem to belong to the same family of stories as the rest of the nineteenth century accounts, we can make some parallels with a few later legends of single black dogs. I said before that single dogs did not become popular until the twentieth century but there are sufficient references from earlier centuries to show that they have always been around, and these references are closely aligned with stories of packs of dogs. The hound itself is not described in the folklore in any detail but from Bray's later description of it, it appears to be more red like the 'Cwn Annwn' than it is black like the typical Dartmoor beasts. Although it has a muscular body and strange-coloured eyes, these are not red. It being a bloodhound is interesting, as is the creature's similarity to the original dog in 'The Hound's Pool', including the motif of the impossible task and the transformation itself.

It is also interesting that modern versions of the folklore have changed so little over the years since then. There is a very great discrepancy between the hound in *Fitz of Fitz-Ford*, and the hound recounted by Bray in her notes. However, all of the later legends follow the version described in Bray's notes, supporting the idea that she was drawing on a real tradition which lingered for at least a century from the time that Anna Eliza Bray first recorded it.

The function of the hound in the story is also peculiar. In *Fitz of Fitz-Ford* the dog is the faithful companion of Lady Howard, but in the legend it is depicted as her punishment, whether she is doomed to become it or to follow it. The dog itself is only present because the lady is sinful, and therefore it is clearly a demonic Hell Hound-like creature rather than a friendly one. The animal's pugnacious attitude in the story may well be a reflection of its nature in the folklore.

The black dog has a long history as an associate of the devil and of sinners. It may be that it only originally symbolised doom when those who saw it knew that their sins had finally found them out, although it now seems to signify universal doom to saints as well as sinners as per the modern 'Grim' of *Harry Potter*.

Modern folklore researchers have tended to separate out depictions of single black dogs and depictions of the hounds of the wild hunt, with some justification. Despite being physically very similar, the solitary hounds in, for example, *The Hound of the Baskervilles*, 'The Hound's Pool', and *Fitz of Fitz-Ford* are something of a different breed to the packs of dogs in accounts of the 'Wish or Wished Hounds', 'Richard Cabell of Brooke', and 'The Devil and his Dandy-dogs'. In this book I examine them all together as I believe that early stories like *A Straunge and terrible Wunder,* have elements of both genres. Perhaps these stories represent a time before the two types of story separated.

Around 1900, the 'pack of hounds' story type seems to disappear from contemporary folklore, and we find the type only in old records of non-contemporary material. After this point we find stories of single hounds increasing, perhaps inspired by the popularity of *The Hound of the Baskervilles*. Although the Legend of Lady Howard is clearly the story of a Phantom Hound, versions of it, like the one presented as the last extract above continue to borrow motifs from Wish Hound folklore for some time to come. In a version of the legend from 1880 we are told:

> *A few years ago two ladies from the North of England made a tour of pleasure into the county of Devon. In their journeyings they rode on the outside of the coach from Okehampton to Tavistock, in order that they might see some portion of the far-famed Dartmoor.*
>
> *Twilight came on whilst they were crossing the moor. Suddenly their attention was aroused by the agitation and excitement of the coachman, who in terror exclaimed, "There, there! do you see that?" On being questioned as to what he meant, he pointed with his whip to some creature that was running along by the side of his horses, saying, "There's the black dog that hunts the moor."*
>
> *Terrified at the sight, he lashed his horses into a gallop in order to escape from the weird "black dog that hunts the moor," which suddenly vanished.*

> *I congratulated my lady friends on their good fortune in having been thus made acquainted with a bit of the "Folk-Lore" of Devon.*[83]

To suddenly find yourself riding alongside the hunt is a motif that has always been common in Wild Hunt legends, and although there is only one hound here, we saw in the last extract above that this has not always been the case. Although *Fitz of Fitz-ford* does seem to represent the start of the Phantom Hound genre on Dartmoor it by no means led to the end of the Wild Hunt, just as in biological terms an evolution does not necessarily signal the end of the life of the original species.

---

[83] Wilkey, J.F. 'The Black Dog that Hunts the Moor' p.100, in: *Report and Transactions of the Devonshire Association, vol.12*, (Brendon & Son, Plymouth)

Interlude – From Dartmoor to Britain

Over the century between 1830 and 1929 we have found twelve definitely attested legends of monstrous hounds. The majority of these are set on Dartmoor, but I have also included two legends set in neighbouring Cornwall, and I have also included the legend of 'Cwn Annwn', which has some claim to be a legend of Dartmoor transported to Wales. These ten stories represent three different genres of Hound legend.

Of these twelve, six of them represent stories of **Phantom Dogs**. 'The Hound's Pool', 'The Ballad of the Hound's Pool' (which we only looked at briefly), *Fitz of Fitz-Ford*, and 'Dando and his Dogs' all represent stories of wicked men and women who have died and then been punished. Weaver Knowles and Lady Howard were turned into Dogs, whereas Dando, and another version of Lady Howard became ghosts who rode about accompanied by dogs. Actually the stories of Lady Howard and Weaver Knowles are especially close since each of these characters has been given an 'impossible task' to complete before they are permitted to rest in peace. This just leaves the final screaming 'black, shaggy dog', mentioned in extract four of R.J.K.'s essay on 'The Wish or Wisked Hounds of Dartmoor, which does have a great deal in common with the dog of 'The Hound's Pool'.

Three of the stories represent more sinister **Hell Hounds**. Although this is quite a diverse group it can be categorised by visions of hounds hunting wicked people to death in order to take them to Hell. Each of the stories breaks the mould in a different way. For example, the legend of Richard Cabell has the man dying naturally, but his burial being haunted by black dogs breathing fire. These hounds are presumably waiting to take Cabell's soul to Hell, and their persistence may have some connection to the legends that Cabell cheated death. The Baskerville Hound meanwhile was brought to Earth by a man so evil that his descendants are also haunted to death despite not being as wicked as their ancestor. Finally in 'Cwn Annwn' we find the motif twisted into the idea of righteous Hell Hounds. These hounds hunt a man's spirit across the moors, but they are summoned by a helpful druid and seem to come from the Otherworld rather than the Underworld. Perhaps the growing scepticism nineteenth-twentieth centuries made this genre unpopular as all the stories seem to twist the mould in some way.

That leaves just three legends which can best be described as **Wild Hunt** legends. In all three the Wild Hunt seems to come from Hell, and this is best demonstrated in 'The Devil and his Dandy Dogs', which has a man being hunted across the moors until he prays and is delivered from evil. The other two of these both depict the so-called Dartmoor 'Wish Hounds', although they are almost incidental to the plot of 'The Farmer and the Black Hunter', where a farmer is rude to a huntsman and later finds his son was killed earlier that day. Hunting and killing children seems to be a frequent concern of the Wild Hunt, but to some extent this story is a hybrid between the Wild Hunt and Hell Hound genres, especially since the death of the boy may have been in part due to this father's rudeness. Finally the 1847 seminal study of the Wild Hunt by R.J.K. has the Wild Hunt at its centre. It is difficult to see with this essay where the folklore ends and the author's speculation on the folklore begins but the various talismans against the Wild Hunt are interesting and probably genuine.

As I have said, the story of Lady Howard from 1830 is the earliest full-length legend of Dartmoor's Beasts. There may be older legends, but the increased popularity of folkloric research and the value and interest in folk-tales acted as a catalyst to make the genre more popular. Increased popularity not only set more people to recording local legends but also, conversely, increased the number of legends actually being composed: Increased availability of legends inspired new legends and the increased interest of the rich in legends must have made legend-writing both fashionable and profitable, inspiring creativity even more.

This story also seems to represent the earliest extant story in the genre of the Phantom Dog. I say extant, because it is clear that legends of single ghostly dog figures are clearly around earlier than Lady Howard. Perhaps their origin is in the so called 'Kirk-Grims' called by Baring-Gould the 'goblin apparitions of the beasts that were buried under the foundation-stones of the churches'.[84] Perhaps their origin is in one or two of the sixteenth century pieces of folklore we have yet to see. In any case it does seem to have been *Fitz of Fitz-Ford* which brought the genre into the mainstream, and it is this genre which seems to lead slowly towards *The Hound of the Baskervilles* and even the modern Beast of Dartmoor.

However, this was certainly not the inception of the genre of mysterious beasts and Monster Dogs. If we widen our focus to the whole of Britain we find a vast range of legends, representing the other two of the three genres (Hell Hounds and Wild Hunts). Many of the stories are so reminiscent that they can almost certainly be considered indirect inspirations or sources for the nineteenth century Dartmoor tradition. Others are less close, and represent perhaps failed innovations in the genre, but even these still often contain certain characteristic features which tie the genre together even across centuries.

The black dog was such an inspiration to the history of literature in Britain that it would be impossible to gather together all mentions to it. However I will attempt to draw together at least a representative sample, with a focus on legends which seem the closest to the modern Dartmoor tradition. After exploring as many such traditions as possible the conclusion will attempt to trace the lineage of the modern Dartmoor stories through time.

---

[84] Baring-Gould, M.A. (1892), *Strange Survivals*, (Methuen & Co., London). p.5.

Monster Dogs of Britain, 1678-c.1127

The Wonders of the Little World, by Nathaniel Wanley, 1678

Introduction

Nathaniel Wanley (c.1633-1680) was an ecclesiastic and scholar of considerable renown in the seventeenth century. He was born in Leicester, attained a degree and a master's degree from the University of Cambridge by the time he was 23 and returned to Leicester. He was due to become curate at Lutterworth in 1662 but ended up becoming Vicar at Holy Trinity in nearby Coventry instead.[85]

He wrote *The Great Duty of Self-reflection upon a Man's own Wayes,* books of poetry and a translation of the Latin text Justus Lipsius, but his most important book was *The Wonders of the Little World,* which he published over the course of six volumes. This book compiles a long list of the various kinds of wonder which can be found about the world, and draws uncritically from a huge range of sources both classical and modern.[86]

Unlike other writers that we have seen and will see throughout the course of this book, Wanley truly seems to have enjoyed his job as a minister. He oversaw repairs to the church and left money to endow a Christmas sermon each year in his will.

Wanley's book is interesting for our circumstances because it mentions black dogs at least twice. Both of these references appear to be borrowed from other authorities, and may not even be set in Britain, but I include them to show how popular and well known the motif of the black dog must have been in stories of the time. Britain was not

---

[85] See 'Wanley, Nathaniells, 0-1676', in: *The Clergy of the Church of England* database, (www.theclergydatabase.org.uk).
[86] West, P. 'Wanley, Nathaniel (1632/3–1680)', *Oxford Dictionary of National Biography,* (Oxford University Press, 2004) (online ed. available: http://www.oxforddnb.com/view/article/28665, 2008)

culturally an island by this period, and although throughout the rest of the book I look only at accounts from Britain, it is occasionally possible to see from books like this that legends of the black dog were a Europe-wide phenomena.

Since the two references are only short I will move through them very quickly:

Text and Commentary
1.

> *Jovius extols the prodigious wit of Henricus Cornelius Agrippa, saying that with immense understanding and vast memory he had comprehended the accounts of all Arts and Sciences, the inmost secrets and highest heads of them all and then adds that not being as yet old, he departed this life at Lions in a base and obscure Inn with the curses of many persons, as one that was infamous, and under the suspicion of Necromancy, for that he was ever accompanied with a Devil in the shape of a black Dog; so that when by approaching death he was moved to repentance, he took off the Collar from his Dogs neck, which was inscribed with magical characters by the Nails that were in it, and brake into these last words of his, Abi perditia bestia, quae me perdidisti, (be gone thou wretched beast which hast utterly undone me.) Nor was that familiar Dog from time forth ever seen more, but with hasty flight he leapt into Araris, and being plunged therein over head, he never swam out again, as is affirmed by them that saw it.*

Heinrich Cornelius Agrippa (1486-1535) was a famous German researcher of the occult as well as a critic of the arbitrary and debate-ridden academic disciplines of the arts and humanities. Rumours about his use of magic, necromancy and demon-summoning, and in particular about his black dog familiar circulated soon after his death, in much the form that they are presented above. The story must have been a familiar one to many households in the seventeenth century.

The dog of this account is explicitly stated to be 'a Devil in the shape of a black Dog'. However the creature is clearly *a* Devil rather than *the* Devil, and seems to function in the story as a kind of familiar.

> 2.
>
> *Crescentius, the Popes Legate at the Council of Trent, 1552, March 25, was busie writing of Letters to the Pope till it was far in the night, whence rising to refresh himself, he saw a black Dog of vast bigness, flaming eyes [and] ears that hung down almost to the ground, enter the room, which came directly towards him, and laid himself down under the table.*
>
> *Frightened at the sight, he called his Servants in the Antichamber, commanded them to look for the Dog, but they could find none. The Cardinal fell melancholy, thense sick and died at Vetona: on his death bed he cryed out to drive away the Dog that leaped upon his bed.*[87]

The second extract from Wanley comes from slightly later in his book, but forms the story of a contemporary of Cornelius Agrippa's. The black dog seen by Crescentius is far more like a 'grim' or black-dog-shaped omen of death than the outdoor, hunting-hounds we have seen in the Dartmoor legends. The animal could only be seen by Crescentius and seems to have come to escort him to his death.

However there are some similarities between this creature and the Dartmoor hounds of later times. Physically the vast, black dog with flaming eyes is familiar to us. Further, long ears are one of the defining features of the bloodhound breed which we have already seen to be one of the most common types of dog depicted. Better still, if Crescentius was a sinful man the story becomes one of a hound from Hell come to take the sinner away, especially given the dog's move towards him on his death bed. There is little direct evidence of this in the text, but when it was published in 1678, Britain was in the grips of the 'Popish Plot'; a widely held belief that the Catholics planned to assassinate King Charles II. One of the outcomes of the Catholic Council of Trent in 1552, to which Crescentius was an aide, was to condemn

---

[87] Wanley, N. (1678), *The Wonders of the Little World Or a General History of Man*, (T. Basset, London), pp.518, 611.

Protestant beliefs. With these events in mind it is easy to imagine Crescentius as a villain in the atmosphere of seventeenth century Britain.

Commentary

Wanley's dogs are merely the tip of the iceberg with regards to popular depictions of sinister black dog legends from the early-modern period, but, as stated in the Introduction, they do demonstrate how the view of dogs as a progression from old to new may be an oversimplification.

Both the story's dogs are alone, and both are black and otherworldly. Cornelius Agrippa's dog has a collar covered in arcane glyphs, presumably to control it, and is depicted straightforwardly as 'a Devil in the shape of a black Dog'. At the end of the text it seems to drown, much like the demon Legion in the Bible.[88] In the Crescentius story, the dog is huge, and has flaming red eyes which, as we have seen, are fairly typical of the later supernatural hounds of Dartmoor.

The function and *modus operandi* of the hounds in these seventeenth century legends differ from those of the hounds in the later Dartmoor legends. Cornelius Agrippa's hound is his familiar, and he is quoted as claiming that the dog 'perdidisti' (ruined) him. If he was talking spiritually, perhaps he was supposed to mean that he was soon to go to Hell after signing a contract with the beast or being tempted into the occult. In any case, it is clear that the dog was not there to take him to Hell after death but to accompany him in life, so it has very little in common with the later Dartmoor beasts, despite its physical appearance.

On the contrary, although Crescentius' hound clearly is there to accompany or bring him to Hell, its actions are still very strange. First the very invisibility of this dog to anyone else searching for it is a strange feature. On the one hand, the Dartmoor hounds tended to be visible to anyone when they are seen at all, but on the other hand if the dog was invisible to anyone else, this suggests that it held a personal message to Crescentius, which would agree with the idea that it foretells his death. The second interesting feature is the creature's

---

[88] *Mark* 5:1-11

patient waiting under a table. The civilised dog that would wait quietly in the corner is certainly a long way from the terrifying chase which seems to be the hallmark of the hounds in later tradition. Ultimately, beyond its physical appearance, the Crescentius hound too has little in common with the later Dartmoor legends.

Huge black dogs with sinister intentions are found frequently in literature from all over early-modern Europe. A record much closer to home comes from a short pamphlet from 1683 called *A Narrative of the Demon of Spraiton*, which is set in Spreyton, just a few miles north of Dartmoor. The shape-shifting spectre of this legend appears 'like a monstrous Dog, belching out fire' at one point.[89] Clearly the shape of a monstrous, fiery dog was commonly thought to be an unnatural one, but, just as clearly, the ghost is not supposed to be a hound after the fashion of the Wisht Hounds of Dartmoor.

Another often quoted example was published in a booklet called *Observations upon Prince Rupert's White Dog called Boy* in 1643. Although this dog was white and not black it is said to be invulnerable to bullets, able to turn invisible, able to prophesy and speak many languages, (most especially a 'mixt language, somewhat between Hebrew & High-dutch'). The booklet ends by denouncing the dog as a witch. It is tempting to see this as some seventeenth century version of a tabloid newspaper or gossip magazine, but the book had a serious and political point. It was written in an attempt to try and undermine respect for the Royalists of the English Civil War. The Cavaliers were either High Anglican or Catholic rather than Low Anglican and this was deeply suspicious to the average Englishman of that time. An answer to the book, called *A Dialogue, or Rather a Parley, betweene Prince Ruperts Dogge whose name is Puddle, and Tobies Dog whose name is Pepper* was published in 1643 which did not reject the charges. The idea that a supernatural dog was assisting Prince Rupert must have had some value to the author. All this shows clearly how important the motif of the supernatural dog was, even in the seventeenth century.

The legends we have been looking at since the interlude can be characterised by a national British rather than a regional Dartmoor

---

[89] Anon. (1683), *A Narrative of the Demon of Spraiton*, (Daniel Brown and Thomas Malthus, Temple Bar and Poultry). p.5.

focus. In our search for animals closer to the mould of the Dartmoor Beast we can probably contain our search mainly to legends original to Britain. However at the same time we cannot be sure that the British legends are the only influences, or indeed influences at all. The *Narrative of the Demon of Spraiton,* and the various dialogues with Boye/Puddle above, for example, probably did not affect the later regional Dartmoor legends at all. There are other British legends however which are much closer to the Dartmoor vein.

A Straunge and terrible Wunder, by Abraham Fleming, c.1577

Introduction

A Straunge and terrible Wunder is the contemporary account of a sixteenth century disaster in the parish churches of Bliborough and Bongie, Norfolk, on Sunday the 4th of August, 1577, between 8 and 9 P.M. The form of this disaster was a thunder storm, with bolts of lightning which shook the earth. These disasters were accompanied by a black dog that killed two people and left another scorched and shrunken. The account was preserved in a British Museum book[90], but was considered of such interest in the nineteenth century that it was copied and republished with a new cover in 1820.

---

[90] I have been unable to view the original personally, but the original title page is presented here. The reprint is Fleming, A. (1820 ed.), *A Straunge and Terrible Wunder,* (J. Compton, London)

A straunge

and terrible Wunder wrought
very late in the parish Church
of Bongay, a Town of no great di-
stance from the citie of Norwich, name-
ly the fourth of this August, in the yeare of
our Lord 1577. in a great tempest of violent raine, lightning, and thunder, the
like whereof hath béen sel-
dome séene.

With the appearance of an horrible shaped thing, sensibly perceiued of the
people then and there
assembled.

Drawen into a plain method according to the written copye.
by Abraham Fleming.

The 1820 edition also quotes another account of the same disaster by John Stow in what has become known as 'Holinshed's Chronicles', a highly influential antiquarian project of the sixteenth century which set out to describe and illustrate the history, geography and cultural curiosities of the world at the time. Stow's description need not concern us much here. It confirms the date and time of the incident and also that two people were killed, but instead of death by encounter with black hound it instead states that they were struck by lightning in the bell-tower. Stow's account agrees perfectly with the account given of the storm in the register books of St. Mary's parish church, although it gives fewer details than Fleming's.[91]

Considering the agreement in the other sources it seems probable that this account of the event was only invented long after the fact, and was not the way the story was told at the time.[92] Whether the story of the dog at the church was invented by Abraham Fleming, or whether it was a piece of folklore generally believed in 1577 need not concern us here however. All that is really important to know is that if no forgery has taken place, this folklore is from the sixteenth century and yet, as we shall see, still corresponds with the folklore of the nineteenth century.

The writer, Abraham Fleming (1552-1607) was ordained in 1588 after taking a degree from Peterhouse College, the University of Cambridge. He was then made a deacon and priest and served as chaplain to the Countess of Nottingham until 1593 when he became a Reverend of St Pancras in Central London.[93] If the 1577 date assigned to the text is correct then Fleming wrote this book when he was 24 or 25 before joining the clergy. It is important to note that not only does he himself does not claim any connection to Norfolk, what we know of him does not suggest any connection either. This means on the one hand that his story is unlikely to be forged, since a forger would surely have picked an identity with better links to the subject area, but also that his story is based on second hand testimony at best. The language of the text is consistent with a sixteenth century date.

---

[91] See: Suckling, A. 'Bungay', pp.119-61, in: *The History and Antiquities of the County of Suffolk, vol. 1.* (1846). Pp.124-6.
[92] See Westwood, J. 'Friend or Foe? Norfolk Traditions of Shuck', pp.57-76, in: Trubshaw, B. (ed. 2005), *Explore Phantom Black Dogs*, (Heart of Albion Press, Loughborough).
[93] See *The Clergy of the Church of England* database, (www.theclergydatabase.org.uk).

The text begins with a preface that I have not quoted below, it draws a comparison between natural disasters which the author calls 'signes from heaven' and human beacons, which were large fires on hills made by humans which were lit in times of danger. When danger threatened one beacon was lit and this could be seen by other people on nearby beacons who would light their own fire, thus passing a message across the countryside. The author's suggestion is that the natural disaster 'lately wrought in Norfolke' is a sign 'no doubt of Gods iudgement, which as the fire of our iniquities hath kindled'.

Following this is an account of the disaster itself which I have presented in full below. After the end he also presents 'A Necessary Prayer' to stave off God's wrath. Nevertheless, the author's moralising was to some extent only a flimsy pretence for publishing this booklet. The author expends 644 words giving a moral frame to his account of the disaster, but 1,147 describing the disaster itself, and it is clear from the author's lively prose style that to some extent the supernatural nature of the disaster was exciting to the young man who wrote this book.

Text and Commentary

1.

Sunday, being the fourthe of this August, in ye yeer of our Lord 1577, to the amazing and singular astonishment of the present beholders, and absent hearers, at a certain towne called Bongay, not past tenne miles from the citie of Norwiche, there fell from Heaven an exceeding great and terrible tempeste sodein and violent, between nine of the clock in the morning, and tenne of the day aforesaid.

This tempest took beginning with a rain, which fel with a wonderful force, with no lesse violence than abundance which made the storme so muche the more extrem and terrible.

This tempest was not simply of rain, but also of lightning, and thunder, the flashing of the one wherof was so rare and vehement, and the roaring noise of the other so forceable and violent, that it made not only people perplexed in minde and at their wits end, but ministered

> such strange and unaccustomed cause of feare to be conceived, that dumb creatures with ye horrour of that which fortuned, were exceedingly disquieted, and senselesse things void of all life and feeling shook and trembled.
>
> Therr werr assembled at the same season, to hear divine service and common prayer, according to order, in the Parish Churche of the said towne of Bongay, the people thereabouts inhabiting, who were witnesses of the straungenesse, the carenesse, and sodenesse of the storme, consisting of raine violently falling, fearful flashes of lightning, and terrible cracks of thunder, which came with such unwonted force and power, that to the perceiving of the people, at the time and in the place above named, assembled, the Church did as it were quake and stagger, which struck into the harts of those that were present, such a sore and sodain feare, that they were in a manner robbed of their right wits.

Our first extract sets the scene but also the tone for the events. On Sunday the 4th of August 1577, in Bongay, near Norwich there was a sudden storm, beginning with heavy rain followed by bright lightning and loud thunder. This weather caused animals to be 'exceedingly disquieted' and even inanimate objects 'shook and trembled'. In the church a congregation of local people were gathered for the usual evening service, and they felt the church shake around them and were 'robbed of their right wits'. If we were inclined to try and trace an 'origin' for this folklore, it is easy to imagine such circumstances triggering a mass-hallucination.

On the other hand, the way Fleming describes these events is clearly not factual and rational, it is more like he is telling a ghost story. Once anticipation is built up to its highest levels he continues:

2.
> Immediately herrupon, there appeared in a most horrible similitude and likenesse to the congregation, then and there present, A Dog as they might discerne it, of a black colour; at the sight wherof, together with the fearful flashes of fire then were seene, moved such admiration in

> *the minds of the assemblie, that they thought doomes day was alreadly come.*
>
> *This Black Dog, or the Divel in such a likenesse (God hee knoweth all who worketh all) running all along down the body of the Church with great swiftnesse, and incredible haste, among the people, in a visible forme and shape, passed between two persons, as they were kneeling upon their knees, and occupied in prayer as it seemed, wrung the necks of them bothe at one instant clene backward, insomuche that even in a moment where they kneeled they strangely dyed.*
>
> *This is a wonderful example of God's wrath, no doubt to terrifie us, that we might feare him for his justice, or putting back our footsteps from the pathes of sinne, to love him for his mercy.*

The second extract of our story introduces the 'Black Dog' which is accompanied by 'fearful flashes of fire'. This detail seems intended to confirm to his audience that the dog is intended to be 'the Divel in such a likeness'. The creature runs very fast among the people, and apparently wrings the necks of two of them. This detail at least seems to have been suggested by the real event, since other accounts of the disaster also put the death toll at two, but suggest that these were struck by lightning and fell from the bell-tower.

At the end of extract two, the author returns to his moralising, but after his evocative description of 'the great swiftnesse and incredible haste' of the hound it sounds even emptier than it did in his introduction.

> 3.
>
> *To our matter again. There was at ye same time another wunder wrought: for the same Black Dog, still continuing and remaining in one and the self-same shape, passing by an other man of the congregation in the Church, gave him such a gripe in the back, that therewith all he was presently drawen togither and shrunk up, as it were a piece of lether scorched in a hot fire; or at the mouth of a purse or bag, drawen togither with a string; the man, albeit he was in so straunge a taking, dyed not, but, as it is thought, is yet alive: whiche thing is mervellous in the*

> *eyes of men, and offereth muche matter of amasing the minde.*
>
> *Moreover, and beside this, the clark of the Church being occupied in cleansing the gutter of the Church, with a violent clap of thunder was smitten downe, and beside his fall, had no further harme: unto whom beeing all amased, this straunge shape, wherof we have before spoken, appeared, howbeit he escaped without daunger; which might, peradventure, seem to sound against trueth, and to be a thing incredible; but let us leave thus, or judge thus, and cry out with the prophet, O Domine, &c.! O Lord, how wonderful art thou in all thy works!*
>
> *At the time that these things in this order happened, the Rector, or Curate, of the Church, being partaker of the peoplees perplexitie, seeing what was seen and done, comforted the people, and exhorted them to prayer, whose counsell, in such extreme distresse, they followed, and prayed to God as they were assembled together.*

In the third extract the dog attacks another person, biting them on the neck. The man shrivels up 'as it were a piece of lether scorched in a hot flame'. The dog also appears separately to the Parish Clerk who falls from his ladder in shock but is otherwise left alone by the dog. Amusingly Fleming states that the first man did not die of being shrivelled but is still alive, and his account at this point is so specific that it begs the question of whether this part of the story has been inspired by real eye-witness survivors of the disaster.

Extract three ends with the rector of the church exhorting the people to prayer. At this point the dog leaves the story, so perhaps, just like in the case of 'The Devil and his Dandy-Dogs', the prayer stops the creature from hurting anyone else, once again reinforcing its demonic identity.

> 4.
>
> *Now for the verifying of this report, (which to some wil seem absurd, although the sensiblenesse of the thing it self confirmeth it to be a trueth,) as testimonies and witnesses of the force which rested in this straunge*

shaped thing, there are remaining in the stones of the church, and likewise in the church dore which are mervelously renten and torne, ye marks as it were of his clawes or talans. Beside, that all the wires, the wheeles, and other things belonging to the clock, were wrung in sunder, and broken in peces.

And (which I should haue tolde you in the beginning of this report, if I had regarded the observing of order,) at the time that this tempest lasted, and while these stormes endured, ye whole church was so darkened, yea with such a palpable darkensse, that one persone could not perceive another, neither yet might discern any light at all though it were lesser then the least, but onely when ye great flashing fire and lightning appeared.

These things are not lightly with silence to be over passed, but precisely and throughly to be considered.

Fleming's evidence for his story consists of marks on the church door and the breaking of the church clock. The church's clock was probably broken by lightning but has since been repaired. But many others since Fleming have been inspired by the events of August the 5th of 1577. The fame of this account has spread, and the town today has many pubs named after the animal. The other church named in the legend, the church of Blythburgh Holy Trinity still retains the marks on its doors as a tourist attraction to this day (see the following picture).

'The Devil's Fingerprints' on the north door of Blythburgh Holy Trinity Church, picture by fourthandfifteen (www.flickr.com/chelmsfordblue)

5.

On the self same day, in like manner, into the parish church of another towne called Blibery, not above seven miles distant from Bongay above said, the like thing entred, in the same shape and similitude, where placing himself uppon a maine balke or beam, whereon some ye Rood did stand, sodainly he gavie a swinge downe through ye church, and there also, as before, slew two men and a lad, and burned the hand of another person that was there among the rest of the company, of whom divers were blasted.

This mischief thus wrought, he flew with wonderful force to no little feare of the assembly, out of the church in a hideous and Hellish likenes.

These things are reported to be true, yea, by the mouthes of them that were eye witnesses of the same, and therfore dare with so much the more boldenesse verifie what soever is reported.

Let us pray unto God, as it is the dutie of Christians, to woork all things to the best, to turne our flintie harts into fleshlie hartes, that we may feele the fire of God's mercy, and flee from the scourge of his justice...

In our fifth and last extract Fleming briefly notes that the black dog also visited Blibery, where it terrorises the congregation, kills three people, and burns the hand of one man. In John Stow's account (mentioned in the introduction to this chapter) lightning hits this church first, but Fleming seems to consider the events at Blibery as decidedly secondary in interest to those at Bongay he has already described.

Many people were also 'blasted' by the dog in Blibery, but this is unlikely to have been serious — Fleming is unlikely to be using the modern technological meaning of the word suggesting the people were hurt with fire, and more likely to be referring just to the people being bowled over by the dog.

He finishes by starting his prayer to stave off God's wrath. I have not quoted the main body of the prayer since it offers no new details and seems to be merely provide a frame and rationale to the main body of the text.

Discussion

Overall *A Straunge and terrible Wunder* is very different indeed from both our nineteenth and twentieth century hound legends and the earlier medieval material. Most obviously, instead of the hound being a hunting dog, perhaps sent by Hell, the dog in Fleming's story seems to be the Devil himself in dog form. Throughout the text the form of the dog is never described precisely. The animal is black, but other details are vague. It is often described as a 'straunge shape' rather than explicitly as a dog and it is easy to get the impression that the creature does not actually have a fixed form. The 1577 figure in the artwork shown in the introduction has horns, which is not something we have seen on phantom hounds before now.

Given the location of the sighting in Norfolk, and the Hellish black dog shape of the apparition, this story is sometimes called the earliest evidence for the 'Black Shuck' legend. It certainly had a strong influence on later versions of the folklore but the dog in the story is never called a shuck, and in later versions of the story the shuck is not supposed to be just a form of the Devil like it is in this version.

At the same time, this story is very different to later accounts of the Hounds of Dartmoor as well. The dog is alone, which we only find in the latest Dartmoor legends, and seems to be in the world as a force of nature or warning of God's anger along with the storm, as opposed to the Dartmoor legends where the creature has a mission to hunt down evil-doers and bear them to Hell.

On the other hand the hound of this story embodies a very familiar paradox. It is the Devil, or at least a creature of the Devil, and yet it is being sent into a holy place as an embodiment of God's wrath. The unstated answer to the paradox here, as elsewhere seems to be that since the Devil could not act with God's permission, God must intend the hound to be present in the church. This issue arises again and again in our search, and it may well be that some of the early popularity of the hound legends was because they allowed people to grapple with complicated theological and philosophical issues like the existence of evil in the face of a benevolent omnipotent Creator in a concrete form.

The Devil-dog of *A Straunge and terrible Wunder* is remarkable for (i) its association with natural disasters and God's wrath, (ii) its terrorising of the good church folk and (iii) the fact that it actually physically kills people by wringing their necks and biting them. Clearly it has not been a strong influence on the later Dartmoor hound legends, but at the same time there are things about the story which are familiar. The dog is pure-black, terrifying and travels alone, much like what is perhaps the most famous Dartmoor Beast, Sherlock Holmes' Hound. Whilst the dog of our present story had little direct influence on today's Beast of Dartmoor, we can find similarities which probably stem from it being based on the same classic English sources as the Dartmoor hound legend. The next text we are going to examine could well have inspired both the *Straunge and terrible Wunder* and our more familiar Dartmoor legend.

'Jacob's Well', from Salisbury MS 103, written in Sussex, c.1425

Introduction

'Jacob's Well' or 'Fons Jacob' is a series of Catholic sermons based around one single convoluted metaphor of cleaning out a well. This well represents each person and the sediment and polluted water in the well represent sins and other things which stop humans being spiritually close to Heaven. A Christian needs to painstakingly remove the polluted water, cleanse the sides of the well, re-wall the well with faith, then fill up the well with grace and prevent the well becoming re-polluted. Throughout the text the dangers of becoming corrupted by sin and of dying unredeemed are illustrated with examples, especially at the end of each sermon-chapter, and our extract comes from an example of the dangers of lechery.

Information about the original author is hard to come by, but Leo Curruthers has published a paper assessing the probable date and location of writing. Books based around metaphors like this were fairly common in the fifteenth century, although our text is drawn-out longer than most of the others. 'Jacob's Well' itself is probably based on the 'Speculum Vitae', an important English version of the 'Somme le Roi', although this older text does not contain any Hellhounds. It may have had its origin in a real series of sermons, delivered by the writer to a local congregation. It is also clear that the manuscript, written c.1450, is a copy of an earlier version, although we can only guess at when the manuscript was written. Curruthers puts it c.1400-1425.

Although the surviving manuscript was acquired by Salisbury Cathedral somewhere in the middle of the seventeenth century, and is now named after the Cathedral, it was not created there. The language is mainly in the dialect of Suffolk (between Bury St. Edmunds and Ipswich), but there a few more northern features, perhaps from North-Norfolk, Lincolnshire or the North-East Midlands. Since scribes tend to 'modernise' texts when they copy them it is probable that our scribe was from Suffolk, and either the whole of the original text, or some of the borrowed passages, were originally written in a more northern dialect.

The stories at the end of the chapters are not at all original either, although the manuscript does not cite any source for our particular story. The hounds in our extract may have been based on local folklore, or another Latin or English source, but in some ways the author's source for the story does not particularly matter, as the hounds have the typical features of both their successors and their predecessors.[94]

Only the first half of the manuscript has been published for modern readers, but thankfully that half includes the part we are most interested in. Middle English of the fifteenth century is quite easy to read, and the *Early English Text Society* version of the text that I have used below is very well edited anyway. However since these texts are mainly aimed at academics I have made our extract still more simple to read by replacing the Middle English letters (thorn (þ) and yogh (ȝ)) with their modern equivalents and occasionally adding letters in brackets. I hope that these changes will mean that even readers who have never read any English of this date before should have no problems so long as they read slowly (preferably out-loud). The first paragraph is the most difficult.

Text and Commentary

1.

[She was] a leccherous womman all her lyve, [and] on her dede[-]bedde sche dyde her clowtyn a peyre of schooen[s], & badde her freendys that sche schulde be schod therwyth & beryed. Sche was beryed therwyth.

In the nygt folwyng, be[y] the mone-lygt, a knygt of that same toun cam rydyng homwarde wyth his man. Agens hym kam this deed womman crying, & seyde,

---

[94] See: Carruthers, L. 'Where did Jacob's Well come from? The provenance and dialect of MS Salisbury Cathedral 103, pp.335-340 in: *English Studies, vol. 71, no. 4*, (1990).
Brandeis, A. (ed. 1900), *Jacob's Well*, (Early English Text Society, London). Pp.i-xiii.

> *'Helpe me knygt!'*
>
> *The knyjt [a]lygt doun & made a sercle wyth his swerde & took to him that dede womman into that sercle, wyth her smok & clowtyd schoon. He knewe her wel. Sche tolde hym that sche was deed & feendys pursewyd her. Thei herdyn fro [a]ferre the voys of feendys lyche the voys of hunters & of [t]her houndys, wyth 'orryble hornys & cryes.*

Our first extract introduces the text as being the story of a wasteful, lustful woman who died unrepentant, and asked to be buried in a pair of shoes rather than in humble burial shrouds as was the ordinary Christian practice of the time. The night after her death and burial a knight riding by found her calling for help, above ground. The woman apparently knows she is in danger even at this point. The knight dismounts and the woman explains to him what is wrong. In the text this happens after he has already started to protect her, but this might be just a mistake.

In order to protect her, the knight draws a circle in the ground with his sword and pulls the woman inside with her hair wrapped around his left arm to prevent her from leaving the circle. This is interesting as a magic circle used to ward off evil spirits is a typical feature of modern ceremonial 'magick', as popularised by the secret organisations of the nineteenth and twentieth centuries like the *Heremetic Order of the Golden Dawn*, but also as used by modern practicing Wiccans. Its appearance in this text suggests a great antiquity for the practice.

The actions of the knight here, even apart from using magic are peculiar. It seems probable that the knight grabbed the woman's hair to prevent her leaving the circle. This suggests that he knew she would be tempted to try to escape when she became frightened. Did he believe that his circle would ward off Hellhounds though? In our other early texts where Hellhounds hunt the dead, they are implacable and it seems impossible to stop them, but in the later Dartmoor legends they could be prevented from hunting the living by keeping doors shut and hiding crusts of bread under pillows, or by praying to God. This text seems more reminiscent of the later tradition in this respect. It is also possible that the knight did not grab her hair to keep her safe, but to keep her for himself. She is technically a spirit herself, and magic circles in modern times are traditionally not only used to protect those inside, but also to summon and control spirits. This interpretation would lend a much more sinister tone to the story.

The sound of the hunt is that of horrible horns and cries, which is very reminiscent of how the wild hunt is described in both earlier and later legends, except that the howling of the modern Dartmoor hounds is replaced by the sounding of horns.

This extract is also especially interesting since the word 'dede[-]bedde' for 'death-bed' is a northern dialectal form of the term 'death-bed' strongly indicating that this part of the text has a more northern origin, perhaps belonging to the North-East Midlands, north Norfolk or Lincolnshire rather than Sussex[95].

2.

Sche trem[b]elyd for drede & told the knygt:

'Now come feendys to have me to Helle for synne of leccherie, & for pride, envie, slouthe, coveytise, glotonye & hate!'

The knygt took his hors to his man & helde his swerd drawyn in his rygt hand & he helde her in his left hand be[y] her heer woundyn aboutyn his left arm. The Helle-huntere wyth his Helle-houndys com ny[gh]. The dede womman seyde to the knygt:

'Late me renne! Lo, thei come!'

The knygt helde her stylle. Sche drewe harde & ofte to gon fro the knygt. At the laste, sche gaf a brayde that her heer lefte aboute the knygtes arme, & sche ran away. The feendys huntedyn after & all for-rentyn her, & for-brentyn her & leydin her over-thwert on a brennyng feend, & so, wyth horrible cry born her into Helle.

---

[95] Carruthers, L. 'Where did Jacob's Well come from? The provenance and dialect of MS Salisbury Cathedral 103, pp.335-340 in: *English Studies, vol. 71, no. 4*, (1990). P.339.

Our second extract shows that the hounds terrify the woman, just as the knight seems to have expected. She first asks the knight to let her flee, then pulls away leaving all of her hair behind, despite the knight's best efforts. Immediately after this she is torn apart by the 'Helle-houndys' and dragged to Hell by the hounds and the 'Helle-huntere'.

Could she have been kept in the circle by force? It is not clear, so perhaps wicked souls cannot be saved after all. Other folkloric stories of how Death or the Devil reaps souls have the spirits almost hypnotised like scared rabbits, or sometimes even dancing in a procession straight into Hell. We will consider this idea in more detail in the Discussion.

3.

On the morwe, the knygt dyd opyn her grave & fond the heer of her heed plukkyd of[f] & put the heer that was abowtyn his arm to her heued & seyde to the peple,

'This was her heer.'

& he tolde [t]hem all togydere how sche mette hym, & how the feendys born her to Helle for her leccherie & othere synnes because sche wolde nogt leve her synne & dyed uncontrite.

The next day the knight went to the graveyard, opened the grave and found her body there without any hair. This part of the story works better if you do not think about it – was the woman that the knight met supposed to be a (corporeal) spirit or the corpse itself? If a spirit, why did the body lose its hair? If the whole body, why was the body returned from Hell to her grave?

The plot holes are not really important here though. It is more worthwhile to point out that the Hellhounds are called fiends and that they only chased her because she was sinful and doomed to Hell. The Hellhounds are clearly here working as agents of fate, even though they are part of the Helle-huntere's hunt.

4.

Therfore, caste out this wose of synne wyth a skete of contricyoun, wyth a scavel of confessioun, & wyth a schovyl satisfaccyoun, of whiche thre[e] I schal telle yow another tyme! For whoso castyth out synne, wyth thise thre[e] instrumentys of penaunce, synne schal voyde, grace schal entre, & þe kyngdam of heuene schal reyghin.

'Penitenciam agite, appropinquabit enim regnum celorum.'

(To this kyngdom brynge he you & me, / that for us deyid on rode-tre[e].) Amen[96].

The last extract contains the author's moral for the story; that people should not be sinful. If the main part of the text was being copied from elsewhere, it has clearly come to an end at this point, and these words are the author's own. The author urges people to cast out sin and continues the metaphor that they should clean their wells (see the Introduction to this chapter - in this text individuals are represented as impure wells) using three pieces of specialist equipment, a 'skeet', 'skavel' and shovel.

The moral message given here is so straightforward that the complex story was probably unnecessary to illustrate it. I would suggest instead that the moral only provides a pretext, and that the real reason for the author to include the story was simply for the fun of being scared, or to please listeners or readers. If this is true it suggests that hound folklore was in use and popular at least as far back as the fifteenth century.

Discussion

The folklore of the fifteenth century 'Jacob's Well' text, is highly reminiscent of the nineteenth century Dartmoor Hound texts, despite being written almost four centuries before them. The hounds are

---

[96] Brandeis, A. (ed. 1900), *Jacob's Well*, (Early English Text Society, London). Pp.166-7.

barking and one of the hounds at least is 'brennyng' (burning) in the text, which is reminiscent of the burning eyes and teeth and even burning coat of Sherlock Holmes' Hound The hounds are multiple, and they are followed by a master, the 'Helle-huntere' who owns the hounds which chase the woman.

One of the central difficulties with the text is whether the hounds are servants of fate, or just demons from Hell. Supporting the latter argument, in the text the hounds are called 'Helle-houndys' and 'feendys' and it is clear that they have come from Hell, and later bear the soul to Hell after tearing it to pieces. If the hounds were agents of fate they would be implacable and impossible to fool, but the knight of the story seems to believe he can defeat them and ward them off with his circle and perhaps the might of his arms alone. This is reminiscent of 'The Devil and his Dandy-hounds' where the hunt was defeated simply by the hunted man praying in 'the old language'.

However, at the same time the hounds are no mere demons, they are clearly agents of fate as well. The woman is only being hunted because she was sinful during her life, so she is doomed to go to Hell – the knight was not harmed even though he must have been very close by because he is destined for Heaven. The hounds terrify the woman because she knows she cannot avoid them, and even though she seems to know it cannot succeed she has an uncontrollable desire to flee from the hounds. Considering what happened to the man in 'The Devil and his Dandy-dogs' to the man who did not flee but instead confessed his sins, it seems probable that everyone who is actually killed by the Hellhounds flees from them. Perhaps in a way the victims are fleeing from their own sins, since it is their sinful nature that guarantees their death. If this is the case, then the woman's urge to flee is almost ritualistic in nature – the hounds cannot hunt if no-one flees from them.

Ultimately the case for the hounds being servants of Hell is stronger than the case for them being servants of fate, but perhaps in some ways they are both. In medieval Christianity it was generally accepted that the Devil is given the power to hurt people by God, and all human punishments are thus foreordained, and are the natural consequence of sin rather than an unpleasant and avoidable side-affect. Whatever the case, the presence of this story under such a dubious moral pretext in this fifteenth century manuscript clearly indicates that the story of implacable hounds from Hell must have had some currency in Britain even four hundred years before our earliest explicit record of the hounds of Dartmoor.

'The Desputisoun Bitwen the Bodi & the Soule', in the Auchinleck Manuscript, c.1300.

Introduction

'The Desputisoun Bitwen the Bodi & the Soule' (more commonly called 'þe Desputisoun bituen þe Bodi & þe Soule' in older orthography), contains an account in Middle English of a dreamed debate which took place between the soul and body of a dead man post mortem. The two debaters each place blame on the other for all that has gone wrong, and both gleefully insist that the other will be punished for the crimes during their lifetime. The body is doomed to rot in the ground and the soul is doomed to be tortured until Judgement Day. Variant versions of this story can be found all over Europe, and can be traced back to medieval Egypt. 'The Desputisoun' itself is really an adaptation of the Latin 'Dialogus inter corpus et animam' of the early twelfth century, with some input from 'Nuper huiuscemodi uisionem somnii'.[97]

Our version of the story comes from the Auchinleck Manuscript, an anthology created in London which contains a range of material, especially poetic narratives which were circulating in the 1330s. The manuscript is more likely to have been a commercial venture than a religious one, and a number of names are written in the margins which have been interpreted as a list of the manuscript's owners over the last 700 years[98].

Even though the manuscript itself was commercial product, the 'Desputisoun' text we are interested in is a highly Christian story and it

---

[97] This text is also called the 'Visio Philiberti'. For more see: Matsuda, T. (1997), *Death and Purgatory in Middle English Didactic Poetry*, (D.S. Brewer, Cambridge), p.132-139; Justin Brent, J. 'The Eschatological Cluster', pp.157-176, in: Bell, K., J.N. Couch, (2011), *The Texts and Contexts of Oxford Bodleian Library MS Laud Misc. 108*, (Brill, Leiden), Pp.170-6

[98] Wiggins, A. (2003), 'The Auchinleck Manuscript: Importance' and ': History and Owners', in *The Auchinleck Manuscript* (National Library of Scotland, (http://auchinleck.nls.uk/editorial/importance.html)).
I did not have time to consult the slightly earlier version of the text in Laud misc. 108 ('L') before time of press but believe it to be identical apart from the placement of the first verse.

is probable that it was originally produced earlier than this by a person with an ecclesiastical or monastic background. Indeed, the story is also present in incomplete form in the earlier attested Bodleian Library MS 1486 (Laud misc. 108) which was written somewhere c.1275-1325.

Our extract comes near the end of the text (lines 448-487) when the debate is over. In all previous versions of the story in the genre the soul is borne off, often using pincers, to be tortured with molten lead and barbed hooks. However in the 'Desputisoun', for the very first time in the genre the soul is borne to its punishment by Hellhounds rather than just fiends. The way these Hellhounds are described is very interesting, as we shall see.

I have edited the text to make the orthography easier for those who do not read Middle English. The words which are ~~crossed-out~~ can be replaced by those [in square brackets] after them, and I have added letters to words in the same way and these are added for modern clarity.

Edited Text and Commentary

    1.
    'Bodi, Y may no lenger duelle,

    To stond for to speke with the[e];
    Helle houndes here Ich yelle,
    & f[i]endes mo[re] than y may se[e],
    To com to feche me to Helle,
    & Y [know] not whider Y may fle[e];

    & [but] thou schalt com with flesche & felle
    At Domesday & speke with me.'

The first stanza of our extract sees the Soul give up its argument with the Body since it observes that the 'Helle houndes' with 'fendes mo than y may se' are drawing near. It bids farewell to the body which it will be reunited with on Judgement Day before it goes to Hell for the last time.

> 2.
> Hadde he no ~~rather~~ [sooner] this word y-seyd,
> It ~~wist~~ [knew] never whider to go,
> It was y-hent in a brayd
> With a thousand f[i]endes & yete mo[re].
> & when thai hadde on him y-layd
> [T]her scharpe hokes al[l] tho,
> It was in a sori ~~playd~~ [plight]
> Y-toiled bothe to & fro.

Stanza two describes fiends which come and bear the soul away with their sharp hooks. It seems probable that the term 'fendes' here includes also Hellhounds, since they are clearly present in stanzas one and three. Fiends are more commonly depicted as deformed humanoids in appearance, so it is interesting that those in this part of the story may be more canine than anything else. With this in mind the 'scharpe hokes' may well be intended to be the claws of the Hell hounds.

> 3.
> Sum were rogged & rowe tayled,
> With brode bo[l]ches on [t]her bak[s],
> Scharpe clawed & long nailed;
> ~~Nas~~ [There was] no lim[it] withouten lak.
> Rewefully he was aseyled
> With many a f[i]ende, [dark] blo & blak;
> 'Merci!' he crid, & litel [a]vailed,
> When God wald take his hard wrak.

Stanza three contains the best description of the Hell hounds. The 'tayled' nature of the fiends makes it probable that we are still talking about Hellhounds rather than traditionally humanoid fiends. They coloured dark blue or black, are rugged and rough-tailed and with bulging hunchbacks and sharp claws. Many such creatures assail him, and although we cannot know how many of these are dogs and how many are fiends, the picture that emerges is more disturbing and horrific than intimidating in a more traditional sense.

> 4.
> Sum the ~~chauel~~ [jowl] al[l] to-thrast
> & goten in the le[a]d al[l] hot,

> *& bad[e] he schuld drink fast,*
> *& birly about al o brod.*
> *A fende ther com atte last –*
> *Maister he was, ful wele Y wot*
> *A ~~colter~~ [plough-blade] glow~~end~~[ing] on him cast,*
> *That thurth the he[a]rt the point it smot[e].*[99]
>
> *5.*
> *Glaiues glowend to him thai sett*
> *To bac, to brest, in [ea]ich a side,*
> *That at the hert the pointes mett,*
> *& made [in] him woundes depe & wide;*
> *& than thai asked how that he let*
> *His hert, that was ful of pride;*
> *gif he hadde any thing that him hett*
> *More schame him schuld bitide.*

Stanzas four and five move focus from the Hellhounds to the beginning of the soul's torment. I am not clear what the hounds are thrusting with the jaws at the beginning of verse four but clearly the soul has been led to the punishment arena where it is forced to drink molten lead and is stabbed with a 'colter' by the master-fiend. Clearly the job of the Hellhound-fiends here was to locate and bring the soul to the place of punishment, where it could be tortured (partly by them but then by others).

Stanza five is chiefly interesting for our purposes because it has the Hellhound-fiends speaking to the man and asking him why he sinned (a question aimed at the story's audience more than at the man himself). Since ordinary dogs cannot talk, and no-where else do we find Dartmoor hounds speaking this is clearly a peculiarity of this text alone, but it does suggest that these hounds are no mere animals but demons in animal form.

Giving the fiends the shape of hounds would have mirrored in the minds of a medieval audience the hounds which track game and lead mortal men to where they could kill deer, boar and other venery

---

[99] Burnley, D., Wiggins, A. 'THe Desputisoun Bitven the Bodi & the Soule' in *The Auchinleck Manuscript* (online edition, (http://auchinleck.nls.uk/mss/bodysoul.html), 2003).

animals. The difference is that the Hellhounds in this text bring the soul to Hell rather than leading hunters to it. This may have been inspired more by hare coursing where greyhounds were expected to catch and kill the animals before humans can reach them[100]. Hounds do lead huntsmen in both later and, indeed, in earlier texts, but hounds also hunt on their own in other texts, so both variants seem to be accepted forms of the legend.

Discussion

The Hounds of this text are explicitly Hellhounds rather than Wild Hunt hounds, sent to take the souls of sinful people after they die in order to bring them to be tortured by demons. These Hellhounds act independently and intelligently and seem to be demons in hound-form rather than animals, especially since they speak at one point. As agents of fate they are more than simply demonic, but they are also clearly servants of Hell since they take delight in torture. This lack of ambiguity is familiar from other later texts which have hounds as servants of the Devil.

At the same time it is not at all clear that the fiends are even physically entirely canine. They are only described once in our extract as Hellhounds, and it is possible that they were imagined as half-human-half-dog rather than fully hound. That the term 'Helle houndes' was not being used figuratively is clear from an elsewhere in the text where the Hellhounds are mentioned again. Near the end of the text the other demons (which are also called fiends) 'Helle houndes to him lett', so that the dogs could torture him more. More importantly though, earlier in the text we find the soul speaking a very telling couple of lines about the Hellhounds to the body:

> '*Helle houndes com sone,*
> *& y no may nougt fram hem blenche [shy-away].*'

This helps corroborate the evidence that the job of the Hellhounds is especially to seek and retrieve wicked souls, rather like human's

---

[100] This is clear from medieval hunting manuals, See Baillie-Grohman, W.M.A. and F. (1909), *The Master of Game*, (Chatto &Windus, London). p.186

hounds. Hellhounds clearly have a formidable reputation if the soul does not even try and escape from them, although this might be more because they are agents of divine, implacable fate more than independently awe-inspiring creatures.

The physical description of these hounds is at once familiar and alien. They can be black and ragged like more modern hounds, but they can also be 'blo' (bilberry coloured) rather than black. They are ragged, rough-tailed and have bulging hunchbacks and sharp claws. As I said earlier this seems far more disturbing than the large modern pedigree beasts which terrorised Dartmoor in later centuries.

Ultimately, as we have seen, the innovations introduced by the 'The Desputisoun Bitwen the Bodi & the Soule' are not preserved in later texts, and nor are they seen in earlier texts. Although hounds do occasionally roam by themselves, seeking victims to pull down to Hell they are more often accompanied by at least one huntsman until the era of the solitary hounds much later on.

'Sir Orfeo', in the Auchinleck Manuscript, c.1300

Introduction

Near the end of the Auchinleck manuscript which contained 'The Desputisoun' is another text, the much more famous and influential Middle English 'Sir Orfeo'. This is a kind of verse romance which tells the story of the knight-king, Sir Orfeo, and how his wife was kidnapped by a fairy king. This sets the scene for the rest of the story which is about how Orfeo rescues his wife. The text has aged much better than 'The Desputisoun', and can still be enjoyed by modern readers today after they have become accustomed to the peculiarities of the language. The text calls itself the translation of a Breton lay in the introduction, and this could be true. The existence of an Old French version of the story is corroborated elsewhere. Certainly the story is not original to Middle English romance. There is a very famous legend called 'Orpheus' in Ancient Greece which tells precisely the same story, and Orpheus was venerated as a religious icon in the Greek mystery cults for a long time from the first millennium B.C. to the early first millennium A.D.

The Middle English text of 'Sir Orfeo' is usually dated c.1275-1325, with the manuscript date of c.1330-40 acting as a 'terminus ante quem' (latest possible date) for our existing version of the story. The author of the story is unclear, but it is written in a dialect roughly attributable to the Westminster-Middlesex area of England near London. Our interest in the story is only limited and comes from just after when Orfeo has left to pursue his wife Heurodis. He is wandering the land, clad in beggars' clothes with only his harp to console him. He lives in the wild, and he sees many strange things while he wanders. One of these seems to be a sort of Wild Hunt, a hunting expedition led by the King of the Fairies.

Once again I have adapted the language of the text making it more familiar to modern English speakers by crossing out archaic words and replacing them with modern translations in brackets, and by supplying additional letters when words are hard to understand in the Middle English form.

Edited Text and Commentary

> He might se him bisides
> Oft in hot ~~undertides~~ [noon-times]
> The king o fairy with his rout
> Com to hunt him al about
> With dim cri and bloweing
> And houndes also with him berking
> ~~Ac~~ [And] no be[a]st thai no ~~nome~~ [caught]
> No[r] never he ~~nist~~ [knew from] whider they bi-come

Our only extract from 'Sir Orfeo' is very short and concerns the Wild Hunt which the main character sees. He sees the King of the Fairies more than once, hunting during the hottest part of the day with shouts and blowing of horns. This is interesting partly because the hottest part of the day is when we might expect the least hunting to take place. Perhaps by making the fairies hunt at this time, the author is just showing off how different to humans they are.

It is also interesting that the Fairy King never catches any animals, despite hunting 'oft[en]'. I can think of three possible explanations for this. First, it may be simply that this was another way to separate the hunt from ordinary mortal affairs, just like the timing of the hunts. The editors of the text note that when Orfeo visits the Otherworld he finds that life there is almost in suspended animation, nothing new ever takes place, so perhaps the endless hunts can be interpreted like this.

However, when the fairy women came out later to go hawking for waterbirds, these actually are killed. Perhaps it is the manner of the prey which is important. In 'Pwyll', a slightly earlier Welsh text which we shall move on to when we have finished with 'Sir Orfeo', a large part of the plot is the conflict caused when the King of the Fairy-realm decides to hunt in the normal world at the same time as the local lord. The right of chase and ownership of the important venery animals was an important legal issue in the medieval period, and since Orfeo was actually the local king, perhaps the Fairy King knew that if he hunted in Orfeo's land, Orfeo would have legal recourse against him. This interpretation is supported by the fact that Orfeo finds the fairy-world as a consequence of and directly after seeing the women hunting water birds.

Another possible explanation which has parallels in the other texts we have looked at is that the Fairy King was not hunting for animals but on a wild hunt for wicked humans. Although the Hellhounds searched for humans by themselves in the 'The Desputisoun Bitwen the Bodi & the Soule', the hounds were accompanied by hunters in their search for wicked humans in 'The Devil and his Dandy Dogs' and also in the earliest text which we shall come on to later, the Peterborough version of the 'Anglo-Saxon Chronicle'.

The hounds themselves are not special at all in this text. The sound associated with the hunt is of the blowing and horns and barking of dogs, just like in our nineteenth century Dartmoor stories, but these sounds do not have any terrible significance or terrifying nature like they do in later stories.

Finally it is worth pointing out that there is still some ambiguity about whether this hunt has come from the Otherworld or the Underworld, or whether these are different names for the same place. Later in the story when Sir Orfeo finally does visit the court of the King of the Fairies, he finds it full of dead people, but it is also: 'fair cuntray / as bright so sonne on somers day' (lines 350-1, 385-). In the original Greek version of the story, 'Orpheus', the hero's wife (called there Eurydice) is clearly held in the Underworld by Hades and Persephone. This is not a bright place at all but misty and gloomy, so the either the Middle English translator or their source tradition must have made the innovation that it is the King of the Fairies who stole Heurodis.

Discussion

Although our extract from 'Sir Orfeo' is very short, it does provide a number of interesting features, which are made more interesting by the links between 'Sir Orfeo' and its manuscript companion the 'Desputisoun'.

The hounds themselves in 'Sir Orfeo' are apparently so ordinary that they were not considered worth describing in any great detail. Although they are heard barking, this bark does not appear especially ominous, and it is clear that the hounds here are far from the disturbing, terrifying and more familiar hounds of the 'Desputisoun'.

The leader of the hunt being the King of Fairies is also interesting compared to the 'Desputisoun', where the hounds were independent and their aim was to bring back the soul to its first place of punishment. The confusion about whether or not the hounds are accompanied by huntsmen remains contentious in our Dartmoor legends from the nineteenth century.

Similarly, the ambiguity in 'Sir Orfeo' about whether the hounds are from the land of the dead or the land of the fairies, and whether these two places are separate also continues to be an issue in the nineteenth century. If we did not have both of these stories, dated to approximately the same time period it would be natural to assume that the one which we did have was a typical depiction of the hounds from c.1300. As it is though, it is clear that very different depictions of supernatural hounds were possible even in this period. Clearly Wild Hunts and Hell Hounds were completely different breeds of dog and inhabitants of different genres even in 1300. Although the two genres are much closer in the later Dartmoor folklore, the rift between them is still visible as we have seen.

'Pwyll', in the White Book of Rhydderch, c.1200 A.D.

Introduction

Of all the texts which I present, the Middle Welsh 'Pwyll' is the most difficult to date. It is present in two main manuscripts, the White Book of Rhydderch and the Red Book of Hergest. Since both of these manuscripts are datable to the fourteenth century, it might seem most likely that the story of 'Pwyll' itself is not much older, but actually this is unlikely. 'Pwyll' is the first of the 'Four Branches of the Mabinogi', and fragments of other branches can be found in manuscripts from the mid-thirteenth century onwards. The language evidence supports the theory that the stories were first written down in their current form approximately 1200-1250 A.D. [101]

'Pwyll' is also mentioned in older texts like the more archaic seeming 'Preiddeu Annwfn' meaning that the story might have existed earlier than the earliest surviving version, whether as an oral 'fairy-tale' or just an older form of the tale which was updated and has not survived. The description of the hounds in the story may be a traditional one therefore, which has an even earlier antiquity than the earliest recorded version of the story as a whole.

The section of the story we are most interested in comes right at the very beginning of the first of the 'Four Branches'. While out hunting one day, Pwyll, the lord of Dyfed (one of the medieval kingdoms of Wales), finds some hounds which have just hunted down a stag in the woods. He chases off the other pack and feeds his own hounds on the stag, but this turns out to be a mistake. The master of the other hunt comes to him and complains. At first Pwyll is not sure he has done anything wrong since he is a lord with hunting rights over the woods. However he soon finds that Arawn, the master of the hounds outranks him as the crowned king of Annwn (the Welsh Otherworld). Pwyll's

---

[101] A good discussion of the date of 'Pwyll' is found in Rodway, S. 'The Where, Who, When and Why of Medieval Welsh Prose Texts: Some Methodological Considerations' pp47-90, in: *Studia Celtica 41* (2007), pp.58-60; 68-70

desire to redeem himself lends impetus to the rest of the plot, and the consequences of his actions are even felt in the later 'Branches of the Mabinogi'.

Translated Text and Commentary

1.

Pwyll, Prince of Dyfed was Lord over the seven cantrefs of Dyfed. Once, he was in Arberth, a chief court of his, when it came to his mind and to his thoughts to go hunting. Here is the part of his realm that he thought to hunt: Glyn Cuch, and he set off that night from Arberth, and he came up to Pen Llwyn Diarwya, and there he [stayed] that night.

And after that night, early the next day he arose, and he came to Glyn Cuch and sent-off his hounds under the [canopy of the] trees. And he sounded his horn and began to muster the hunt and walk after the hounds, and he lost his companions.

The first section localises the text in Glyn Cuch in Dyfed, south-west Wales. Like the other medieval stories we have looked at I do not believe that the author knew anything about Dartmoor, but, as we shall see, Dartmoor's hounds do borrow some of their distinctive features from the Hounds of Annwn.

2.

And while he was listening for the cry of the pack, he heard the cry of another pack, and it was not the same cry, and that [was] coming towards his own pack. And he saw a clearing in the forest of a level field, and while his pack was just coming up to the side of the clearing, he saw a stag in front of the other pack. And towards the middle of the clearing, behold, the pack that was after [the stag] caught up with it, and they struck it to the ground.

And then he looked at the colour of the pack, without bothering to look at the stag. And of [all] the World's

> *hunting hounds he had seen, he had not seen [any] hounds the same colour as those. This was the colour on them: gleaming shining white, with their ears in red. And just like the whiteness of the hounds gleamed, so gleamed the redness of the ears. And with that he came up to the hounds, and sent-wandering the pack that had killed the stag, and fed his pack himself from the stag.*

Here we get a close look at the Hound of Annwn, and we find they are very different to even the hound pack found in 'Cwn Annwn', which is supposed to be another Welsh form of the legend. The hounds are physical, and their prey is a normal one for hunting hounds.

The colour of the hounds is singular. They are completely white with gleaming red ears. There are many parallels for this colouring as we shall see later, but for now it is interesting that despite their strange colouring Pwyll is not warned-off or intimidated and still pushes them aside to feed his own dogs. This is completely different to the fear with which Dartmoor's hounds are almost unanimously met with. As we shall see, it may suggest that Pwyll saw the hounds as only pedigree-coloured rather than actually otherworldly.

3.

> *And while he was feeding the pack, he saw a rider coming after the pack from on a great, dapple-grey horse with a playing horn around his neck and a garment of light grey cloth as [his] hunting clothes. And with that the rider came towards him, and spoke like this to him:*
>
> *'Chief,' he said, 'I know who you are, and I will not greet you well!'*
>
> *'Well,' said Pwyll 'Maybe you have [such] rank that you should not.'*
>
> *'By God,' he said, 'It is not the level of my rank that restrains me from it.'*
>
> *'Chief,' said Pwyll, 'what else?'*
>
> *'Between me and God', he said, 'your ignorance yourself and your arrogance.'*

'What arrogance, Chief, have you seen in me?'

'I have n[ever] seen more arrogance in a man!' he said, 'than to drive wandering the pack that has killed the stag, and to feed your pack yourself on it! That,' he said 'was arrogant, and although I will not take revenge on you, between myself and God,' he said, 'I will do dishonour on you to the value of one-hundred stags!'

'Chief,' said Pwyll, 'if I have done wrong, I will buy your peace'

'In what manner', he said 'will you buy it?'

'Up to whatever may be your rank, but I do not know who you are.

'I am a crowned king in the land I come from.'

'My Lord,' he [Pwyll] said, 'Good day to you, and what land do you come from, for your part?'

'From Annwfn,' said he, 'I am Arawn king of Annwfn.'[102]

The last section we will examine of 'Pwyll' is a repartee between the hero and Arawn. Although Arawn knows that Pwyll has committed a crime as soon as he sees him feeding his hounds, Pwyll himself does not know that he has until Arawn reveals his identity. It is only at this point that Pwyll's mode of address changes. He no-longer calls Arawn 'unben' (chief) but 'arglwydd' (my lord). He may have suspected it before, especially when Arawn refused to greet him, but his answers are still a tentative 'if I have done wrong'.

Looking at 'Pwyll's mistake it is interesting to see that some comparison can be made with the plot of 'Dando and his dogs'. In both cases the greed of the main character gets him in trouble with an otherworldly figure. In Dando's case the hounds are his own, which become ghosts after he is pulled into Hell, but although Pwyll has his own hounds, it is the hounds already possessed of the Lord of Annwn which the text focuses on. Some comparison can also be made with 'Sir Orfeo', where the King of the Fairyland goes hunting but does not

---

[102] This is my translation of 'Pwyll' from the White Book Welsh of Sir Ifor Williams. The end of it has already appeared in *Aliens in Celtic History and Legend*.

take any animals, perhaps in order to stop King Orfeo from having a legal recourse against him.

The description of Arawn himself here is interesting for how it compares with later descriptions of the Master of the Hunt. Arawn rides a light grey horse with light grey hunting clothes and a horn around his neck. We can perhaps trace in this description the dark clothing and real horns which dress the Master of the Hunt in later stories but again the description is very different.

Discussion

The white, physical, stag-hunting hounds of 'Pwyll' are very different from the huge, terrible, fiery-black, human-hunting hounds of the later legends. Intriguingly the Master of the Hounds has changed over the years much less than the hounds themselves. The Otherwordly master in 'Pwyll' with his horn and grey cloak who seeks to address the moral shortcomings of the hero of the story is actually in many ways reminiscent of the later stories.

The colouring of the hounds is their only feature which may have influenced later legends. The bright red colour of the hounds' ears might have in turn inspired the singular bright red hounds of 'Cwn Annwn', especially since that story is set in Wales and is supposed to have been influenced by Welsh folklore.

However even the hounds of 'Cwn Annwn' are different from the hounds of 'Pwyll'. The former are ghostly, hunt the dead and breathe smoke. The hounds of 'Cwn Annwn' are completely normal other than their otherworldly master and origin.

There is even some indication that the strange colouring of the hounds might not have been considered so unusual by 'Pwyll'. In the story he displays no fear of the hounds at all and even physically pushes them away to feed his hounds. Just how unusual the readers themselves might have found the hounds is debatable.

On the one hand, it is also true that some animals may well have been pure-white with red ears in the medieval period. Some of the most common animals described in this fashion are cattle, and today we still find 'wild' cattle, untouched by the selective breeding of the nineteenth and twentieth centuries. Some of the last of these are at Chillingham, just north of Newcastle, and although there is no evidence that the breed of cattle is any older than the eighteenth century, if they or a similar breed were around in the medieval period perhaps medieval audiences would have had no trouble imagining dogs of these colour. They were unusual and of high-pedigree but not supernatural.

On the other hand, it is true that all otherworldly animals seem to have this very same colouring in Welsh literature[103]. From that perspective, perhaps the colour of the hounds is a plot device to build tension so that the audience know that the hounds are otherworldly, even if the main character does not. Considering both how commonly the colour-motif is used with supernatural creatures and how at ease Pwyll seems with the hounds perhaps both explanations are admissible.

Ultimately, although 'Pwyll' may have proved an inspiration for later legends of supernatural masters of hounds, the physical description of the hounds themselves does not appear to have had a strong influence on the development of the later Dartmoor folklore.

Intriguingly though, the corporeal shape, rational prey (stags) and harmless sound of the dogs in this early folklore from c.1200 is more reminiscent of our semi-modern, c.1900 versions of the folklore, than other versions nearer to the time which have supernatural hounds. The only real difference between the accounts is in the number of animals (the large single Monster Hound of Sherlock Holmes vs. the entire pack of the 'Cwn Annwn') and colouring. Perhaps in order to enjoy stories of ghostly creatures a certain suspension of disbelief is required which did not yet exist around 1200 A.D., and which stopped existing around 1865.

---

[103] See for example Hemming, J. 'Bos Primigenius in Britain: Or, Why do Fairy Cows have Red Ears', pp.71-82, in: *Folklore, vol.113, no.1*, (2002)

'De Nugis Curialium', by Walter Map, c.1181-84

Introduction

Walter Map (1140-c.1210) is the earliest author we can identify with any certainty. He seems to have been of Welsh origin, but wrote in Latin and came to the English court around 1162 after attending the University of Paris for a while. He was made 'household clerk' and later Archdeacon of Oxford but must have embraced life as a courtier, as he was made the King's representative at the Third Lateran Council, and the title of his only securely attested book is 'De Nugis Curialium' or 'Trifles of Courtiers', and was clearly written for courtiers in the time of Henry II (1154-89).[104]

The part of the text we are most interested in is one of the first stories of the book. It is the tale of 'King Herla', a king of 'antiquissimorum Britonum' (the most ancient Britons), referring to the people who spoke the British language (the ancestor of Welsh) before the arrival of English into the country, about seven centuries before Walter Map's time. Although set mainly in this time, right at the end events are brought up to the twelfth century and it seems clear that the story was one original to the twelfth century, and simply set in the ancient past like we might tell stories of the Tudors.

'De Nugis Curialium' is a lengthy text and was probably written over years, but the story we are most interested in is found in the 'first fragment' which can be dated fairly accurately to 1180-1184 by various internal references to courtly life. I have also included a second version of the same story which was probably written originally as a kind of draft around 1181.[105] In some ways we might view 'De Nugis' as the opposite of 'Jacob's Well'. The former text is an anthology of different

---

[104] Macpherson, E. 'Walter Map' in: *The Catholic Encyclopedia. Vol. 9*. (Robert Appleton Company, New York, 1910), (available online: http://www.newadvent.org/cathen/09635a.htm).
[105] Hinton, J. 'Walter Map's de Nugis Curialium: Its Plan and Composition', pp.81-132, in: *PMLA, vol.32, no.1* (1917). pp.94-7, 109-11.

stories and has a single moral message as a kind of justification for writing, whereas the latter is mainly made of moral messages.

Although the hounds of this story are fairly minor characters the story seems worth mentioning since it is so early, and since King Herla gives his name to the Herla-king troop or 'Harlequin' troop, which is a common name for the Wild Hunt, especially in later French literature.

Translated Text and Commentary
1.

An earlier draft of the story - from dist. iv, chapter 14

The assembly and night time companies which [people] called the Herlethings too were sufficiently famous in England until the time of our current lord, King Henry II. Forever wondering, lost, on insane marches and in stupefied silence, in these [companies], many appeared alive that are known to have died. Regarding these Herlethings, their kind was last seen marching in Wales and Hereford, [during] the first year of the reign of Henry II, around midday. We travel by the [same] method [as] theirs with cart and with sumpter horses, with saddle bags and with riding satchels, with [hunting] birds and with hounds, with men and women together.

Back then, those who first saw [them] roused all in the vicinity with shouts and pipes. Then, as is the code of that most vigilant people, many companies arrived straightaway, equipped with all kinds of weapons. And because they were not able to extort a word from them with words, they prepared to hurl a response at them with missiles. But they [the Herlethings] rose up into the air and suddenly disappeared.

From this day, this troop has not been seen anywhere, as if they have given up to us fools those wanderings of theirs by which we wear out [our] clothes, devastate kingdoms, we break our bodies and those of our mounts, and we have not time to seek remedy for [our] poor souls. Naught of use comes to us without work, nothing of profit is given to us if losses are considered, we do nothing by

> *plan, nothing accidentally. Empty to us and unfruitful [is] so much hastening, we are carried on insane [courses]...*

Extract one provides a good contextual introduction for the main part of 'King Herla', and is taken from a later chapter in 'De Nugis Curialium' which seems to have originally been a sort of draft for the main chapter. The way it is written seems to help make sense of the first sentence of the main chapter of 'King Herla'. In the later chapter Map seems to be referring to the popular medieval idea seven centuries earlier popularised by St. Augustine of Hippo in his book *De Civitate Dei* (the City of God) that all Christians are citizens of a single, eternal heavenly city, which is opposed to the earthly city of the Pagans. Comparison of the king's court during King Henry's time and Hell is a central premise of 'De Nugis' which Map returns to repeatedly throughout the stories. Map seems to believe that the court of King Henry was madly and aimlessly galloping with no plans or goals and was doomed to collapse just like the court of King Herla.

The justification for recording the story of King Herla at all is to provide a moral warning to the court of Walter Map's own time that they needed to place their trust in the Kingdom of God rather than any secular kingdom. However, just like we saw later in the *Straunge and terrible Wunder* of 1577, Map's warnings here are something of a flimsy pretence of a justification. The dramatic and sensational elements of his story cannot have been unintentional, and nor can he have missed the effect they would have on an audience. The way the story is written makes it clear that it was written to scare, entertain and please more than it is written to drive home a religious point.

On the other hand, after the end of the extract I have presented here, Walter Map continues with a long list of what he considers to be the failings and hardships of the court in his time, most of which he feels the court shares with the mythical court of King Herla. You can see the beginning of the list with his idea that the people of his time do not have time to plan or take stock, they work too hard and gain very little from their work. This list may well strike a chord with a number of readers today who will be familiar with the poem 'Leisure' by William Henry Davies starting:

What is this life but full of care?
We have no time to stand and stare.[106]

This poem was first published in 1911, and so we can see that Walter Map's concerns are a perennial issue. Map's list stretches on for two pages and therefore it is clear that to some extent Map truly believes that the story of 'King Herla' is a valuable tool for understanding the problems in his own age, as well as a fine and dramatic story.

2.

About King Herla

The stories have it that there was one [court] however, and only one, which was similar to our own court. They say that Herla, a king of the most ancient Britons, was involved in negotiation with another king, who appeared as a pigmy from shortness of stature which did not exceed a monkey's. According to the story, the dwarf approached [him] seated on a goat of the hugest size. The [dwarf-]man can be described as resembling Pan, bright of face, with the hugest head, [and] a long ruddy beard reaching the chest. [There he wore] a bright fawn-skin of stars [but had] a hairy belly and legs which degenerated into goat-feet.

Section two begins looking at the main part of the text, and immediately we find the pigmy king described in great detail. He is a ridiculous character, short with goat legs, wearing a deer skin which does not hide his hairy stomach. However, King Herla appears not to notice the oddness of his opposite's appearance and greets him in exactly the same way regardless. It seems clear that we are dealing with an Otherworldly figure in the pigmy king rather than a terrible Underworldly one, despite Walter Map's intention to compare his court to the Devil's own. This text may also have proved an inspiration to the odd seeming figures in 'Pwyll' and 'Sir Orfeo', who are also treated seriously by their human counterparts in their own stories.

---

[106] Davies, W.H. 'Leisure', (1911).

3.

Herla and [the man] spoke together alone. The pigmy said:

'I am king [over] many kings and princes, and an innumerable and infinite population, I am sent and I come from them to you freely. To you indeed [I am] unknown, but [I] exult in the fame which exults you above other kings, since you are both the best and closest to me by blood. You are also worthy of inviting me to gloriously grace your wedding when the King of France's own daughter is given to you, which he has arranged, although you are not aware. And behold, the messengers will come today.

And let there be an eternal agreement between us that I shall come to your wedding, and you [shall come] to my own one a year from the day.'

Having said this, he turned back from him quicker than a tiger and he removed himself from his [King Herla's] vision.

Therefore next the king, with fits of astonishment, received the ambassadors, and accepted the [marriage-]price. As he was solemnly occupied in his wedding, behold, the pigmy before the first dish, with a great multitude of [people] very similar to him with tables, so that the tables were filled and more were sat outside than inside, in the pigmy's own pavilions [which were] pitched in a moment. Waiters jumped out from these with sound vases of precious stones fitted together by inimitable craft. They filled the palace and the pavilions with gold and precious stone utensils. Nothing in silver or wood was used or set down. Whenever they were wanted they were there, and they served nothing from the royal or other stores [but] all they produced all from their own [store] and by themselves they delivered everything exceeding request and demand. What Herla had prepared was saved, his waiters sat relaxing (people don't serve without being asked). The pigmies were all around, pursued by the thanks of everybody, with costly, gemmed clothes lit up like the stars preceding all others. They did not bore anyone by word or deed or presence or absence.

> *Then the king in the middle of the labour of his waiters spoke to Herla thus:*
>
> *'Best of kings, with the Lord as my witness I am at your wedding according to our pact. However if you are able to wish anything else more than you see here then ask it of me [and] I shall carefully supply it for free, if not, do not delay when you repeat this honour yourself.'*
>
> *Without awaiting a reply to these words he immediately then returned to his pavilion, and around cock-crow he left with [his people].*

The beginning of our third extract is taken up by the King of the Pigmy's speech. He reveals that despite his odd appearance he is a very great over-king of a large area, again much like Arawn of Annwfn in 'Pwyll' and the King of the Fairies in 'Sir Orfeo'. Unlike these figures he can also vanish on command, the text reads literally 'se rapuit ab oculis eius' (he removed himself from his [Herla's] vision).

Perhaps more impressive than his invisibility though, is his mystical way of knowing that King Herla will soon be wed, although whether this is through human means or supernatural ones is not specified.

Most interesting of all, the pigmy king admits that he considers Herla 'the best [king] and closest to me in blood'. We might draw parallels with more modern fairy-tales here. The King of the Pigmies appears to be acting like some distant fairy godmother, but also apparently makes a pact with Herla, something which we often see from more sinister fairy figures like the antagonist of 'Sir Gawain and the Green Knight', or in modern times like the deal made with Rumplestiltskin in his story.

Indeed this parallel is made stronger when the pigmy king carries out his side of the bargain. His role in the king's wedding is perfect, and his pigmy 'ministrī' (usually translated 'servants', but here 'waiters' seems more appropriate) are highly regarded by all the guests. Even the cutlery and crockery used is very fine, being made out of gold, silver and precious gems. The Otherworld in the medieval period was known to be filled with amazing and impossible artefacts, and I have written on this motif before.[107] Herla has done very well out of this deal, but

---

[107] See 'Cases of Strange Artefacts' in *Aliens in Celtic History and Legend*.

medieval audiences knew just as well as modern ones that if something seems too good to be true then it probably is. The penultimate sentence of our extract sounds very much like a warning or threat, and provides foreshadowing of the dangers to come.

4.

After a year he suddenly requested the presence of Herla to maintain his pact. He assented, and supplied [himself] with enough to repay the debt, he followed [where] he was led. Then he entered a very high cave in a cliff, and after a considerable darkness, [they came] into the light which was not seen from the sun or the moon but from many lamps. They crossed to the home of the pigmies, a fine mansion by every quality like the palace of the sun Ovid described.

There he celebrated the wedding, and repaid the pigmy fittingly according to his debt. He was given permission to return, laden with burdens and gifts of horses, dogs, hawks and all things that seem to be proper to hunting and falconry. The pigmy conducted them straight into the darkness, and presented [Herla] with a small blood-hound to hold, forbidding that anyone in the whole company should dismount anywhere, for any reason, before the dog itself jumps away from its bearer. Having said farewell he returned to his country.

The text begins to move very fast in the next section, and everything appears to be going perfectly according to plan. We can't be sure how Herla managed to repay the pigmy king fairly for all wedding assistance, but we are told that he did, and the pigmy king seems completely satisfied with all his assistance, sending him home with large amounts of hunting and falconry equipment. Only his odd present of a bloodhound gives away that anything might still be wrong.

The bloodhound itself is an interesting creature. The Latin term used is 'canem modicum sanguinarium' (lit. small dog of blood), and although this has usually been translated as bloodhound, a bloodhound would ordinarily be much too big to fit on a horse's saddle in front of a knight. Perhaps there was originally some other reason it was called a blood hound, it may have been blood red coloured, agreeing with our 'Cwn Annwn' text or it may be that the wild hunt dogs were then supposed to be bloodhounds, and Walter Map just wanted Herla to be holding one. On the other hand, bloodhounds are probably the most frequent breed chosen as monstrous dog breeds right up until the *Hound of the Baskervilles*, so perhaps we need look no further than the traditional translation.

The fact that the otherworldly mansion is inside a cave through a cliff is also interesting, since it exactly parallels the description of the otherworld in 'Sir Orfeo'.

5.

After a short time Herla [too] returned to the light of the sun and his own country. He spoke to an old shepherd, asking for news of his queen by name. Then the shepherd with astonishment answered, saying:

'Lord, I [only] understand your language with difficulty, since I am a Saxon and you a Briton, but I have not heard the name of that queen except that the name is said to be given to a queen of the most ancient Britons who was wife of King Herla, who is said in story to have disappeared with a certain pigmy into this cliff. He has not been seen anywhere after that above earth. Actually, having expelled the natives the Saxons have held this country now for two hundred years.'

The king was stupefied by this, since he [had] thought the period was only three days, he scarcely stayed on the horse. Some others of his companions themselves, forgetting the order of the pigmy, dismounted before the dog and they immediately changed to dust. For this reason the king, understanding the reason behind his command, prohibited touching the ground under pain of death before the dismounting of the dog. The dog however has not dismounted.

Thus the story has it that King Herla wanders forever on infinite marches with his retinue, riding on madly without ever resting or staying [anywhere]. Often [there are] many who have seen the retinue, as they claim. Finally however, as they claim, on the first year of the coronation of King Henry, our king, [the retinue] stopped frequenting [the area] like they used to visit before. Then also it was seen by many Welsh people sinking into the River Wye in Hereford.

The fantastic ride quieted from that hour also, just as if they had given up their wonderings to us to quiet themselves. But if you should like [more] to listen [to stories about] how deplorable things are becoming, not only for us but for almost all powerful courts, you certainly bid me be silent, justly and fairly. I'll bet you want to give ear to [more] recent news for a while.[108]

The fifth and last extract, is where King Herla at last comes to the slow, horrific realisation that he has travelled through time, and that everyone he knows is dead. This is a frequently seen motif in medieval literature: Accidental time-slippage or unwitting travel into the future is a common side-affect of visiting the fairy-realms, where it is said that time travels far more slowly. The motif is so well known that the audience would have known exactly what was happening, whether they were reading or having the text read to them. Knowing what will happen sometimes doesn't stop a thing being horrific though, especially when a bad thing is happening to a good character. Herla's fate was sealed as soon as he made a deal with a being from another world since it is well known that fairies of the otherworld will usually doom a person in time.

It is also worth noting the truly lacking part that dogs have to play in the story at all, and it seems likely that in the earliest legends, the Wild Hunt may not have always included dogs. There is a similar account, for example, in Shakespeare's *The Merry Wives of Windsor*, where Herne the Hunter (the leader of many later hunts in folklore) is described without any dogs accompanying him.

We discussed the 'blood-hound' in the previous section and the animal is no easier to understand here. It seems to be a special magic dog, and

---

[108] Translated from James, M.R. (1914) *De Nugis Curialium*, (Clarendon Press, Oxford) pp.11-16; 186-7.

it is certainly a peculiarity of this story to find a hound riding a horse at all.

After finishing the main story, Walter Map once again discusses the Wild Hunt's presence in the real world like we saw in the draft version of the story which I presented in extract one. He opines that the Wild Hunt were not seen in the world after the coronation of Henry II, which is a strong claim, considering that the folklore continues to repeat itself for the next eight hundred years!

Discussion

The story of 'King Herla' is another very anomalous one from the point of view of the later Dartmoor folklore. The legend has a troop which cannot stop or rest from their riding for fear of death, together with the greyhounds and hawks and hunting equipment they have brought from the otherworld. It can be compared best with the Cornwall story of 'Dando and his Dogs' as a kind of origin legend for the wild hunt phenomena. Interestingly though the tale also tries to present a kind of death-legend, suggesting that the Wild Hunt is no longer seen since the coronation of King Henry. On the one hand this may have been written to ingratiate himself with the king – he is saying that the king's reign is so righteous that the hunt has stopped visiting. However on the other hand the story also suggests that King Henry II's court is now exactly like the cursed Wild Hunt which is certainly not much of a complement.

The troop of King Herla was changed by its visit to the otherworld, but although the pigmy king of the story has goat feet and his realm is clearly subterranean, he does not seem especially Devil-like. Herla himself does nothing especially sinful, and is a tragic figure in the story, so clearly we have here an early example of the Hunt being Otherworldly rather than Underworldly, much like we found in the Welsh story of 'Pwyll' in the last chapter. The way the court is described; with men and women riding together and with sumpter (baggage) horses as well as hunting hounds and hawks, make the Hunt of the story sound far more like a real-world court than a supernatural host of dangerous creatures. Indeed, from the way the Herlething is described there seems to be very little reason to fear them hurting anyone. They are more like ghosts than like demons, despite the oddly demonic form of the King of the Pigmies. The only exception to this is that when, in the author's own time they were attacked, they levitated into the air. Their ability to do this shows that they have supernatural qualities beyond their appearance and their origin story. Clearly there are already two sides to the Hunt even at this early stage, and by the time of the nineteenth century Dartmoor legends it seems to have been natural to fear them.

The term 'herlethingi' used in the introductory section is a borrowing from an Old English term, Herles-þing, (Herla's Court), with the plural Latin case ending 'i' at the end of the word. The use of an Old English term here strongly suggests that Walter Map was not making everything about his story up by himself, the term Herlething must have been created before his story by someone speaking Old English, and perhaps the story of the Herlethings was well known to English speakers of the time. The way the Herlethings are talked about, this term is more likely to have been used for Herla's court after they came back from the Otherworld and started their wild riding.

There are several hounds in the story, but they are not really familiar from the point of view of the later traditions. There is one very small 'blood-hound' which may be a blood-coloured hound rather than a bloodhound. If this dog is red, it would agree with the Welsh 'Cwn Annwn' story from the modern period, although this is not the way the term 'canem sanguinarium' is usually translated. The role of this hound is that of the 'psychopomp', a creature intended to guide humans between this world and another. Alby Stone has pointed out how well this fits in with millennia of stories from tales of the canine Annubis and Cerberus, gatekeepers of the Underworld in Egyptian and Greek mythology, to Finnish, Irish and Indian mythology.[109] Admittedly it's easy to find details of stories which are the same from any traditions, and these certainly do not indicate a shared origin or consciousness about these stories, but the similarities are striking nevertheless.

The blood-hound is a magic creature, but beyond this dog we also find that the troop is given many hounds and hunting hawks to accompany

---

[109] Stone, A. 'Infernal Watchdogs, Soul-Hunters and Corpse-Eaters', in: Trubshaw, B. (ed. 2005), *Explore Phantom Black Dogs*, (Heart of Albion Press, Loughborough).

them back to the world. We do not get many indications of how the Herlething were seen after their return from the Otherworld, but the presence of all of these hunting creatures raises the possibility that they were added to the story to explain the presence of dogs along with sightings of the Wild Hunt.

We now move on to what is widely agreed to be the oldest version of the hound legend in Britain, written in the time of King Henry II's grandfather, King Henry I. This time the narrative is written in Old English, so I have translated it completely instead of editing it.

The Peterborough 'Anglo-Saxon Chronicle', c.1127.

Introduction

'The Anglo-Saxon Chronicle' is one of the most important medieval sources from Britain, as it gives a medieval account of the country's history, detailing what happened in each year from the first Roman invasion of Britain by Julius Caesar in 60 B.C. through to the mid-medieval period. Up until around 600 A.D. there are very few records in *The Chronicle,* and even after this none of the records are 'contemporary' (i.e. written at the time they were supposed to have happened) for another three centuries. The beginning of the 'Chronicle' was probably first written during the rule of King Alfred the Great, c.892. From this point onwards the text is 'contemporary' and events of great importance were recorded only shortly after they happened.

Although all the surviving manuscripts of the 'Chronicle' agree more-or-less exactly about what happened in the years before 892 A.D., after this year they sometimes differ about the information they contain. This is a natural result of the 'Anglo-Saxon Chronicle' being copied and updated in different places. The various versions of the 'Chronicle' that survive were started in the tenth and eleventh centuries, and were abandoned one-by-one from the eleventh century onwards. Copied versions would have contained all or much of the same information up until the year they were copied, and then would give independent or only-semi dependant accounts after this year, as different scribes took up the story.

Unfortunately sometimes versions of the 'Chronicle' seem to have been compared and additional information was added. This makes it harder to reconstruct the relationship between the surviving versions. Sometimes different versions of the 'Chronicle' were synthesised with each other or with other lost sources, and sometimes events were left out if the scribe found them distasteful to their political or personal sensibilities. Modern scholars are not all in agreement about the relationships between the surviving versions of the 'Anglo-Saxon

Chronicle'. Even if they were, it is clear that the Chronicle is not always reliable. Signs from heaven, for example, are often inserted or augmented for dramatic affect when recording the events of any given year. Since scribes are unlikely to have witnessed the year's momentous events themselves, the chronicles tend to be heavily based on hearsay and rumours. The entries sometimes resemble early, incipient folklore more than what we would today term serious history as I have argued previously[110].

The version we are interested in is variously called 'Recension E', 'The Laud Chronicle', or, most frequently, 'The Peterborough Chronicle'. It gets this last name from its preoccupation with events in and around Peterborough town and Peterborough Abbey in the east of England, and it was the last surviving version of the 'Chronicle' to be started. It was probably started shortly after a fire destroyed the Peterborough monastery and perhaps an earlier version of the 'Chronicle' there in 1116, and gives an independent account of events from 1121 until 1154. Since it was written so late the language of the text is almost Middle English rather than Old English and melds the northern and eastern dialects. However I have still translated the text for ease of reading, since even in modern English the church terminology of the extract we are interested in is fairly complicated.

Translated Text and Commentary

1127 A.D.

This same year he [King Henry I] gave the Abbacy of Peteborough to an abbot who was called Henri of Poitou, who [still] held his Abbacy of Saint-Jean-d'Angély in his possession. And all the archbishops and bishops said that it was far from right and that he should not hold two abbacies in his possession [at the same time]. But that same Henri gave the king to understand that he had given-up his abbacy because of the great unrest that was

---

[110] A more in-depth analysis of the folklore of strange shapes and lights in the sky in the 'Anglo-Saxon Chronicle' and especially the Peterborough version can be found in *Aliens in Celtic History and Legend,* 'Cases of UFOs in 'The Anglo-Saxon Chonicle''. Also see the online .xml edition and description of the 'Anglo-Saxon Chronicle', (http://asc.jebbo.co.uk/intro.html).

in that land. [He also said] that he [had] done this by the Pope's counsel, and by leave of Rome, and by [the counsel] of the Abbot of Cluny, and by [the fact] that he was legate of the Rome-scott [tax]. But it was not true at all; he wanted to hold both [abbacies] in his possession and he held [these] for as long as God's will was. As a cleric he was [the] Bishop of Soissons, afterwards he [was] a monk at Cluny, after [that] a prior in that same place and after that he was a prior at Savigny. Thereafter, through [the fact] that he was a relative of the King of England and of the Count of Poitou, the Count gave him the abbacy of Saint-Jean-d'Angély-minster. Afterward, through his considerable scheming, he obtained the position of Archbishop of Bensançon and held it in his possession for three days. Then he rightly lost it because previously he had obtained it wickedly. After that he obtained the position of Bishop of Saintes which was five miles from his abbacy. He had that nearly a week in his possession. The Abbot of Cluny brought him [from] that like he did Bensançon earlier. Then he thought that if he might become rooted in England, that [then] he might have all his will. Thus he sought-out the king and said to him that he was an old and a broken man, and that he could not endure the great wickedness and the great unrest that was in their land. He earnestly entreated that by hi[s own merit] and by the names of all his friends [the king should give him] the Abbacy of Peterborough. The king gave it to him because he was his relative and because he was the foremost person to swear and to bear witness when the Count of Normandy's son and the Count of Anjou's daughter were divorced for consanguinity. Thus wickedly was the abbacy given [away] between Christmas and Candlemass [February] in London. Thus he went with the King to Winchester and then he came to Peterborough, and there he lived just like [bee-]drones do in a hive. All that bees drag towards [the hive], drones devour and drag [away], just like him. He took whatever he could from within and without, from clerics and the laity and he sent it overseas. He did no good there nor did any good leave there.

We are interested in only about half of the material from one year of the Peterborough version of the' Anglo-Saxon Chronicle'. This year is 1127, only six years after the 'Peterborough Chronicle' was restarted. Even from the short extract above it is clear that the 'E' recension of the 'Anglo-Saxon Chronicle' does have a preoccupation with the events of Peterborough, and the scribe's own personal and political biases are also quite obvious.

The subject-matter of this introductory part of the extract is dry and repetitive, and all that it is really important to take from the first extract is that Abbot Henri of Poitou has just taken over Peterborough Abbey. He previously held a variety of monasteries and ecclesiastical positions in France (in 1127 Normandy and England were still both ruled under King Henry I). While he was Abbot of Peterborough he also continued to be the Abbot of Saint-Jean-d'Angély in France. He was allowed to do this because of his relation to the king and his important friends. According to the 'Chronicle' he took all that he could from the Abbey of Peterborough and himself did not do any good there. If the 'Chronicle's harsh condemnation is to be believed, there was a general feeling that Henri's position as abbot of two monasteries was unfair. This is one of the only times in any of the surviving 'Chronicle' texts that any living person is criticised

In the time before sugar was imported, honey was a treasured sweetener and bee-keeping was much more common. In those times presumably the analogy of drone-bees would have been much more widely understood. Nowadays in colloquial speech 'mindless drone' might mean roughly the same thing as 'worker-bee', but among bee-keepers the difference is still understood. To explain it simply, drones are those bees whose primary function is to mate with the queen. Ordinary worker-bees are infertile but drones are not. Since they have this important task they do not assist with gathering nectar or pollinating flowers. The scribe of the 'Chronicle' is describing Abbot Henri as someone who takes all the profit but does not help with the work of the abbey.

> 2.
>
> *Let no-one think it [too] amazing that we are telling the truth, because it was known fully over all the land that as soon as he came there (that was the Sunday [in Lent]*

> *when we sing 'Exurge quare obdormis, Domine?') then, soon thereafter, many people saw and heard many hunters hunting. The hunters were black and huge and horrible, and all their hounds were black and broad-eyed and horrible. They rode on black horses and on black bucks. This was seen in the deer-fold itself in the town of Peterborough and all the woods that were from the town itself to Stamford, and the monks heard the horn-blasts that they blew at night. Reliable people who observed them at night said that they thought that there might well be about twenty or thirty horn-blowers. This was said and heard from the [time] that he came here, and all that Lent-time and onward to Easter. This was his arrival. About his departure, we cannot yet say anything. May God provide!* [111]

Our second extract from the text follows immediately on from the first and is much more interesting in content. The scribe seems to realise that he is speaking very strongly and feels the lack of any evidence beyond hearsay for future readers who might not know about the events. As evidence he produces what has been called 'the earliest account of a Wild Hunt in English'.[112] The fact that a supernatural hunt rode through the local area is supposed to be evidence of Abbot Henri's wrongdoing, but why? We could just interpret the story as meaning that because the abbot was sinful, the land which the abbot controlled suffered and the abbey stopped being a stronghold of righteousness. However there is another interpretation which may be even closer.

A clear parallel can be drawn between this hunt and the nineteenth century legends like 'Dando', the 'Cwn Annwn' and the 'The Devil and his Dandy-dogs'. In the 'Peterborough Chronicle' version a group of black riders on black horses with black dogs hunted through the area around Peterborough blowing horns. From these signs alone people at

---

[111] This is my translation of the year 1127 of the 'Peterborough Chronicle'. It is a translation from the online edition of the Old English text by Tony Jebson, 1996-2007 (http://asc.jebbo.co.uk/e-L.html).

[112] Rooney, A. (1993), Hunting in Middle English Literature, (D.S. Brewer, Cambridge). p.35. Rooney's assertion that 'no particular victim is identified' is incorrect, the object of the hunt is clearly supposed to be Abbot Henri.

the time would have realised they were supernatural in nature. It is clear that they are hunting something, and have not yet managed to find it. The last two lines of the extract give a clear clue as to what the hunters are hunting. The riders arrived around the same time as Henri did, and it seems that they are following him. The most probable explanation is that the riders are hunting Abbot Henri for his sinful ways, and they will take him to Hell if they catch him. The scribe writing the chronicle knows this, and seems to believe that Henri deserves it. The final words 'May God provide!', suggest that the scribe believes that the hunt is a kind of divine retribution against Henri's use of the abbey for personal profit.

The hunt also chases sinful humans in 'Dando', 'The Devil and his Dandy-dogs' and in the other slightly later medieval English text, 'The Desputisoun Bitwen the Bodi & the Soule'. The human only escapes in one of these stories, 'The Devil and his Dandy-dogs', and then only because when he prays the hounds from Hell cannot reach him. In 'Cwn Annwn' like in 'The Desputisoun', two humans are chased by hounds, first a maiden by ordinary, if terrifying, bloodhounds and then a knight by Hell Hounds. The knight when hunted is already dead, but when caught, its soul will be dragged to Hell and the hunt will be over. Although none of these stories are actually set on Dartmoor, these stories are those which most inspired the nineteenth century stories of the Monster Dogs of Dartmoor.

Discussion

It is interesting quite how little the legend changed in the seven hundred years between the twelfth century and the nineteenth. The hounds of the 'Peterborough Chronicle' remain black, horrible, and even have very wide eyed (lit: 'brad[-]egede' – broad-eyed), like the 'saucer eyes' of those in 'The Devil and his Dandy-Dogs'. The following huntsmen are still black and larger than ordinary humans, and they still blow horns. There are more huntsmen in this early story than in later legends which tend to have many more hounds than huntsmen, and the hounds do not howl especially or have glowing red eyes, but the descriptions remain very similar just the same.

This is contrary to the vastly different hounds we found in 'Pwyll' which were white and red, not frightening at all, and not interested in attacking humans. It seems clear that our later Dartmoor legends are far more based on the medieval English tradition than the medieval Welsh. Even stories like 'Cwn Annwn', which are supposed to be solely based on the Welsh hound folklore borrow strong elements from the English version.

It is also interesting that it is a living person, Abbot Henri who being hunted in the 'Peterborough Chronicle'. Most other versions of the legend, including 'The Desputisoun Bitwen the Bodi & the Soule' have Hellhounds seeking out the souls of wicked sinners. The 'Peterborough Chronicle' makes it clear that the idea of the hounds seeking the living is not a new one.

The physical characteristics of the hounds are also interesting. Although they are wide-eyed, black and horrible, they do not breathe fire or have red eyes in this text. The story of the chronicle does not get its power from terrifying descriptions of hounds, it gets its power from the un-stated implication that the hounds are a force of God's vengeance, and that if they ever catch Henri they will take him to Hell. It is possible that the hounds only needed to be described as horrible when their function was forgotten. Only after their significance is forgotten are stories made of the horrible sight or sound of the hounds, without knowing why they are hunting.

Ultimately, even in the earliest version of the legend and the earliest possible source for the modern legend we still find physically similar horrible, black and broad-eyed hounds. This shows that even though they are left out of some legends of the Wild Hunt, they are actually an integral part of even the earliest versions of the story. Even leaving aside the physical similarities, these hounds hunt wicked humans to drag them to Hell, which is again a motif found in several nineteenth century versions of the folklore. Even though the Hellhounds of the 'Chronicle' are not described any differently than a human hunter's hounds might be, they are still clearly agents of divine wrath and therefore also clearly supernatural. This sets them in contrast to the Hounds of Annwn in 'Pwyll', where the dogs were so ordinary that the hero could push them away to feed his own hounds while out hunting.

Conclusions

The Sample

Fellow researchers may rightly object that I have failed to reproduce every single version of the folklore of the black dogs or the hounds of the wild hunt from the history of British literature. To this I answer that some pieces of folklore have been purposefully left out. For example, the reader will find no references to the dispute between Sir William de Tracy and Thomas Becket, since although these characters are historical, I have not been able to find any reliable references to their ghosts having hounds before the late twentieth century.

Stone has suggested that Grendel, the first monster fought by Beowulf might be a monster hound based on the etymology of his name.[113] If true, this would be the very earliest reference to a monster hound in British literature. The date of Beowulf is a deeply vexed issue but it is certainly earlier than the Chronicle in the preceding chapter. Unfortunately though, the idea of a canine Grendel is quite impossible. Although Grendel is described as a 'wolf' and 'wargh', these terms are generally used in Old English just to describe fierce, formidable opponents. Wolves were thought of as dogs of war, delighting in battle whoever won since they got to eat the corpses of the slain. Grendel and his still more terrible mother both live underwater, and although they are not fully described they walk bipedally, wrestle, have arms and legs and could wear armour if they chose to (although they spurn it). Clearly they cannot be seen as dogs.

Likewise I have left out the famous Shakespearian reference from *The Merry Wives of Windsor*. In this story, Mistress Page describes how Herne the Hunter, an old keeper of Windsor Forest haunts an old oak tree each night. Knowing that many still believe this folklore she seeks to have Falstaff meet her by that tree one night to manipulate his fear of the unknown. It is a great story but the Herne of the story is not

---

[113] See: Stone, A. 'Infernal Watchdogs, Soul-Hunters and Corpse-Eaters', in: Trubshaw, B. (ed. 2005), *Explore Phantom Black Dogs,* (Heart of Albion Press, Loughborough). p.46

mounted, or accompanied by dogs. Indeed he seems to be more of a spirit or god after the manner of Pan than he does a member of the Wild Hunt:

> *There is an old tale goes, that Herne the*
> *Hunter (sometime a keeper heere in Windsor Forrest)*
> *Doth all the winter time, at still midnight*
> *Walke round about an Oake, with great rag'd-hornes,*
> *And there he blasts the tree, and takes the cattle,*
> *And make milch-kine yeeld blood, and shakes a chaine*
> *In a most hideous and dreadfull manner.*
> *You haue heard of such a Spirit, and well you know*
> *The superstitious idle-headed-Eld*
> *Receiu'd, and did deliuer to our age*
> *This tale of Herne the Hunter, for a truth*[114]

The entire reason the folklore is frequently quoted seems to be that of the name "Herne" comes to be attached to the Wild Hunt motif, rather than that the text itself has any real claim to fame among students of Monster Dogs.

I do not doubt that I have also overlooked some pieces of folklore, perhaps even earlier references to the hounds of Dartmoor, although I hope not too many. My aim with this book has been to present at least a 'representative sample', and to demonstrate that the Dartmoor hound folklore of the last two centuries is inspired by a diverse and rich nation-wide folklore of ghostly black hounds from across Britain. The most immediate question for now is how well I have succeeded in this.

Analysis of Pre-Dartmoor Results

In the Interlude between accounts of the Hounds of Dartmoor, and accounts of the Hounds of the rest of Britain I suggested that the legends of the hounds we had seen up to that point could be divided into three types. There were stories of Phantom Dogs, stories of Hell Hounds and stories of the Wild Hunt. Going back further in time from the nineteenth century, it is possible to continue to fit the stories prior to the modern period into almost the same categories, with the exception that we have no more stories of phantom dogs:

---

[114] Shakespeare, W. *The Merry Wives of Windsor,* Act 4, Scene 4.

Monster Beasts Categorised – c.1678-1127 A.D.		
Wild Hunt	**Hell Hounds**	**Miscellaneous**
'Sir Orfeo'	*The Wonders of the Little World* – 'Crescentius'	*The Wonders of the Little World* – 'Cornelius Agrippa' -Dog familiar
'Pwyll'	'Jacob's Well'	*A Straunge and terrible Wunder* - Devil in dog form
'De Nugis Curialium'	'The Desputisoun Bitwen the Bodi & the Soule'	
	'The Anglo-Saxon Chronicle'	

Helpfully, this evidence lines up perfectly with the answer to the question we have been asking throughout this book, where do the hounds come from:

Do they come from the Underworld or the Otherworld? 1678-1127 A.D.	
Underworld	**Otherworld**
The Wonders of the Little World (x2)	'Sir Orfeo'
A Straunge and terrible Wunder	'Pwyll'
'Jacob's Well'	'De Nugis Curialium'
'The Desputisoun Bitwen the Bodi & the Soule'	
'The Anglo-Saxon Chronicle'	

In the nineteenth and twentieth century folklore from Dartmoor, both Wild Hunts and Hell Hounds came from Hell, and could be stopped by praying, Eucharist bread, etc. However in the earlier stories this is not the case. There is a perfect distinction between Hell Hounds, which all come from Hell and stories of the Wild Hunt, which typically start in the Otherworld.

So far so good: We have clear evidence of two separate genres of Monster Dog story. There are legends of Otherworldly wild-hunts, which in the medieval period are not even frightening, and legends of Underworldly Hell Hounds which are always terrifying and seek to drag evil souls to Hell. The two latest stories (The Wonders of the Little World (1678) and A Straunge and terrible Wunder (c.1577)), both seem to be of devils in dog form, and need only attest to the popularity of stories of the devilish Hell Hounds.

However when we look at the evidence more closely, some of our conviction seems misplaced. For example, although I have categorised the story from 'The Anglo-Saxon Chronicle' as being about Hell Hounds since the hounds seem to be waiting to pull one man to Hell, actually it is more often categorised as a Wild Hunt legend. It describes a hunt with horses and hunting hounds with horns haunting the woods which is seen by many people in the area. The monk writing the 'Peterborough Chronicle' probably did not realise it, but what he created in 1128 was a hybrid between stories of Hell Hounds and stories of Wild Hunts.

In the years after the twelfth century our stories seem to separate much more easily so that we can much more definitively identify the hounds in 'Pwyll' and 'Sir Orfeo' and 'De Nugis Curialium' as being about Wild Hunts rather that Hell Hounds. However it is interesting to note that the genres seem to be re-merging by the nineteenth and twentieth centuries so that all the Wild Hunts in this period come from Hell, and some of the Hell Hounds are accompanied by a huntsman. Ultimately the 1127 'Chronicle' is probably one of the closest of our legends in plot to the nineteenth and twentieth century Dartmoor tales, despite the being the furthest from the Dartmoor legends in date.

This can all be seen much more clearly when we arrange the stories as a kind of family tree or 'stemma' diagram. This sort of diagram is usually intended for variants of the same text, but we can use it to show how the legends evolved over time, and which texts are most likely to have influenced which other texts:

192

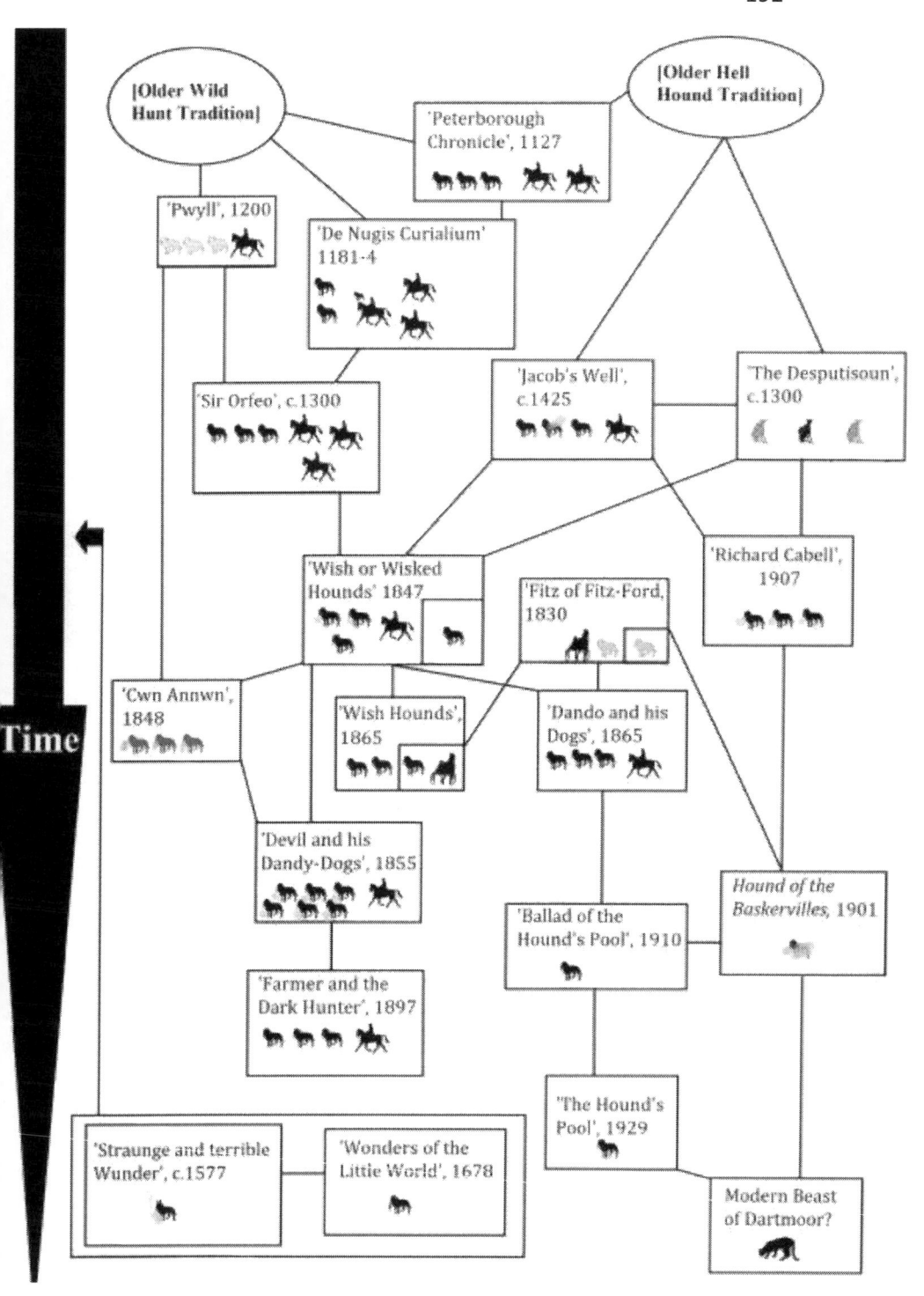

[Older Wild Hunt Tradition]

[Older Hell Hound Tradition]

'Peterborough Chronicle', 1127

'Pwyll', 1200

'De Nugis Curialium' 1181-4

'Sir Orfeo', c.1300

'Jacob's Well', c.1425

'The Desputisoun', c.1300

'Wish or Wisked Hounds' 1847

'Fitz of Fitz-Ford, 1830

'Richard Cabell', 1907

'Cwn Annwn', 1848

'Wish Hounds', 1865

'Dando and his Dogs', 1865

'Devil and his Dandy-Dogs', 1855

'Ballad of the Hound's Pool', 1910

Hound of the Baskervilles, 1901

'Farmer and the Dark Hunter', 1897

'The Hound's Pool', 1929

'Straunge and terrible Wunder', c.1577

'Wonders of the Littie World', 1678

Modern Beast of Dartmoor?

Time

Stemma Diagram and Full Analysis

The above diagram includes all of the sources in approximate order of date from top to bottom. Sources with two different versions of the same legend are either split up like Hunt's *Popular Romances of the West of England* or have the variant form in a small box like *Fitz of Fitz-Ford*. In order to fit all the texts into on page the scale has had to be very compressed in places. In particular the reader should note that the two texts at the bottom-left, the 'Straunge and terrible Wunder' and the 'Wonders of the Little World' are only placed there since they do not appear to influence or be influenced by any other texts, and in order to conserve space in the centre of the diagram.

The centre of the diagram is so cramped because, as I have noted before, in the nineteenth century suddenly the Hell Hound and Wild Hunt genres join into descriptions of the Phantom Hounds: At this point, although the Wish Hounds are led by a single, sinister huntsman like the Hell Hounds, they also hunt everyone rather than just sinners like the Wild Hunt. They even seem to threaten everyone in some early nineteenth century versions of the folklore, which is something none of the Wild Hunt packs seem to do before that point except that found in the Peterborough Chronicle.

There are some other differences between the Dartmoor and British Monster Dogs too. The innovation of presenting only a single hound instead of a hound pack is the most important of these, and comes with the start of the Phantom Hound genre in Fitz of Fitz-Ford. This genre seems mainly due to an embellishment first noticed and reproduced by Anna Eliza Bray, who gave her ghost of Lady Howard a ghostly dog companion. From a nation-wide perspective, the sudden appearance of a the Phantom Black Dog phenomena in Victorean Britain has previously been suggested by Jeremy Harte, but here for the first time we can trace the antecedents and slow evolution of the legend into this form[115].

A second important innovation came when the hounds themselves start to become less normal looking and more supernatural. Most of the dogs start off large and black, but they are not feared or

---

[115] Harte, J. 'Black dog studies', pp.5-20, in: Trubshaw, B. (ed. 2005), *Explore Phantom Black Dogs*, (Heart of Albion Press, Loughborough).

necessarily seen as anything other than phantom hounds until 'The Desputisoun' c.1300, when they are described as fiends. Even then they do not actually start to breathe fire until after the end of the medieval period, with the 'Straunge and terrible Wunder' c.1577. This really appears to be more symptomatic of the nineteenth and twentieth century legends. Even then only five of the eleven sources we look at actually breathe fire or smoke. Some stories like 'The Farmer and the Black Hunter' even draw some of their dramatic tension from the observer not understanding what the hounds represent, although to be fair some of the other stories have large enough and terrifying enough hounds in their packs to show viewers fairly quickly that they are not normal. Early on I hypothesised that this was due to the increased rationalism of the nineteenth and twentieth centuries, which led some of the stories from c.1900 to closely resemble the earliest Monster Dog stories of Britain. Harte has examined this evolution in the folklore and he suggests the late innovation may have been influenced by the growing popularity of stories of human ghosts. This may appear speculative but it might explain the way some of our phantom hounds suddenly blink out of existence.[116]

After the nineteenth century we only ever see one human hunter accompanying the Monster Dogs at any one time, even in the stories where a large pack of hounds feature. It is difficult to say if this is an innovation of that era. In the earliest stories we have seen, the earliest Wild Hunts have multiple hunters whereas the earliest Hell Hounds are followed by one hunter at most. There is one exception to this rule in the shape of 'Pwyll' which sees only one hunter following his otherworldly hounds, but it is fairly clear that this element of the text was not accepted by later authors in the genre. This suggests that even though the Wild Hunt and Hell Hound genres stayed relatively separate in the nineteenth and twentieth centuries, they were still able to influence each other even then.

In the stemma diagram above I have given all of the hounds a black colour except where the text explicitly gives the dogs other colours. This is based on an assumption that the dogs would normally be

---

[116] Harte, J. 'Black dog studies', pp.5-20, in: Trubshaw, B. (ed. 2005), *Explore Phantom Black Dogs*, (Heart of Albion Press, Loughborough). P.17-18.

considered as black if not described, but how accurate is this assumption really? If we look at each of the texts in turn we find the following:

What colour are Monster Dogs?

Text	Colour
'Peterborough Chronicle'	Black
'De Nugis Curialium'	Not described
'Pwyll'	Pure white with shining red ears
'Sir Orfeo'	Not described
'The Desputisoun'	Black and blue
'Jacob's Well'	Not described
A Straunge and terrible Wunder	Black
Wonders of the Little World	Black
Fitz of Fitz-Ford	Sandy-red
'Wish or Wisked Hounds'	Black
'Richard Cabell'	Black
'The Wish Hounds'	Not described
'Cwn Annwn'	Red
'Dando and his Dogs'	Not described
'The Devil and his Dandy Dogs'	Black
'The Farmer and the Black Hunter'	Not described
'The Ballad of the Hound's Pool'	Black
The Hound of the Baskervilles	Black and glowing

| 'The Hound's Pool' | Black |

Overall ten of our sample of nineteen (52%) are explicitly described as black, six (32%) are not described and only three (16%) are other colours. This might seem quite shocking, given that I have coloured in all the dogs black on the stemma diagram, but actually the difficulty with the texts is that a large percentage of them are simply too short to describe the hounds in any detail at all. This is equally the case in the nineteenth and twentieth and the pre-Dartmoor tradition. The percentage of black animals is approximately the same in each, and so is the very low percentage of animals which are given a different colour.

One way we might be able to fairly decide what colour the non-described hounds were imagined to be, is to briefly consider only those stories which describe the colour of the dogs. Of these, ten (77%) are black and three (23%) are not. Given these figures, where the dogs were imagined to be any special colour it is probably safe to assume that people hearing or reading these stories would usually have imagined the dogs to be black. For this reason I have decided it would be more deceptive to leave the dogs on the stemma diagram above uncoloured than to colour them in black.

Final Comments: do these tales lead-up to the Dartmoor Beast?

'If enough circumstantial evidence exists to link the Black Dogs of the past with the black cats people see now and then today, then it opens the gates for other exciting possibilities...'[117]

In the Interlude I spoke about the Phantom Dog genre which seems to have been a late development of the Wild Hunt and Hell Hound legends. On the stemma diagram I have made the brave claim that this genre, together with the ever-present influence of the *Hound of the Baskervilles* legend, made possible the mental creation of the modern Beast of Dartmoor. But how likely is this really?

---

[117] Francis, D. (1983), *Cat Country,* (David & Charles, Newton Abbot). p.16.

The Cultural Source Hypothesis, that sightings of the Beasts of Britain could be a cultural phenomenon and a subjective experience, was considered briefly by Merrily Harpur in her book *Mystery Big Cats*. She discarded the idea since her witnesses all seemed so sure of what they were seeing, and some of them only came to the realisation that they were not looking at bin bags or domestic cats after sustained contact.[118]

I do not wish to cast aspersions on the reliability of big cat witnesses, but it is a well known fact that 'even Homer nods'. The contagious and subjective nature of the Monster Dog folklore at least can be seen from the similarity of the sources we have looked at, and it is also probable that the Phantom Dog genre around 1900 had definitely developed the basic elements which we see in Big Cat folklore today. Phantom Hounds appear alone, they are deep-dark black in colour, they are seen only by a few but everyone knows about them, they have favourite haunts and although they are not from either the Underworld or the Otherworld, they were also something more than ordinary. The Beast of Dartmoor still has many of these characteristics today, and certainly had more of them when it was first being seen in the 1980s.

Di Francis considered the evidence of Monster Dogs and their influence on Mystery Cat legends in her book *Cat Country*. She noted especially the confusion which witnesses seemed to show about whether they had seen a cat or a dog in her accounts from the 1960s-early 80s. Her conclusion was that perhaps people seeing big dogs over the last centuries had actually been seeing big cats instead, but been too embarrassed to believe their senses.[119]

Francis' note about the confusion in early reports between dogs and cats is very interesting, and it is true that to this day big cat witnesses continue to compare the size of their sighting to a dog. I only disagree about the significance. To me it seems more likely that the legend evolved, and the accounts followed the legend, than that people were simply mistaken about what they had been seeing for centuries before the 1980s.

---

[118] Harpur, M. (2006), *Mystery Big Cats*, (Heart of Albion Press, Loughborough). Chapter 19.
[119] *Cat Country*, (1983). Chapter 4.

On the other hand, it must not be forgotten that cats, cat scats (faeces) and cat hairs have unmistakably been found across Britain over the last century. Police forces still take the media frenzy of cat "flaps" seriously to this day, and even though it is rare to find a real Beast at the bottom of these scares, that is little consolation to sheep farmers who have lost expensive livestock to the animal.

Perhaps the most likely solution lies in a theory which embraces multiple explanations, as Bob Trubshaw has suggested[120]. Although there are now no wolves in the British wilderness, there are other paws that stalk at night, other voices that cry out and other teeth that bite. Some of them are real, and some of them are imagined and some of them are mixtures of both.

Perhaps it was sightings of real, unmistakeable big cats in the British countryside that helped accelerate the shift from Monster Dogs to Mystery Cat. The influence of *The Hound of the Baskervilles* in 1901 had already made it more popular to see a single, natural dog rather than multiple hellish creatures and from there the legend needed only a catalyst like a few sightings of real big cats to move from describing a black phantasmal dog to describing a mysterious black cat.

Philosophers and psychologists both will tell you that people don't see stark reality: External stimuli are changed to recognisable patterns in our mind so that we can understand them.[121] Think of when you use a computer or watch a film. Human vision automatically narrows so that you do not "see" what is around the screen's edge and in the room, only what is happening within the frame. Physically the light from outside the frame probably still reaches your brain, and if something moves in the background you will still see it, but if nothing happens you only "see" what is on the screen.

In the same way, the stories of Dartmoor's Beasts which we have looked at are part of the culture which English speaking people in general and South-West-born people in particular grow up with, even

---

[120] Trubshaw, B. 'Phantom Black Dogs: an introduction', pp.1-4, in: Trubshaw, B. (ed. 2005), *Explore Phantom Black Dogs,* (Heart of Albion Press, Loughborough)

[121] This explanation for the Black Phantom Dog is best advocated by Simon J. Sherwood in his 'A Psychological Approach to Apparitions of Black Dogs', pp.21-35, in: Trubshaw, B. (ed. 2005), *Explore Phantom Black Dogs,* (Heart of Albion Press, Loughborough).

if they never read them. It is often said that culture is a lens through which we perceive the world, but it is true nevertheless.

Where in 1900 someone seeing a dark shape on Dartmoor might have imagined that they were seeing a black hound, now they see a black cat. Whether this dark shape is actually a dog or a cat, or a rock is almost unimportant. The reason for it remains debateable, and is perhaps unimportant anyway.

Perhaps the most important thing we really learn from our study is how fickle a thing our worlds can be, and how subjective human experience really is. But that's nothing new. People have said that reality is what you make of it for a long time, and Edgar Allen Poe surely wasn't the first to wonder:

> *Is all that we see or seem*
> *But a dream within a dream?* [122]

---

[122] Poe, E.A. 'A Dream within a Dream' (1849)

Printed in Great Britain
by Amazon